BY MATT COSTELLO

Rage
Doom 3: Maelstrom
Doom 3: Worlds on Fire
King Kong: The Island of the Skull
Missing Monday
Artifact
Unidentified
Maelstrom
SeaQuest DSV: Fire Below
See How She Runs
Garden
Day of the Snake
Homecoming Caught in Time
Darkborn
Wurm
Child's Play 3
Hour of the Scorpion
Time of the Fox
Child's Play 2
Midsummer
Wizard of Tizare
Beneath Still Waters
Fate's Trick: In the World of Robert Heinlein's Glory Road
Revolt on Majipoor
Sleep Tight

With Craig Shaw Gardner

The 7th Guest

With F. Paul Wilson

Masque
Mirage

Writing as Chris Blaine

Drowned Night

Writing as Shane Christopher

Nowhere
In Dreams

MATTHEW COSTELLO

BALLANTINE BOOKS • NEW YORK

A Del Rey Trade Paperback Original

Copyright © 2011 by id Software LLC, a ZeniMax Media Company
All rights reserved.

Published in the United States by Del Rey, an imprint of The Random House Publishing Group, a division of Random House, Inc., New York.

DEL REY is a registered trademark and the Del Rey colophon is a trademark of Random House, Inc.

RAGE and its logo are registered trademarks of id Software LLC, a ZeniMax Media Company.

ISBN 978-0-345-52936-7
eBook ISBN 978-0-345-52935-0

Printed in the United States of America

www.delreybooks.com

2   4   6   8   9   7   5   3   1

Book design by Christopher M. Zucker

Dedicated to the entire team at id Software.
Your creative vision and passion made
this new world come to life.

APOPHIS 99942

ONE

THE HOOK

Raine looked up from his beer as the bartender raised the volume of the TV.

The newscast showed rioting in the streets of Kabul, then a jump to another reporter atop a hotel roof looking down at a Baghdad filled with fires.

"The effect of the United States Armed Services complete withdrawal continues to destabilize the entire region. The violence now threatens to spread to neighboring states. Secretary of—"

"Turn that crap off, will ya, Eddie?"

The sound disappeared.

Raine picked up the near-empty shot glass next to his beer and drained it.

Funny, to sit here in this Red Hook dive appropriately named The Hook, just as his old man used to do when he retired to his old neighborhood in Brooklyn. His dad—a lifer in the Marines—was a man who had only one vision for his two sons.

Not just to enter military service.

Both would go into the *Corps.*

No question about it.

And Nicholas Raine didn't even question the idea of following his brother Chris.

Ultimately, that meant following him to the never-ending training missions and covert ops that made up the constant war of the twenty-first century.

Then things changed.

Probably on the day his brother got caught by an IED. The grim reality of these forever wars hit him.

And worse, the old man died, his heart hitting him harder than any man would ever dare to. He hadn't been well for a while, not after years of hard living and drinking and too much time on his hands. Chris's death seemed to deal the final blow.

That attack didn't kill the old man. But the chaotic Veterans Hospital in Bay Ridge didn't have any miracles in its pouch to save the old sergeant.

Yet—he himself soldiered on.

It's what he knew. What he *could* do. It had become . . . all that he was good at.

He tried to remind himself that his father believed in all this "serving God and country." That "Semper Fi" was more than a gung-ho motto.

So he soldiered on. That is, until the order came to leave. Seemingly out of the blue, whole units and commands vanished overnight.

And now he bided his time here—holed up in a dingy one-bedroom in Red Hook, this bar his *office*—waiting to see if his country had any more need of him.

"Goddamned soldiers just gave the hell up anyway."

Raine heard the words.

Said too loudly to just be a private comment. The customer in broadcast mode apparently.

Then again: "All those years, all our fuckin' money, and then they just up and run? God—damn."

The bartender, Eddie, shot Raine a glance. Not that they had spent these nights sharing their life histories.

Not that they were pals.

But like any good bartender, Eddie had antennae.

Eddie moved down to the end of the bar. To the customer with his loud opinions on the fighting men and women. On what happened and how they just left the area.

The implication: *like cowards.*

Raine turned to watch Eddie, seeing his head bob. Telling the guy, just barely audible, "C'mon, can that stuff, okay, Mikey?"

The guy on his stool looked down at Raine, putting pieces together.

"I'm entitled to my opinion. It's my damn opinion. We went over there and then after decades, after freakin' *decades,* we just leave? Tell ya, the troops, these new guys, they just couldn't cut it."

Raine was already off his stool.

Moving down the long wooden bar.

Monday night. So quiet. A few people shooting pool in the back, oblivious.

A couple sitting in a booth, talking, possibly taking note, thinking they should have selected a better spot for a romantic meeting.

As Raine got close, he sized up the guy.

A giant bowling ball of a head that melted into absolutely no neck, as if his skull had been glued to a barrel-chested body. Massive Popeye arms. Maybe a dockworker. Big powerful guy.

Good.

That would make this even better.

Raine didn't say anything. After all, what was there to say?

Instead his right hand shot out like a projectile, targeting the man's right hand as it closed around a beer glass.

Raine's grip tightened on the man's wrist and squeezed. The guy's glass rolled free as Raine pressed the hand flat, now splayed against the sticky wood of the bar.

At the same time, his other hand went to just under the man's chin. Because even though it didn't look as though the man had a neck, of course he did. Sure. Buried somewhere in the jowly fat and muscle.

Raine's fingers closed tight. The man now had two amazing sensations of pain coursing through him at the same time: the hand, which was being squeezed so hard it felt like it would pop off, and the agony from his throat.

The fat, drunken, self-appointed military historian couldn't breathe; his eyes bulged out.

Finally, Raine spoke.

"Listen. If I ever hear you say a word criticizing our military—even a single word—then that hand you have there will become useless. And whether you will be able to speak—"

A little tightening of his grip on the man's fat-covered throat.

"—that would be anybody's guess." He paused. "Got it?"

The bug-eyed man nodded.

Raine released him and walked back to his stool.

The TV had been changed back to the Monday night game.

Giants. Minnesota.

His shot glass had been filled.

But maybe he'd rather catch the game back in his apartment a few blocks away. Sitting here, tonight at any rate, had lost its appeal.

He slid off the stool, threw a few bucks on the bar, and walked outside.

A chilly fall night, and Raine zipped his jacket tight, collar up. He didn't even see the black vehicle, engine idling, sitting outside The Hook. Didn't register it as something out of the ordinary until a window rolled down and someone called out to him from the passenger seat.

"Lieutenant?"

Raine stopped and turned around, now noticing the limo-like vehicle. Not exactly the usual wheels found in this neighborhood.

He stood there while the passenger door opened and a man in a suit got out.

"Yes?"

Raine saw that the man held a large envelope in one hand.

"Lieutenant, I have orders for you. Here."

Raine laughed. "Orders. From whom? I've been told that it would be quite a while before my country needed me. In fact, I was banking on it."

In answer, the man simply extended the envelope.

For a moment he didn't take it. But in the end he was a soldier, a *Marine,* and when a man said "jump" . . .

He undid the clasp and took out a single piece of paper. The man from the black car helpfully pulled out a small flashlight and pointed it at the document.

He looked up at the man. "Says here . . . I'm supposed to get in the car—right now, all due speed—and go with you to Floyd Bennett Field where a plane is waiting. And that's . . . it?"

The man said nothing.

"Not one for talking, hm?"

"Lieutenant, I've just been told to hand this to you and have you come with me. You can see that it is signed by General Mc-Williams. Everything is in—"

"I know. 'In order.' I don't get it. Can I at least go back to my apartment, grab a bag, some things?"

The man shook his head. "No, Lieutenant. *My* orders are to see that you come directly. No stops, no bag."

"*Your* orders? Who you with? NSA? CIA? Any of the A's?"

Again the man said nothing.

"I'll tell you one thing, whoever you are. It's something my dad drilled into me. Reason I joined the Corps. Stayed in the Corps. And that thing is respect for orders, respect for command. That's how you save lives. So this—"

Raine waved the sheet of paper.

"—actually *means* something to me. And if I'm supposed to—God knows why—go with you, then that's what the hell we will do."

Raine guessed he might still be amped by his bar scuffle.

In answer, the man opened the back door.

Raine got in, and with his escort sliding back in the passenger seat, the big black car pulled away from the front of the dive bar.

Out to a sleepy Flatbush Avenue.

It was getting late, so only a few places were now open as the dense area of Brooklyn gave way to open spaces near the Atlantic, places with tall grass, and what Raine thought had been the abandoned airfield named Floyd Bennett.

Been a while since he'd been out this way. Back then it was to Riis Park and sunny days at the beach. When Brooklyn was at its best.

At one time Raine knew there had been plans for housing to go up here, to transform the field—the historic airfield that once saw Amelia Earhart and Wiley Post fly away to smash world records—into a development.

But the economy, and then the history of the place, saved it. No money for development, but enough for a National Landmark designation that preserved many of the hangars and even kept a few airstrips in place. But nobody—military or commercial—used it.

Or so Raine thought.

They passed the Belt Parkway, to the beginning of the field. The fence on the side of the road showed the lack of attention. Weeds, debris. No money or nobody cared? Both probably.

"Why here?" Raine asked.

The driver didn't say anything.

The escort did, though, turning around. "I don't know, Lieutenant."

Great help, that guy. Loaded with information.

He wished he hadn't had that last beer. It would be nice to be totally clearheaded for whatever this thing turned out to be.

They stopped and turned at the entrance off Aviation Road. A pair of army soldiers stood guard, the wide gates swinging open just as the black car reached it, then quickly shutting behind them.

When they reached the runway, Raine leaned forward, looking for what he guessed would be a military transport. Instead, off at one end, he spotted the lights of a small jet.

As they got closer, Raine could see nothing military or commercial about it. Rather, it looked exactly like some fat cat's private jet. A jet a businessman might use to run down to Palm Beach. Catch some rays in January. Play with the mistress. Rub in a rival's face.

Not what he expected at all.

The driver pulled the car up to the side of the plane. On cue, the door of the plane opened, stairs gently tilting down to the tarmac.

The car stopped.

"Here we go, Lieutenant."

The escort got out and Raine followed him.

WELCOME TO BUCKLEY

The small jet seemed to leap into the night sky, then took a sharp angle that had it first racing out to the nearby Atlantic before banking and heading west.

Not going to Lejeune, then, Raine realized, thinking of the base in North Carolina he had been stationed out of before being sent home. *Interesting.*

He looked down and saw the lights of Coney Island. Another abandoned project. Somehow, the planned renovation of what they used to call "America's Playground" never happened.

When there's no money, things don't happen.

Still, in the reflected glow of the lights left on at night, he saw the tall, always imposing spire of the parachute jump. Inactive for, what . . . sixty, seventy years? The once breathtaking ride had long been an inoperative landmark, a skeleton, a monument to times when such thrills could be created.

A time of great amusement parks and world's fairs. His father used to talk about a place in Coney called Steeplechase.

"Nicky, I tell ya—you kids would've *loved* it. Crazy rides. Horses that raced around the perimeter. Made your heart race. And safe? Fugeddabout it. But now? All gone. Everything's gotta be so damn safe these days."

All gone.

One of his father's favorite sayings.

This restaurant, that movie palace, his favorite fishing boat in Sheepshead Bay.

All gone.

Then his wife—Raine's mom—died, and he hit his ultimate "all gone."

Became a changed man. Quiet. Stayed to himself. As if he had given up. And when Chris came home in a box? The military escort. The salutes. The flags waving, and Raine fighting to keep from breaking down. His father had sobbed uncontrollably, showing Raine another part of what it meant to be a man.

All gone.

Raine had made a pledge to his brother then. A promise to keep fighting—to make sure that he never had to say "all gone."

I'll keep on for both of us, Chris. I'll go back. I'll do what they sent us over to do. Don't you fucking worry about that.

And he would keep that promise until someone decided that whatever we were doing to keep the world free and safe was over.

He had to.

What was the expression? Ours not to question why. Ours but to do—

Coney and the coast faded into the background, the jet still climbing sharply.

"Lieutenant Raine?"

"Just Raine, Mister . . ."

"Raine it is. I'm Jackson. The plane has sandwiches and beverages. Maybe a beer?"

"Got any of those little packs of peanuts, Jackson?"

The joke finally made the man in a suit smile.

Barely.

"Don't suppose you can tell me where we're headed?"

"Actually, my orders allow me to now that we're airborne."

Raine raised his eyebrows.

"There really *is* a need for all this security, Lieutenant. I imagine it will be made clearer to you soon."

"I hope so. The destination?"

"Buckley Air Force Base."

"Colorado? Really? Pretty damn far away." He shook his head. "And what awaits me in Buckley?"

Jackson stood up.

"Let me check on those peanuts."

The night deepened. A moonless night, the stars bright and nearly unwavering in the cloudless sky. And every now and then Raine saw *one*.

A yellow-red streak in the sky.

For a week or so they'd been visible each night, this sporadic meteor shower connected to the asteroid—Apophis 96 . . . 95 . . . something—still way out there in space. Apparently a bunch of debris ran well ahead of it, hitting the atmosphere.

It was a big asteroid, too—nearly the size of the city. Good thing it was going to give them a miss.

There—another streak. This one turning fiery before it disappeared.

Giving us a miss.

Lucky thing. Because, after all . . . despite Hollywood's mad plots of diverting a major asteroid, just what the hell would we really do?

Still—he had to wonder why we were getting so many of

these meteorites. Seemed strange. Then again, what he didn't know about astrophysics could fill a lot of books. And had, he thought.

He put his head against the porthole window, wedging a pillow into the crack between the window and the seat.

The window—cold, but soothing.

He shut his eyes.

He felt a change in angle.

He opened his eyes, and for a moment didn't have a clue where he was. Totally disorienting, waking up on a plane. He wasn't complaining, though—traveling this way was a damn sight better than bouncing around on a military transport.

He looked over at Jackson, who was looking out a window on the other side. Raine looked out his own window and down. There wasn't much out there. The dots of houses and lights on the roads took on an eerie yellowish cast when seen from a few miles up. After a few minutes he could see an airstrip ahead.

Had to be Buckley.

Jackson looked over.

"Seat belt on?"

"Learn that in flight attendant school?"

Another small smile. Maybe this guy enjoyed knowing things that he didn't. Something that security and spy types liked. Secrets. They were all about their damn secrets.

Raine wasn't too big on secrets.

"We'll be down in a few minutes."

"And my magical mystery tour continues."

"Right."

The smile on the man's face had faded, replaced by something else, something in his eyes. Concern? Sadness?

Raine had led men into situations that could only b

scribed as hell. Into actual hell—no exaggeration—and he had brought a lot of them out again. In that time he had learned to check their eyes. To catch the fear sitting there. The concern. The telltale anxious signs that someone might crack. That someone might just freeze up.

And a few words—of support, of connection—could make the difference.

Humans are funny. They have a lot of needs. But maybe the one need they have above all is communication.

Does someone understand me?

Is someone listening?

The plane leveled off some. Slowed.

Raine stretched, arching his back to shake off the effects of hours sleeping crumpled up in a chair—albeit a fairly luxurious one. At least the beers and shots had lost most of their edge.

Good. Especially if he was going to get his orders.

He looked back out the window and noticed the planes on the tarmac getting bigger. The small jet circled hangars, some of them spilling out F-16 fighters into the early morning Still, it looked pretty quiet here, even if it was an hour or so before dawn.

He guessed the time.

About 4:30 A.M.

He looked at his watch: 5:07.

Not bad. Still, the sky should be turning light, no?

Then he remembered the time difference. *Mountain time here.*

He pressed a button of his watch and moved it back two hours: 3:07 . . . 3:08 A.M.

He relaxed—he never could explain it, but it was strangely relieving to have the right time on his wrist.

• • •

The screech of the jet's tires hitting the runway.

A tilt as the nose touched down.

The scream of the engines in reverse, brakes.

That crazy feeling of having your body pasted against the seat.

The jet slowed. As it taxied to wherever it was going to discharge Raine, he thought of something that hours ago hadn't seemed too odd:

He brought *nothing*.

No uniform. No change of underwear, no running shoes. No toothbrush, no personal effects. Nothing but what he wore to the bar, and a wallet filled with too little cash. The idea hit him full force.

It's crazy. To fly out here with nothing. Sure, orders are orders . . .

But he didn't have a clue what it meant.

The plane slowed some more. Raine unbuckled his belt while it still taxied. When the jet stopped, he listened to the small sounds of the engines slowing, quieting. Bright lights came on in the cabin.

Jackson stood up before him.

"Welcome to Buckley, Lieutenant."

He went over to the small jet's door and pulled a wide metal latch to the left, unlocking it. And like some magical portal, the door popped open, sending stairs down to whatever waited outside.

THREE

HANDLING
THE TRUTH

Raine walked out into the cold mountain air, where an Air Force jeep stood by, engine running.

"I assume that this jeep is for us, Jackson?"

"Yes."

Raine walked over and got in the back while his escort went around to the front passenger seat. The jeep pulled away fast, before Raine even had time to get settled.

"We late or something?"

No response. *Of course not.* Raine looked out at the quiet airfield, the hangars with bright lights inside showing massive bombers and jets as if on display. A few ground crew walked around, but other than their arrival, there didn't seem to be much happening at the base.

He looked over his shoulder at the small jet. Already it had started taxiing, turning in the other direction.

Time for its next pickup?

As the jeep raced toward a distant corner of the base, Raine felt his apprehension—if that's what it was—grow.

He had been thinking what this might be about. Being picked up in the middle of the night. Flown here. The private jet. Not getting anything from his apartment.

It would be as if he had simply vanished.

Not that there was anybody to notice. With his family gone, and his last attempt at a relationship crashed months ago on the reality of his steady deployments, who'd really be looking for him?

The landlord maybe. For rent. But even that was automatically sucked out of his checking account.

So what was this?

He didn't know; but he knew one thing. Whatever this was about, he would be finding out shortly.

Raine looked down at his hands: clenched tight, resting on his knees.

Relax, he commanded them. *Ease up.* Whatever the U.S. government had planned for him was—quite literally—out of his hands.

The jeep streamed on, and they'd soon left the main part of the base with its hangars full of expensive hardware. A massive building loomed in the distance, four, five stories tall. It looked like something NASA might need, but prefab and put up fast.

Raine leaned forward as the jeep went straight to that structure in the early Colorado morning.

The building was surrounded by a fence topped with concertina wire, and at the gate post, four soldiers stood with their M16s at the ready.

And inside the fence—in case no one got the point—an

Abrams battle tank, another soldier manning the .50 caliber from the open turret.

Probably more security inside the building itself. Raine's intrigue was growing. Something pretty important was happening there.

The jeep screeched to a halt, and he didn't need to be told this was their next stop. He opened the jeep door.

"Thanks for the ride," he said to the driver.

Following Jackson, he went to the gate. Jackson flashed something from his back pocket, one of the soldiers gave a signal, and the gate opened.

Raine came up beside him. "Y'know, stopping for a warm coat might have been a good idea."

Jackson was dressed only in his suit.

"Tell me about it."

A joke? Interesting.

Jackson led the way to a side door. Raine could see this building had giant hangar-sized doors as well. Something big was going on in there.

Or was going to come *out* of there.

Another solider at that door, but he already had it open, and the two men walked in. Raine noticed that Jackson walked with the quick, direct stride of someone who knew where he was going.

He'd been here before.

He made a sharp right at entering and went down a long corridor with corrugated metal walls on either side. It seemed to Raine that there was no way to go deeper into the building.

But then the corridor turned left, and right again, like a maze. Jackson moved quickly, leading him down a warren of hallways before they came to an open service elevator. It was a wire mesh frame, designed to get big things up and down. Jackson slid it open, the elevator's gate rattling.

Raine looked up, the roof of the building high above them, then at the elevator keypad.

After a zero, all *negative* numbers.

"We're going down?" Jackson nodded as the elevator gate closed. He slid his card in front of a reader—too fast for Raine to see—and a light turned green. The elevator started down.

And it kept going down for what seemed a long time.

When it stopped, someone was there to greet them.

"Lieutenant Nicholas Raine. How are you, Lieutenant?"

Raine looked through the mesh and saw his old captain.

"Captain Hill?" Raine saluted.

Hill opened the gate. At first he was surprised to see his captain, but then Raine noticed the scene behind Hill, and it seemed the surprises might only have begun. It resembled Hollywood's fantasy version of a war room. Banks of computer screens, some showing images, other data. People walking around quickly with a grim sense of purpose. And toward the back, a raised stairway up to a door.

Two more soldiers at that door.

Raine walked out of the elevator. "Didn't expect to see you here, Captain."

Captain Stephen Hill, a man Raine had always respected even if he didn't always agree with him, laughed. "To be honest, Raine, never expected to see you here as well." The smile faded. "In fact, I never expected to see you again."

"I—um—"

"I know. You've got questions. Well, I've got answers. I have an office down here. It's small and a bit of a mess, but it will serve." Hill took a breath.

"I'm ready to tell you everything."

Hill had his eyes locked on Raine's.

Like—he's sizing me up.

For what?

"I think I'm ready for that."

A bit of a smile returned.

"So, Lieutenant, you think . . . you can handle . . . the truth?"

Such a line. An old movie scene that every officer Raine ever knew could quote verbatim.

"Always preferred truth to its opposite, Captain."

"Yeah. I know that about you. Okay—follow me and we'll get started. 'Cause, you see . . . you don't have a lot of time."

As they walked toward Hill's office, the captain pointed to a little kitchenette off to the side. "Coffee? Glass of water?"

"No, sir. I'm fine." *Why is he stalling?*

They reached his office, and Raine took a seat facing Hill's desk. It was piled with papers, stacks of photos, and an open laptop. Behind the desk, another computer screen. On it was a paused video, cued to run.

"Tell me, Raine. What do you know about Apophis 99942?"

"Asteroid. Doing a flyby of our planet. Big. Seen the pictures."

"Right."

Hill hit something on his computer, and the frozen video on the screen began running. It showed a massive object moving through space. The asteroid.

"That animation?"

"No. Real. We've had some deep solar system projects out there. Not public knowledge, but they do intersecting loops of our solar system. Give us video feeds. Mainly to watch what other countries might be doing in space. At least, that was the idea."

"Jesus, Captain. That is mighty big."

Raine stared at the live image. This careening hammer threatening to destroy anything in its path.

If this rock from space actually was to hit Earth, we wouldn't have a chance.

"God. The size of a city. Over three miles wide. Good thing it will miss—"

"But here's the thing, Raine. It's *not* going to miss. It's going to be a hit. A direct hit."

The words hung in the room like the pronouncement of a death sentence.

Because in that instant . . . Raine knew that's exactly what they were.

"An asteroid that big? It would be—"

"A slate wiper."

The screen changed. Now it *was* animation, showing the asteroid plummeting through the atmosphere, a massive shock wave racing before it, walls of ocean water rising up, screaming away from the impact well before the asteroid hit.

Then—*impact.*

No sound. But there might as well have been, as the animation showed an explosion that seemed to bite off a massive chunk of the planet, sending country-sized pieces of Earth flying upward.

Hill touched his laptop.

The animation paused.

Raine shook his head. Hill had been his captain for two major counterinsurgency efforts, a by-the-book officer who stood by his men, and definitely stood by the truth.

So Raine didn't question what he'd just been told.

But it seemed unbelievable, unreal . . . *impossible.*

"I don't get it," he said. "The whole world thinks we're safe. They've been told."

Hill nodded, and gestured to the control room they had passed.

"See out there?"

"Couldn't miss it. Like Canaveral."

"Yeah. This is just one of many sites with a similar purpose. Here in America, and in other countries, too. Apophis is coming, and there's not a goddamned thing we can do about stopping it."

"So . . ." Raine took a breath.

The whole mad night had turned surreal. Maybe he'd blink, wake up, and find himself sleeping off the boilermakers from The Hook.

". . . we're doomed?"

Hill sat down. He leaned close. Raine thought—*God*—that he saw something in the captain's eyes he'd never seen before. Not in all the bloody streets and valleys of Afghanistan and Pakistan, as bad went to worse.

Were his eyes watering up?

"We couldn't stop Apophis," Hill said. "But that didn't mean we couldn't do *anything*."

He had looked away, and only now looked up at Raine.

A small smile, and Hill looked away again.

Something else was going on inside his captain, Raine realized.

"Ready for your orders?" Hill said.

Raine actually hesitated before responding. He was a soldier, though, and an officer was about to give him a mission. Somberly, professionally, he said, "Yes, sir."

Hill stood up.

"C'mon, then."

And Captain Hill led the way out of the office.

FOUR

THE ARK

They walked up the stairs behind the bank of workstations, toward a door Raine had noticed when he first descended into this command center. The way was illuminated by a mammoth screen that hovered above everything. The only thing on it was some sort of timer: *2d4h37m37s*.

The seconds rolling back, flying away, the time left until Apophis hit.

The time left until doom.

The two guards at the door moved aside as Hill waved a pass and the door opened.

"What you're about to see is not something a lot of people have."

Hill went in and Raine followed.

And what was there —Raine couldn't even put a name to it.

He and the captain stood side by side at a railing, looking down at a dark, massive object. One end came to a cone-shaped point. The sides had razor-toothed metal tracks, like what you'd see at a mine operation, ostensibly for digging into the ground and moving rock.

The base looked flat, and wider, like the bottom of a mammoth bullet. And—at that base—a door.

"Captain, I have to admit: I don't know what that is."

People in white coats walked around, holding tablet computers, touching them, looking at other screens.

And—surrounding the room—were the ever-present soldiers in full combat gear, holding their machine guns at ready.

As if they were expecting a raid.

"You're not supposed to," Hill said. "C'mon—I'll show you." He led Raine down another flight of stairs, so that they were on the ground next to . . . whatever it was. With it looming above him, Raine was impressed by just how tiny it made him feel. They walked around it, and he noticed little details without knowing what they were for. Finally, they completed their circuit.

"It's called an Ark, Lieutenant."

"Like Noah?"

"Yeah, I guess that's why they picked the name. The French call it L'Arche, the Chinese—with no connection to Noah—a *chun jia*. Means 'life pod' or something."

"Everyone has these?"

"Those with the tech. Those that the scientists who discovered the truth about Apophis 99942 thought could be trusted. Lot of countries still don't know. They still expect the flyby."

"An Ark. You're going to put people in there?"

Hill turned to him. "People *are* in there. Deep cryo. This one's hours away from insertion."

"And that means?"

"Each Ark gets buried somewhere, some nearly a mile deep—depends on the strata and rough predictions of seismic activity over the next century. Each one goes in with the survivors in cryo sleep—"

"Hang on. You call them survivors. This is to save people?"

"Right. Like Noah. Save some of humanity. The best and the brightest. Scientists, doctors, scholars. Each country with an Ark program formed a committee, also top secret." Hill looked at Raine. "I'll tell you—it's fucking amazing no one has found out."

"Sure is."

Hill pointed at the truck-sized Ark in front of them. "This one will get inserted, and it's due to emerge 120 years from now."

"Where—"

"Above my pay grade, Raine. All I know is the timing. It's thought that whatever radiation Apophis releases on impact should have subsided by then. The darkness created by the hit will have also long passed. Life may not survive, but as these Arks come up, they will bring hope for some kind of future for humanity."

"I imagine they carry seeds, tools, things to start again."

Now Hill had his eyes trained on him. Raine was so caught up in taking all this in, the global destruction to come, the Ark Project, this top secret place—that he forgot he had come here on orders.

What the hell could those orders be?

Hill put a hand on his shoulder.

"You see, Raine. That Ark down there has one empty and free cryo chamber. And you, my friend, are going in it."

Raine turned away. *I've been told that it's all over. And that thing down there, that's hope.*

That was his first reaction.

More than a century in the future.

Was that hope? Which was worse? Dying in a flash or emerging from under the ground to what could—he imagined—be hell.

Unlike the rest of the world, he now had an option.

To survive, to have hope, to possibly have a future. "I don't get it, Captain. You said . . . 'best and the brightest.' Pretty sure I don't qualify."

"What will the world be like a hundred years from now? Whole landmasses may have been blown away by the impact, bodies of water disappeared while new ones took shape. Will anything alive have survived? So yeah, we are sending down a lot of scientists. Doctors of all kinds. All the collected wisdom in the world in the Ark computers. But all that knowledge and learning still may need one thing—"

A woman—white coat, chiseled face, blond hair pulled back, librarian glasses—came up to Hill.

"They're ready for you down there, Captain."

She shot Raine a glance. Was that jealousy in her eyes? Envy? Pity?

The scientist turned sharply away.

"They may need some law and order, Raine. Security. Things could get a little hairy. Leadership may be the skill that could make the difference between life and death."

A small laugh. It sounded false.

"So amidst the Arks, we placed a scattering of military, all trained in difficult situations. War, disasters, all kinds of crises. Armed, and with an understanding of their mission: to protect the Ark Survivors, and lead them if necessary."

"Why me?"

"Well, it wasn't going to be you. *I* was supposed to be going.

Not my choice. They brought me in, told me the mission, and I agreed. But then—"

Now Hill looked away.

"They found something during one of the last medical checks. Some cancer. With enough time, treatable. Hell, I might even live. But we didn't have time. So . . ."

Hill looked back to Raine. "Would you send someone who's perhaps dying with cancer into the future? I offered to withdraw before they even came up with the idea."

He took a breath.

"I also suggested my replacement."

Neither said anything for a moment.

"Guess—I should say thanks. But I feel like I don't know enough. Who's in this Ark? What can I expect when it comes out? Where—"

"I know. Lots of questions. Follow me."

Hill moved toward the Ark.

Toward the open door.

Raine had to duck down as he slipped into the Ark.

Inside, in the pale light, the interior was quiet, a hushed temple of technology. Scientists moved around the room, some checking monitors, taking notes, others hitting keys.

Above them, surrounding the room, a belt of large screens mounted to the wall, the telltale signs of a serious computer embedded somewhere inside the Ark's walls.

Suddenly, a gentle female voice filled the room.

"Full system initialization completed."

Raine turned to Hill. "The computer talks?"

"Yes, and you can talk back to it. Ask it questions. When you emerge."

"Talking computer . . . that a good thing?"

Hill grinned. "Might be your best friend when you come out of your pod."

Raine now turned and looked away from the monitors. In a circle, sarcophaguslike chambers sat arrayed like spokes; a dozen such chambers. Almost like a bizarre funeral parlor—more like coffins than anything that might save life.

A spiral staircase curled down. He wondered: storage floors below, holding the tools, the seeds, the bulding blocks needed for a new world? He heard someone come up to Hill. "We're all ready, Captain."

All but one chamber was closed tight. One still lay open, waiting.

"Everyone else is already in cryo, Raine. This Ark is due to leave soon. So to your questions, who these people are—it's all in the briefing you will get when you awaken, during emergence. The computer can answer any questions you might have. It will also be able to give you an update on the outside environment well before you reach the surface."

Raine nodded.

"Guess you're not *asking* me to go."

Hill smiled. "Yeah. It's an order, Raine. Funny feeling, isn't it? To know that the whole world will be destroyed except for you and the other Ark survivors. And yet somehow—it doesn't exactly feel like a gift."

"All the Arks come up at the same time?"

"No. The scientists thought it best—safest—if the Arks came up at staggered periods. That allows for the greatest chance of survival. We don't know what the world will be like. Some come up earlier, others much later."

"And mine—120 years."

"Exactly."

The doctor with the librarian glasses stepped into the Ark. "All set, Captain."

"Okay." Hill turned to Raine. "Lieutenant, as I said, this one is ready for insertion. Just got to get you in there."

"Now?" he asked. Raine hadn't thought it was going to happen so soon.

Hill didn't bother answering. He simply went over to a side wall of the Ark and grabbed what looked like a space suit.

"This—is an Ark suit. Get into it, if you would."

And then he tossed the suit at Raine.

FIVE

THE DEEP SLEEP

Raine lay down on the cool bed of the cryo pod.

A trio of doctors whizzed around him, checking the fit of the suit, looking at the Ark's monitors, then coming back to check small readouts on the suit itself.

Hill had disappeared, and that made Raine uneasy.

None of the doctors said much, just a "lift your arm, please" and "turn to your side."

Their bedside manner sucked.

Finally, Hill came back. Just in time for Raine to notice that something had begun swinging over the cryo pod from the side, resembling a hypodermic with a dozen wires trailing from it.

Except this hypo was the size of a bazooka.

"Mighty big needle," he said.

"Yeah." Hill turned to the doctors. "Can you give us a minute?"

"We don't have a lot of time," one of the white coats said.

"Just a few minutes." His tone didn't leave the impression this was a request. Same ol' captain, Raine thought.

They backed off, busying themselves at the consoles positioned around the perimeter of the Ark.

"In a few minutes this device will implant something in you called 'nanotrites.' Experimental. It's not even something we would use on the battlefield."

"Then why do I want them?"

"Because of their potential. The test cases show that nanotrites do some pretty amazing things. In case of severe tissue damage, organ failure—even a momentary cessation of primal functions—the nanotrites are amazing cellular engines. They promote incredibly rapid tissue growth. They can even restart organ functions."

"And the downside?"

"We don't know all the side effects. Not in the slightest. Could be there's a price to pay for using them, but if there is, we haven't had time to find it. And, they are not the miracle nanomachines we thought they were."

"You're losing me."

"Nanomachines—biologically engineered micromachines. We've been playing with them for decades. *These* seem to work. And because of that potential, we feel it's too good an opportunity to pass up. We don't know what kind of world you're going to wake up to, but we think these nanotrites will be pretty useful. Everyone who went into the Ark has had them implanted."

"I'm guessing I don't have a choice about them. I mean, you said they haven't been fully tested. Could be I'd be better off without them . . ."

"No. You're going, so you get them. Consider that an order."

"And fingers crossed on side effects."

Hill grinned. "Send us a note back."

Raine looked at the doctors, waiting, still standing back.

"Captain . . ." he said quietly.

"Yes?"

"The asteroid. Most of the world predicts a miss. Then a handful of scientists predict a hit. How'd that happen?"

"That's the other thing. Can't say I fully understand it." Hill came a bit closer. "An astrophysicist at Palomar was the first to see something was off about the asteroid, then someone in the London Observatory. They were professional friends, so they communicated their findings to each other, and as soon as they alerted their governments, they were ordered to keep it quiet. More scientists made the discovery . . . all seeing something different than what was predicted."

"Which was?"

"The asteroid acted erratically when it passed close to any zone with a measurable gravitational force. Somehow, that gravitational force, which in most cases should have been insignificant, or at least measurable and predictable, caused a dramatic shift in the asteroid's trajectory, a definite wobble. Most astrophysicists would write it off to random erratic behavior. But for this group, even with Apophis so far away, they saw it as something else."

"Captain," the lead doctor said. "It's time."

Hill held up his hand. "They were finally able to measure it, Raine. Whatever caused the trajectory to wobble and shift . . . could be measured. And all anyone knew was that there had to be something within the asteroid itself, something due to its unknown mineral makeup, where it came from . . . what it was made up of . . ."

"That caused the effect?"

"Exactly. Another unknown, Lieutenant."

"Seems to be all you have to offer today."

"It's time," a doctor said, more firmly. Hill nodded.

Raine, wearing the bulky Ark suit, raised his right hand up as sharply to his brow as he could.

"Last time I'll have to do that, sir."

Hill nodded, grinned, and then saluted back.

"Okay," he said to the doctors. "We're all set."

The long, gunlike device came down slowly, precisely to Raine's neck.

The female doctor gave Raine the play-by-play.

"Lieutenant, you will feel the metal tip press against your neck. The nanotrites need to reach critical velocity within the insertion device. It's really a minicentrifuge. Once they enter, they will travel immediately to your brain stem."

"And you can't knock me out for this?"

A small smile from the doctor.

Guess it's too late to ask her out on a date, Raine thought. Late, by maybe a hundred years.

"For the first moments, you can't have anything in your system to knock you out. No sedation. Full brain activity is required."

"Then full brain activity they shall get."

"Moments after they enter your body, the drip into the suit will pump in the sedative. You won't be awake when the full cryo process begins."

"Which I guess is a good thing, hm?"

"Yeah." A pause. "Good luck, Lieutenant."

Raine felt the metal press against his skin. Cool. Just a bit of pressure.

Then—something sharp.

• • •

A definite prick, much worse than giving blood or an IV.

The needle going deep hurt, but it was followed by a burning sensation that made his eyes water.

It was as if fire filled his throat. He felt it migrate to the back of his neck, near the brain stem.

Then up.

The lights in the room took on an intense brightness. The people in the room turned into ghostly shadows.

He barely felt the injection device pull away . . . because now his entire skull felt that warmth. He had read somewhere that the brain has no nerves, so no feeling there. Probably a good thing. Still, he wanted to scratch his head, covered by the Ark suit skullcap.

But that thought was interrupted as the brightness began to build, turning from a simple fire into a white heat that made him feel as though he lay in the dead center of a massive incandescent bulb.

Then—suddenly—the brightness, the light . . . faded.

The sporadic explosions of heat from his head eased.

He wanted to say something, but saying something had somehow turned impossible. Right, he remembered as the team watched, the sedative . . .

Even thoughts were difficult now. One came to him: *Close my eyes.*

Then another thought: *Sleep would be nice.*

Then: nothing.

SIX

BURIED ALIVE

Hill stood at the door of the Ark, gazing around the vessel with a strange look in his eyes.

The computer spoke in its muted voice. Designed to be soothing, it was anything but.

"Full cryo procedures successfully concluded. Ark 38 is now ready for hibernation."

Then a pause.

"Hibernation procedure to begin in 120 seconds."

The head scientist came over to Hill. "Captain, it's time to leave."

Hill took a last look and walked down the steps out of the Ark.

"Sixty seconds to hibernation . . . fifty seconds . . ."

He joined the full team of scientists ringed around the Ark. The guards—while remaining in position, guns held tight—all now stared at the amazing machine in the center of the room. Hill slipped on an earpiece, his radio link connected to the base's communication network. Totally secure. No one would be able to eavesdrop, to hear the chatter and wonder what the hell the government was so secretly burying in the ground.

"Thirty seconds . . . twenty seconds . . ."

The entire room counted along silently, lips moving.

"Ten . . . nine . . . eight . . . seven . . . "

Hill looked around the room. Did some of these people look at this and think, There goes the only way to survive the coming cataclysm? Wishing that they were inside? Watching all this happen with such torturous, mixed feelings.

Including him.

He had been ready to go. But sometimes nature played tricks. What was the line?

We make plans. So do fools. The gods . . . laugh.

"Zero . . ."

The speakers filled the room with the soft vocal tones of the computer. Then the stairway folded smoothly into the Ark. The door—specially designed to resist extreme pressure from the outside—slid into place and locked tight with a *whoosh*.

The computer grew silent.

The Ark was now sealed tight.

Hill turned away and called out to the guards by the large hangar-sized doors to the side.

"Okay," he said. "Let's go."

Hill sat in the front passenger seat of the Huey Workhorse chopper. A matching chopper flew beside it.

Attached beneath the choppers were two massive chains with giant links strong enough to hold a liner's anchor, or a house, or a stack of cargo containers.

Morning in the Rockies. A beautiful clear sky. A gorgeous blue sky.

Couldn't be more beautiful.

He looked ahead and saw the Ark building. As he watched, the roof of the building began to move. Even over the sound of the helicopters' blades, Hill could hear the sound of metal grinding as the roof panels slid back on their tracks.

His chopper pilot spoke quietly to his counterpart.

"Ready to deploy, Alpha Two."

Hill couldn't hear the other pilot, but he could guess the man said "Roger," because the two choppers—the biggest anywhere in the world—banked to position themselves over the opening.

Hill looked down, into the now gaping maw of the massive building. The Ark sat there, looking like a misshapen black egg.

Not a bad metaphor, he thought. An egg to give birth to humanity's only hope.

If we're not to go the way of the dinosaur.

Which made him pause. He had to wonder: did anyone raise the idea that maybe they were meant to disappear?

Probably had never even been considered.

It was too late to consider now. The choppers were in position.

The pilot spoke again: "Alpha Two—ready to lower on your go." Then: "Lowering now."

And the chain started down, a clanking sound erupting loudly from the rear of the chopper. It was hard to see the Ark now that it was directly under the helicopter, but above the pilot, a monitor showed the progress of the chain and its hook.

Until—

"Turning five degrees . . ."

A small twitch to swing the hook into the top of the Ark.

"And—*locked*," the pilot said, throwing a switch.

The pilot looked over at Hill.

"Got it, sir."

"Pull her up," Hill said.

And together, as if carrying out a carefully practiced ballet move, the two choppers began to rise. After a wobble when the full weight of the Ark hit the two machines—slowing, nearly stopping them—the choppers continued up. The Ark rose out of its birthplace, like dozens of others around the world had already. This was one of the few left to be inserted.

Buried.

Finally, the Ark cleared the top of the building, and the choppers set out on a course to the west. Avoiding towns, highways . . .

Questions.

Some Arks had been transported inside the belly of big transport carriers. Still others in oversized freight train cars. The goal: for nobody to see an Ark.

But here, this late in the game in this part of the West, they would take a course that would give them the least chance of being seen without sacrificing haste.

And for those who did see . . . what would they say?

Besides—in a few days, everyone would have a lot more to talk about.

The asteroid. The Ark Project concluded—and revealed. Doom on its way. Everyone would know the truth.

They roared over the nearby Colorado hills.

The choppers hovered over the site of the excavation, a giant tapered crater in the middle of the desert. The man-made hole narrowed to a point, a massive shaft where the Ark would be inserted—deep, past the bedrock—before being covered with the piles of rubble and dirt by the waiting tractors.

Would it be enough? Hill wondered. Would there be enough protection in the thousand feet of dirt and sand, the massive chunks of granite and basalt piled on top of the sleeping Ark?

It was anybody's guess. The only thing the scientists were clear about was that they couldn't be sure.

"Terra incognita," one said. Estimates of the level of destruction were given with sheepish looks at handheld computers. The numbers seemed to be changing all the time.

No one fucking knew.

"Lowering the Ark, sir," the pilot said.

"Carry on," Hill said. The pilot toggled his radio:

"Lowering Ark station 1138 on my go!" He maneuvered the helicopter, making slight adjustments. "And . . . go!"

The sound of the winch in the belly of the oversized chopper began groaning, the chains rolling out.

The chains so long that they had been rolled on mammoth wheels, the rolled spools stretching from the floor to the roof of the chopper.

Hill got out of his seat.

He walked back to the winch, where he could look down the opening, watching as the Ark moved smoothly down from the sky—with amazing accuracy—right into the crater that had been made for it.

The Arks were designed so they could burrow in either direction. But in this case, this deep shaft had been made well ahead of time.

The scientists' preference.

Let's reduce the chances for a screwup. We'll place the Ark.

So the next time—the only time—the thing would burrow was over a hundred years from now.

The chain kept playing out, and the Ark slipped deeper into the narrow shaft at the bottom of the crater, sliding into it like a bullet into a chamber. A bullet of humanity being shot into the future.

Could have been me down there, Hill thought for probably the thousandth time.

Except—fate had other plans. And what of Raine—was he the right guy? he wondered.

Raine certainly had nothing tying him to this doomed world. No wife, no kids, his own family long gone. Raine kept quiet about whatever passed as his personal life.

For Raine, it was all about the mission.

And what exactly was that mission?

To survive? Yes, but it was more than that. To emerge and locate some of the caches of supplies—the weapons, tools, and precious seeds that might make food on the planet once more.

And foremost, Raine—and the other soldiers on different Arks—were to keep control and protect the survivors.

In case things didn't go right.

In case everything is worse than we ever imagined it could be.

Did Raine know that was the real mission? Face the unknown, and—if necessary—lead what's left of humanity?

The Ark had disappeared.

But the winch kept moving, and the chain clanged its way down into the shaft, link by hefty link. Hill squatted there, peering down, watching its progress.

Until the winch stopped. Then Hill looked up at the machine. There were a few meters of chain left on the spool, but the Ark had hit its final resting place.

Like a strange kind of burial.

He muttered the word to himself. A benediction.

"Amen," he said.

And then he stood up.

Even as the last meters of chain rolled back onto each chopper's winch, a team of bulldozers were already at work pushing the mounds of dirt and rock back into the hole, like planting a bulb.

In hours, it would look like any other spot in the desert.

Back in his seat, the pilot looked over at him.

"Want to stay a bit, Captain?"

"No," Hill said. "I think we're done here."

Only after the words passed his lips did he register the irony.

We're done here.

True fact, he thought. In more ways than one.

"Take us back, Sergeant."

And together, the choppers banked slightly and flew off into the brilliant blue sky.

SEVEN

END OF DAYS

Genereral Martin Cross looked over at Colonel James Casey. They stood in the control room for an Ark station.

Except this was unlike any other Ark station.

Even amidst all the secrecy that surrounded the project—and all the madness, the panic, the rioting that surrounded the revelation of the doom heading toward the planet—there were things people had not been told. Even after people learned of the existence and horrifying implications of the Ark Project, there were still secrets.

Like *this* place.

People, many of them, seemed somehow able to accept the premise of the Arks. Saving those few would guarantee hope for humanity, and deep down—possibly on a genetic level—the biological imperative for the species was kicking in.

But not everyone. One Ark station had been uncovered in

northern Oregon and then overrun. It was to be one of the last Arks inserted, and now the place was trashed: computers and monitors smashed, the innards of the Ark ripped out.

Civilians—self-described militia—had shot soldiers and hung their bodies on the fences as if it was their fault. The Ark and its bank of controlling computers had been totally destroyed. Shockingly, even the intended passengers were executed, as if they had done something wrong.

Still, with locations and the selection process secret, the Ark Project remained largely protected.

But there was one secret that even the military brass protecting those other stations didn't know about. Especially now.

Because it would be like throwing kerosene on a fire.

There would be a few . . . super Arks.

Mammoth, building-sized Arks. Arks designed to hold nearly three hundred people, all selected—and this was the tough part—strictly for their age, gender, and genetic makeup. A pool of people whose genotype would guarantee diversity, enough diversity so that whatever humanity survived would have the full range of genetic components the human species might need.

To survive. To thrive.

Only a couple could be built before the end arrived. But scientists knew that even a few such super Arks could make the genetic difference between the end of humanity or a new beginning.

And so it was here, hidden by a building, that one of the super Arks had been buried. It was limited, of course, by how deep they could place it. One of the scientists had told Cross that it was a "crap shoot."

"We're just not sure it's deep enough," the man had said.

Could be all three hundred people in deep cryo would be crushed when Apophis came roaring down.

A big secret.

But not nearly as big as the one Cross and Colonel Casey had. For like all secrets, there was always one more level. And now it was time for that secret—for that plan—to start.

After all, one look out the windows told everyone that time was clearly up.

Cross watched Casey on the phone, listening.

"Yes, Madame President," Casey said. "I know. We have it on the monitors."

Casey, an adjutant to President Campbell, had been the administration's special advisor on dealing with the dozens of counterinsurgency "wars" that spread from the mountains of Tora Bora to nearly every continent in the world.

Antarctica had seemingly been spared.

And Casey, though an advisor to the President, had begun talking about how things were being mishandled, the country's power squandered—and not just behind closed doors.

Eventually Cross took note, and he started meeting with Casey.

Discussing the failure of leadership. A failure of vision. Of the need for change—and not just another meaningless election.

And this was well before Apophis.

They both realized that what they talked about was treason, revolt. But that was a chance they were willing to take.

Casey became Cross's eyes and ears in the White House. They had formed a bond, shared a vision—even if they didn't know yet what to do about it.

Now Cross looked out the window. He saw daylight, but he also saw the sky filled with the yellow-white streaks, the chunks of the advance meteors racing ahead of Apophis 99942 as if trying to escape its relentless wrath.

Maybe that's what it is, he thought. The asteroid was the avenger of the Almighty. Just payment for a world that wasted an opportunity to master it. It made things easier to think of Apophis that way.

Cross turned back to the monitor.

There it was.

Apophis. Not computer animation, but in wide-screen high-definition. The city-sized asteroid raced toward the planet, its trajectory taking it so close to the moon, which itself would be spared.

Cross looked at the other screens.

And there's humanity, he thought. Humanity responding to the onrush of doom.

People had climbed the Eiffel Tower . . . for whatever reason. Some falling off, others tossing down Molotov cocktails to the crazed crowds below.

Madness.

Beijing police firing into thousands of rioters, mowing them down.

Around the White House stood a wall of soldiers, as the ring of an enraged mob grew tighter around them and the building; the breaking point couldn't be far away.

And on and on.

Streets in Chicago burning like they hadn't since the great fire. Christ, a People's Government had even been set up in San Francisco, claiming to be in charge of the city.

Demanding answers.

Who made the goddamn Ark selections?

Who decided who lived, who died?

Who indeed?

Cross started to turn away when Colonel Casey came over, his last call with President Campbell over.

The President had shown nerves of glass even before this crisis.

Now she was shattered, buried in the White House bunker, grimly awaiting the end.

"So?" Cross said to the colonel.

"Just about done."

"And? She have any clue?"

Casey shook his head. "No. Just a 'good luck' as we sink the last Ark."

"Great. That means we're ready. We should begin then, hm?"

They both looked at the monitor, at the mammoth asteroid.

Not religious at all, Cross said the word:

"God!"

Apophis was due to fly within a hundred miles of the lunar surface. The gravitational pull had been calculated, taking into account the speed and estimated mass of the asteroid. Even entering the asteroid's various course shifts that had occurred in deep space—the cause still unknown—it would only soar close to the moon.

A flyby for the satellite.

But Cross and Casey could see what the satellite cameras picked up—the thing that scared the hell out of them, and had helped force their hand concerning this Ark:

The asteroid seemed to *shiver* as it came close to the moon.

A definite shake, then wobbling, the back-and-forth weaving as if something inside the asteroid reacted to the moon's gravitational force, or maybe whatever lay at the moon's core itself.

In a way no one could have predicted.

Because—they both could see it—the mammoth asteroid tilted slightly toward Earth's moon.

"Christ. It's going to hit it," Casey said. "It's going to hit the goddamn moon."

"That can't be," Cross said.

But it was.

It made no sense. How could that happen? And what of their plans? Did he even *want* Apophis to miss?

And yet what occurred in the next few seconds told him that—if anything—their plans might be more . . . relevant. More important. More vital.

The two men just stood there, both saying nothing.

They watched the edge of Apophis smack into the lunar surface like a jagged-edged cue ball. A chunk of the moon shot out, flying wildly off into space, perhaps to inflict the same damage on another planet that Apophis would soon deal to Earth.

At first Apophis itself seemed intact. But as it flew past the impact gouge—the gargantuan hole it had bitten out of the moon—the asteroid split into three nearly equal pieces, each veering in slightly different directions.

All three smaller pieces still resolutely heading toward Earth.

Other screens showed the mayhem and horror around the world. One by one, as if resigned that human news mattered no longer, the media outlets had all changed to show Apophis, now transformed into three hammers about to fall.

Undoubtedly some crazed commentators—seeing the impact with the moon—started preaching deliverance.

We're saved!

Until it dawned on everyone now that three bullets streamed toward Earth.

Cross turned to Casey. "Let's do this fast, Colonel."

"Yes, General," Casey said.

Cross nodded. Casey had one master. It was not the President, not the head of the Joint Chiefs. Not even his wife, lost to her booze and left behind to die in leafy Georgetown.

"Give the orders," Cross said.

Immediately the troops surrounding this Ark station went into full battle alert. The gates slammed closed. No one would get in or out, no matter what the hell their clearance.

Cross raced ahead of Casey, both dressed in Ark suits.

They had passed into the inner staging area, and once they did that, another phalanx of loyal—if terrified—guards would see that no one got in, and no one got out.

Casey went to the lieutenant in charge of the planned survivors, a respectable list of doctors, scientists, scholars, and even, yes, a theologian.

Theologian . . .

Lot of use that would be.

Casey delivered the order.

"Lieutenant, by order of the President of the United States."

Casey handed the lieutenant the orders on White House stationery, with the recognizable hand of the President.

Perhaps the document wasn't even really needed, not with Casey's say-so.

Still—

"Sir, the Ark passengers—they are to be—"

Casey snapped.

"You can read the damn order, Lieutenant! The situation has changed. The security needs are different. I have alerted the team who will be going in their place."

That team—all handpicked, all military, all knowledgeable about what was happening . . .

All loyal to the core to Cross.

The lieutenant's eyes told of his unasked question.

Any chance. Perhaps. I could—

But Casey needed to keep a squad down below to keep the esteemed guests in order while the Ark and its new passengers got planted.

"C'mon," Cross said. He barely could restrain himself. "Do your goddamn duty, Lieutenant. Same as in war."

Then in a gesture so false that he barely could believe he did it, Cross raised a hand to the young soldier's shoulder.

"None of us wanted this, Lieutenant. This is about the future, about humanity's survival."

The lieutenant nodded. Then, a crisp salute.

"Yes, sir."

The soldier turned and headed down to give the bad news to the once hopeful Ark survivors, now all turned prisoners until the end came.

They walked hurriedly to the Ark.

Casey pressed on his earbud, hearing something.

"Then, yes, yes. We'll be right there." Cross looked at the colonel, questioning. Casey said, "General, something's interfering with communication. Hope we didn't wait too long."

"Less time, less chance of a fuck-up, Colonel."

"The others are getting in place. Cryo procedures begun."

Cross nodded.

Their Ark would enter its shaft right at the Ark station site, close to a massive cache of weapons and supplies.

"Good," Cross said.

He had the thought: this day of global disaster could be the greatest day of his military career.

• • •

Cross watched Casey lay down on the cryo bed.

The Ark door had already been shut. The computer soothingly told them how long until insertion began.

Cross had been hands-on in all the preparations. No bit of tech would screw up his plans. He made one last check to confirm that the date change for emergence had been fully locked into the system.

A tap of the button brought the confirmation of the soothing voice.

"Ark emergence . . . set for 2105."

Cross watched as Casey received the nanotrites injection. The colonel's eyes closed, the deep sleep beginning.

Outside . . . had all discipline begun melting away? Would the guards sworn to protect them hold steady, ready to shoot and kill as needed?

No matter.

In seconds the Ark would lower. In minutes it would be buried.

As Cross lay back, he thought of the one thing that worried him:

Their Ark would emerge first. Years before any of the others.

But would that date be too soon?

Was there any way to know, to even guess?

He felt the needle at his neck puncture his skin, the burning sensation intense as the nanotrites were injected into him.

He felt the heat and then the tingling that the scientists—all watching outside on a monitor—unquestioning, dutiful—had told him about.

Eyes started to close.

He heard rumbling, the Ark beginning its journey down below the substrata of the ground.

He never saw the pod cover close over him.

He never heard the sound of the Ark's drill system taking it ever deeper into the ground at the same time as the excavated rubble buried it, a seal of rock and dirt.

The plan was done. The die cast.

The future, now altered, now something imagined, to be created by the *vision* of one man.

But for now that man slept like thousands of others around the planet . . .

EIGHT

THE CAMERAS

How many cameras around the world were kept running, trying to capture every moment when Apophis hit?

Well before it even got within fifty miles of the surface, advance shock waves had flattened whole forests, created mountain-sized wave surges, triggered violent shifts in geological plates worldwide as tsunamis erupted in all the world's oceans, water and land rising madly to greet the asteroid as it came close.

And still . . . it had not yet hit.

Some people burrowed, some went to high ground. Some got drunk, some made love amidst tears. Others took their own lives before anything happened.

Many did nothing.

And those waiting cameras? Most stopped working well before impact. But a few—specially built and placed in fortified steel bunkers with the same portholes found on the deep submersibles—kept recording and transmitting up to the very last moments.

Apophis had become three asteroids, yet its power had been diminished.

A direct hit could trigger shifts in the undersea mountain ranges, the mid-Atlantic ridge rising as plates violently moved and new volcanic fissures sprouted everywhere.

A direct hit could destroy cities, even entire countries, instantly killing all life for hundreds, even thousands, of miles while changing the very terrain of the planet.

A direct hit could trigger mammoth fissures and cracks in the volatile plates of the Pacific Ring of Fire. Nearly a third of the earth's crust would swell and crash together in just a few violent moments, matched in violence only by the original fiery formation of the planet itself.

Still—a few cameras resisted the first shock waves, the massive blasts of winds that dwarfed hurricane speeds.

They continued to record right up until the moment of impact.

Sending their images out via satellite until that communication link ended, all the satellites rendered useless.

And then at last the cameras would be turned into powder, dust.

Like the billions of people.

Like the millions of buildings.

Like the continent-size swaths of land that, in an instant, turned much of Planet Earth into a landscape that resembled the moon.

Desolation, devastation.

Those last cameras finally vanishing along with it all.

It seemed like the end of the world.

And for most living things, it was.

ONE

THE WASTELAND
≈ 2112

NINE

WELCOME TO THE FUTURE

The first thing Raine felt was a stabbing pain at the back of his neck.

Instinctively, he reached up with his right hand to rub that spot as if it might ease the way-beyond migraine level of agony.

But his hand didn't even respond.

Then, confused by what seemed to be a clear command to *rise*, his hand finally did pop up, as if released from invisible netting.

It rose only inches. Then it hit something.

He realized then that his eyes were shut. It hadn't even occurred to him to open them. If he could make the pain simply stop, maybe he could go back to sleep. Sleep seemed like a good thing, something he wanted, needed. And he couldn't help thinking it would be easier to slip back to sleep if he kept his eyes closed.

But he heard someone talking.

The voice was muffled at first. A woman. Talking to him? A dream? He wondered.

"Emergency extraction of Ark 1138. Revival procedures begun on remaining vital pods."

The voice sounded familiar. He had heard this voice before. Someone he knew. But her words made no sense to him.

None at all.

"Evaluation of pods complete. Pods one through eleven have had essential systems destroyed. Revival impossible. Pod twelve undamaged. Revival progressing normally."

No sense. Wait . . .

Ark. Pods.

Still, the fiber of memory was so *thin*. He could barely connect what those words meant. Ark? Pods? He mulled them over and over.

Until—he opened his eyes.

He saw something only inches above him through the clear protective mask of a helmet. Swirls of smoke, tinged purple and green. And he heard a whooshing sound. On, then off. Then again.

Ark. Pods.

And then he remembered: *I am in a pod. Inside this thing, this Ark.*

He licked his lips and tasted something strange. Something had coated his lips—a slick, metallic-tasting balm.

"Opening pod twelve," the woman said.

Now he remembered that, too. It was the computer.

He heard the sound of things moving. Felt a rumbling under him. Then the thing that had him sealed in here, the cover that restrained his hand from moving up, began to slowly open.

And the sounds suddenly became louder.

• • •

"Caution: emergency fire system in operation. Remain in your pod unit until complete."

Another bit of memory came to him. Along with Ark, pods, computer . . . *I'm Lieutenant Nicholas Raine.*

I was sent *here.*

More *shooshing* noises. Raine turned left, a slight angle of the head, to see a whitish cloud being shot out, aimed somewhere in the back of the Ark.

He tried to sit up.

Again his body seemed glued in place, but eventually he could raise his head, only making the pain at the back of his neck worse.

Then his hand moved over to the edges of the pod. His fingers closed on the edge, grabbing as best they could with gloves on. His actions were deliberate, like his body was planning some terribly complex strategic move.

He lowered his head and then brought it up again, this time pulling himself up, performing the incredible feat of sitting up.

Sparks shot out from a wall ahead of him. From above, a sharp cracking sound. More sparks flew from where he saw exposed wires.

The colored smoke . . . that came from the automated fire extinguishers hitting the fiery spots, picking up the ghostly lights from the computer. Until they stopped.

Pod twelve. That's me, he thought. Pod twelve is okay. Pod twelve survives.

He looked at the other pods. One was cracked, matching a crack that ran straight across the floor . . . and stopped only a foot from his pod.

Another pod was split open. But whoever was in it just lay there. It dawned on him: *I'm the only one alive.*

Something had happened deep underground. The Ark had been damaged, the pods malfunctioning or wrecked by whatever had occurred.

Maybe not a good idea to just stay here, he thought. Despite the computer's advice.

Getting his legs to move, though, was proving to be as difficult as moving his head had been.

But with thinking and planning, he eventually got to a standing position . . . and walked over to the computer.

He opened the face mask of his helmet. The extinguishers putting out the fire had slowed, then stopped completely.

Good—I won't be cooked in here.

The computer talks. And he remembered that he had been told he could talk back to the computer.

"What happened?"

The computer didn't answer. He started to repeat the question.

"What—"

"Seismic occurrence, marked at a depth of 219 meters. Pressure exceeded Ark specifications. Electrical and control systems began to fail. Emergency extraction begun at 0930 hours."

Raine nodded. Guess one didn't have to thank a computer.

"Anyone else survive?" he asked, a question he was pretty sure he knew the answer to.

Another hesitation.

Then:

"No."

Yes, lucky me, he thought. Then, another question:

"The year?"

"By the Julian calendar, June 11, 2114. That calendar is no longer accurate."

The calendar was wrong. How could a calendar be wrong? How could time be different?

What could happen that could change time, days, months?

Then a last word. The last bit of a puzzle. Falling into place in his mind like a wooden jigsaw.

He said the word: "Apophis?"

The computer showed video. Appearing on the big screen high above the pods.

He saw the asteroid racing through space.

The screen went black.

"Attention: systems unstable. Immediate evacuation of Ark 1138 is necessary."

Were there fires still burning somewhere within the Ark? Could this still turn into a tomb for him?

He heard a sound, turning.

The Ark's porthole door was opening. He flipped down his mask. Even with that amount of time passing—accurate calendar or not—he wasn't sure if it was safe to breathe outside. It disturbed him, to think he could have traveled all this time only to die once he stepped outside. Radiation. The air. Whatever the hell the world had been transformed into.

The door kept opening while he stood there, watching, nearly petrified by the idea of leaving this.

Like being born, he thought.

The stairs had cascaded down to the ground. He heard the sound of rock crunching, a grinding noise. The Ark, he noticed, sat tilted at an angle to one side.

Could be goddamn anywhere.

But with the door open, at least he knew . . . *I'm not underwater.*

"Evacuate now. All systems shutting down."

The door to the future—his future—lay open.

With his legs wobbly, his whole body still weak and undependable, he walked out.

Step after tentative step.

The light outside was blinding.

Raine brought a hand up to shield his eyes. His shaky legs were barely up to getting him down the steps, and he felt as though he might tilt forward and fall flat on his face.

He heard his own breathing in his mask.

Heavy, labored sound.

Can all my organs work okay after sleeping for so long? My heart, lungs, everything? What about muscle atrophy? And yet, for someone who just slept a hundred years, he didn't feel too bad. It certainly seemed as though his brain was sluggish to respond, though. Memory shaky. Thinking more cloudy than clear.

It was—

He looked up. No clouds here, just brilliant sun.

A sunny day.

Raine took another step down.

Words surfacing like debris after a shipwreck.

I've been *in a shipwreck,* he thought.

He touched the ground. Uneven, lot of rocks scattered here. The brilliant sun making it hard to take in the full landscape.

Was the sun always this bright?

Or was that new, in this year? Whatever year it was.

He brought his other foot off the step, now fully off the Ark. Fully born into this world.

Seeing nothing around him.

Which is when he felt something wrap itself tight around his neck.

An arm.

• • •

The choke hold closed his windpipe. Another hand ripped off his helmet, exposing his head and throat.

Then before him, the face of a monster blotted out the sun. All he could see were eyes.

A monster, except that he now saw that it actually was someone wrapped in ragged cloth, like a mummy, all the way up to their eyes. Colored splotches like tattoos on the skin. Dark, narrow eyes looking right at his.

Raine tried to free himself from the man behind him, wondering how many were attacking.

But his muscles were too slow, too weak to respond, and the man in front of him—he now knew that the thing in front of him wasn't a monster, but a human—held a knife that caught the shimmering brilliant sun like a deadly jewel.

The man shifted the knife in his hands, enjoying the moment. His eyes on Raine's, the life slowly draining out of them. He brought the knife to Raine's neck.

Didn't last long, Raine thought.

Not much more than the others, all dead, inside.

The blade tip touched skin. Right above the choke hold, under the chin, tip pointing up. Was this a ritual or simply something being enjoyed? The suffocation started kicking in.

Not long now.

"Die, Ark man."

Words. From a human. The first he had heard in such a long time.

One last attempt by Raine to wriggle free, a bit of a kick with one leg. But whoever held him was big, the hold powerful.

Then—a crack.

And instead of the knife slicing up, the man in front of him bloomed a red hole in his forehead.

Another crack, and Raine felt the choke hold magically release as if he were sprung from a trap.

The attacker in front fell forward, coming to kneel in front of Raine. The one in back just stumbled away before falling backward.

Shots, Raine registered.

Someone shot them. Then the sound of an engine, and from the distance—from behind a rocky outcrop, a jagged triangular piece of stone stories high—he saw a car.

Well, not exactly a car.

The thing was open, exposed, and looked more like a cannibalized version of a dozen vehicles than any car Raine could recognize. A pair of metal roll bars were the only protection on the top. It was the strangest thing with wheels he had ever seen.

And yet, driving it, coming straight at him, was someone who looked almost normal.

At least he wasn't wrapped in tattered pieces of cloth from top to bottom. No face painting.

He drove with one hand. His other held a rifle, barrel pointing straight up.

The vehicle sent a spume of dust flying behind it.

Raine waited.

The vehicle screamed to a dusty stop in front of him.

"Better get in, stranger. Unless you want to play with more of them."

Raine looked at the man. Scars. Skin a dark bronze, as if toasted by the brutal sun. He didn't let go of the gun.

"In? Why? Where will we—"

"You got questions. I got answers. Some, at least. But with those two dead, a lot more bandits will be heading here. We got to move. *Now.*"

Raine looked down at the bodies, registering that the man in the crazed vehicle was his savior.

"Get in my damn buggy."

Buggy. That what he calls this thing? This mutated version of what was once a car?

"Right."

Raine stepped into the vehicle, which pulled away the moment his right foot left the ground.

"Hold on. And take this."

The man handed him a rifle. "I'm guessing you know how to use it."

"Yeah." Raine had to shout over the sound of the uncovered, unmuffled engine, animalistic in its deep roar.

"Keep your eyes peeled. Left, right. You see them, take a shot."

The buggy raced over the ground, bouncing crazily with each indentation or pile of rocks it hit, sending Raine shooting up and down.

He felt his stomach tighten, nauseous. An aftereffect of his cryo sleep?

He licked his lips. Thirsty. And maybe, despite the stomach-churning ride, hungry? He didn't know.

" 'Kay, stranger. We got to go through there. That ravine. Quickest way back to my settlement. And I'm thinking . . . quick is good."

"Right," Raine said again, dully. As if it was an obvious fact. *Right.*

"Eyes open. Got it? I'm Dan Hagar." He looked over at Raine and grinned. "Nice to meet you."

"Yeah."

Raine held the gun tight. And now, like some primal memory returning, he let his hand slide down to the trigger. He looked down at the gun. He didn't know the brand, looked almost homemade. Like a standard army issue M16 rifle someone pieced together. But it was a weapon he guessed he could shoot. One that—

(It came back to him . . .)

—he had killed with.

He was good.

A good shot. He remembered that now.

The buggy screamed into the chasm made by two stony fingers of what looked to be the beginning of a pair of mountain ranges.

Raine's hand tightened around the trigger hold.

"Where are we?" he said.

"What?"

Then louder.

"Where are we? Where *are* we—"

"Time for that when we're out of here. Shit—goddamn—"

Raine looked ahead. A ragged metal chain—laced with twisted pieces of sharp metal, a spiky net—suddenly rose up, shutting off passage through the chasm.

Raine glanced up. He saw movement on either side of the ravine.

As they roared into the trap.

"Get that gun up. And . . . hold on."

The vehicle went even faster toward the metal barrier ahead.

TEN

QUESTIONS

The vehicle flew over the pits and rocky outcrops, shaking Raine left and right crazily.

"Hold on!" his savior repeated unnecessarily. Then, despite the roar of the motor, Raine could hear a new sound: the ricochet of bullets hitting the body of the vehicle.

And still the buggy barreled on, and the barrier still lay dead ahead, ready to rip into the tires, chassis . . . and passengers of the car.

Which is when Dan reached down and pulled a lever. The front of his buggy groaned, and a metal flap in front folded forward. A piece of metal with spikes that extended like spears, all protruding from a piece of steel with razor teeth that shot a hundred sparkling reflections of the sun back at Raine.

We're going straight through the thing?

Hold on indeed.

The buggy ran into the suspended grid of twisted wire and hooks, and its strange cowcatcher sliced it in two. The cut pieces snapped back with a howling shriek, flying to either side. As they passed the now useless barrier, Raine saw the bandits racing away from the whiplash of the chain.

And he watched one who wasn't so lucky as the rapid snap-back of the metal trap wrapped itself around him like a snake, swatting him down to the ground while planting hooks into his side. It was gruesome, but there wasn't time to think too much about it, as more gunshots rang out. From the side. Raine looked left. Dan had a handgun out.

"C'mon," he said to Raine. "*Shoot* the goddamn gun!"

In the mad race for the ravine, Raine had forgotten about the gun in his hands. He lifted it and started looking up at the cliffs above them, checking on both sides. Figures scurried along the edge, all holding guns.

Despite the bumping and jumping of the buggy, Raine brought the gun up and fired, and one of the bandits fell off the cliff.

Then another shot. A miss. Return fire sent a bullet flying inches in front of Raine, drilling a hole right down into the floor of the vehicle.

Raine swung his rifle around to the side and started to fire faster. He shot one bandit just as he was taking aim.

"Nice work. Keep it up."

Can't be an endless supply of these bastards, Raine thought.

But ahead, at least two more. Crouched on the rocky ledge, well covered.

"They're going for the tires!" Dan said.

In response, he started swerving sharply right and left anticipating their shots—but also making it nearly impossible for Raine to aim.

Then the buggy steadied, going straight.

Raine didn't need to be told what to do.

The sniper to the left took a shot to the head. Raine wheeled right. A second shooter was firing away, but now with the car going straight for a few precious minutes, Raine took aim.

But Dan swerved again.

"Gave you all the time I could, friend," he said, not sounding all that apologetic. "Try again."

After going right and left, the buggy steadied. And this time Raine fired fast, hitting the rock in front of the sniper. He quickly followed that with another shot, and the sniper was hit, his attempt to hide behind the rock over.

That shooter's gun tumbled from his hands down to the ravine floor.

"Hell. God *damn*. Not bad, stranger."

Dan put his own gun back in its holster.

Unexpectedly, he laughed, the sound echoing with the walls so close.

"Welcome to the future!"

The laughter grew louder, uncontrolled, as if it was some amazing sick joke.

But Raine didn't laugh. Didn't even smile.

Welcome to the fucking future indeed . . .

Raine didn't say anything for a while.

He held the gun, thinking about what just happened. Three . . . four dead men. In a matter of *minutes*. Who were they? What the hell did they want?

And . . . what kind of world was this?

Finally, he spoke, raising his voice to be heard over the engine roar.

"Where are we going?"

"Right. Okay. We're going to my settlement. The Hagar Settlement. My people. Where we live, trade, work, and try to survive."

"I have a lot of questions."

"I bet. And we'll get to them—I told you. But you Ark survivors . . . heard that you're kind of disoriented when you get out. You best take things nice and slow. Let *me* start with a few questions . . . like, what's your name?"

"Nicholas Raine. Lieutenant Nicholas Raine, United States Marine Corps."

After he said the words, Raine realized that the thing he was proudest of, the brotherhood of his fellow Marines . . . perhaps that didn't even exist anymore.

No.

Probably not perhaps.

Probably . . . definitely.

"Raine, hm? Don't get much . . . rain here."

Dan laughed.

"In fact, water is kinda scarce. Like a lot of things are scarce. In fact, if it has any goddamn value at all . . . it's scarce."

"What happened?"

"Hm?"

"Here. When the asteroid hit. I mean, are your people Ark survivors?"

Another laugh. "If Granddaddy Hagar was an Ark survivor, I'd never been born. Talk about short life span. Survivors are captured, then killed or used. That's what the Authority does with them."

"The Authority?"

"Like I said . . . *Raine*. Lot for you to digest. Take it in small bits. Just know this . . . most Ark survivors are gone. Those left, work for *them*. Others tried to escape, but were hunted down. Ones deemed useless—well, they're really *gone*."

"Sounds like a nice group of people, your 'Authority.' "

"The Authority runs things. Or think they do. Out here, in the Wasteland, kinda hard for them to have much control. Too many muties, bandits, groups like us."

"Muties?"

Dan looked over at him. "Okay. You asked about the asteroid? Way before my time. Even before my father's time. *His* father was here. And he said it was supposed to kill everyone. But something happened. It didn't do that. Though might as well have, when you look at what was left. That world. *Your* world. Gone. Cities, even—I've heard—whole goddamn landmasses."

"And time . . ."

"What's that?"

"The computer said time now was different."

"Oh you mean it's off a few days? That sort of thing? Yeah, not the same. Days nearly an hour longer. The asteroid's strike played with the planet's orbit. Really messed with the weather, too. God knows what year it is according to your time. We just date things from when the asteroid hit."

"And muties—what are they?"

"You tell me. The asteroid created pockets of radiation. Where it didn't kill everyone, some survived, but . . . they changed. They became like animals. Living together like rat packs. Breeding like crazy. They feel no pain. Not too hard to kill, but there seems to be a hell of a lot of them. And oh yeah— they can eat just about anything. But they do have . . . their preferences."

Dan paused as if there was something else he was about to add.

"Look, when we get to my settlement you best not ask too

many questions. Not till people get to know you, at least. Get to trust you, know what I mean? They kinda connect questions . . . with the Authority."

Dan spit out the side of his buggy as if the word was distasteful.

"Okay?"

Not ask questions? Raine thought. How else was he supposed to figure out what was going on? After all, if this was his future— what the hell was he supposed to do in it?

But he kept his mouth shut.

"Good, Lieutenant Raine. You'll do just fine." Dan sniffed the dusty dry air. "Or you won't. And there you go, ahead."

Dan pointed.

From out of the cover of low-lying hills ahead, Raine saw something that looked like a town. Except, as they got closer, the buildings seemed pieced together from anything and everything: container cars, metal walls, fencing, tractor trailer bodies sliced in half . . .

And he also saw people with guns on the side of the roadway leading into the heart of the settlement.

"The Hagar Settlement," Dan said quietly.

He looked over at Raine.

"Home sweet home."

He gunned the vehicle then, racing toward the settlement entrance.

ELEVEN

THE HAGAR SETTLEMENT

The vehicle flew over the pits and rocky outcrops. As Dan Hagar rolled passed the guards of the settlement, they lowered their weapons. A slight tip of the head.

Dan seemed to be the person to know, Raine could see.

As they got closer, he could see the strange buildings that made up this world of the Hagars. They had electricity—a few buildings had signs that lit up. Others gushed a stream of smoke into the blue sky.

But it was the way people dressed that had Raine staring.

No one dressed the same, as if their clothes had to be as jumbled and mismatched as the buildings. Then as he passed an old man—who knew how old?—staring at them driving through the settlement, Raine saw that whatever people wore also offered protection.

Layers against the sun, thick padding around knees, elbows, shoulders; some had head gear, a covering that reminded him of an ancient painting he saw in a kingpin general's home in Pakistan.

Skullcaps.

To protect a key organ.

And if no one was making new clothes, did they just piece the material together, stuff handed down from generation to generation? Where did the clothes come from? The ancient material of those who didn't survive?

In which case, were the garments on these people a daily reminder of what had happened to the once great planet Earth?

Dan looked over.

"Everyone's checking you out, Raine. Don't let it rattle you."

Raine thought that he had been the one staring at everyone. Now, when he looked away, he saw that Dan was right. Everyone they passed stared at him, eyes wide.

"Because I'm not from around here?"

Dan laughed. "Right. You're a . . . newbie." Another laugh. "No. Not that, I am afraid. You see, your . . . suit."

Raine looked down at what he was wearing. The smooth contours of the Ark suit. The places where the cryo pod could connect to it.

Looking brand new. Different from anything these people wore.

Except—

Except . . . he remembered someone they had passed. Bits of jacket.

Part of an Ark suit.

And Raine would have sworn that's what one of the bandits wore.

Am I really safe here?

"The reason, Raine, why everyone is staring, is that you are an Ark survivor."

Dan slowed the vehicle in front of a gathering of buildings—or it could have been one building, where a domelike hut meshed with a metal warehouse structure before trailing into a series of smaller buildings.

"Ark survivors—a live one, at least—are mighty rare here."

Dan stopped his buggy and got out.

"C'mon, time you met some of the locals."

Big grin from Dan.

And Raine wasn't sure that meeting the locals was such a good idea.

He followed Dan down a tight alley, two walls of metal making a path between structures before turning and ending at a door.

Raine heard a crackling sound. Small pops. Explosions. Followed immediately by a loud "Damn it!"

Dan knocked on the door, but walked in without waiting for an answer.

"Hold on, Halek," he called out. "You got company."

Raine followed Dan into the room.

Inside, a man was sitting at a bench, his back turned to them, pieces of weapons—barrels, triggers, stocks—spread out in front of him.

He didn't even look up at Dan.

"Halek?"

"I'm busy. Trying to get all this crap you bring me to work. God . . . *damn*." He threw down a piece he was holding. "Junk, so damn old, and you expect me to get it to work, and—"

Finally, he did turn.

"You have got to be kidding me —an Ark survivor? Here?"

Raine first thought that perhaps Halek was impressed. Maybe being a man from the past was important.

But Halek's face, frizzled with spiky hairs sprouting in every direction, and rheumy, bloodshot eyes, didn't look pleased.

He stood up.

"Halek, Lieutenant Nicholas Raine . . . Raine, meet my brother, Halek Hagar."

Raine stuck out his hand. Which wasn't taken.

Halek rubbed his cheek instead, studying him like he was the strange new addition to a zoo.

Then he turned to his brother.

"And you don't think that the goddamn Authority will *know* that you got 'im? That we have him *here*? Do you really think we can afford that?"

Raine wasn't feeling too welcome.

In another world, another time, he would have offered to leave.

But here—*now*—where the hell would he go?

For now, he was tethered to Dan Hagar and this place.

He repeated the two operative words in his head. A personal reminder.

For now.

"I know," Dan was saying, snapping Raine back into the situation, "but they were all dead. The bandits tried to grab him . . . he was the lone survivor. The Authority may think bandits got him."

"You don't believe that, do you? They know the bandits would deal for him."

Halek turned back to Raine. Then he took a step in his direction, the man's smell strong. Was water for bathing in short supply here, or was it just an option Halek chose not to elect?

"Which is exactly what we should do. Tie the bastard *survivor* up and sell him to the next batch of Enforcers that show up."

Dan put a hand on his brother's shoulder. Then he turned to Raine.

"My brother worries about the Authority. A lot."

"Damn right I do."

"But he forgets that we need all the help we can get here. Isn't that right, Halek?"

Dan's brother didn't disagree. But the look on his face didn't appear all that convinced, either.

"And this here *survivor* is a Marine lieutenant." He looked at Raine. "I imagine you've seen things, Raine, hm? Done things? I mean, there were reasons they picked you, right?"

"Guess so. It all happened fast—the selection, that is."

Dan nodded and then looked back to his brother. "I've already seen how good he is with a gun. I wouldn't mind him by my side, especially with the Wasties coming closer every day . . ."

"Wasties?" Rain said.

"The Wasteland bandit clans. What you shot at out there. All independent, but they seem to be converging on our little settlement. Another gun"—Dan took a breath—"another set of *balls*? I definitely could use that."

Halek's tongue did a slow exploration of his lips, around the chapped flesh and cracked corners of his mouth.

"Hell, he might even know something about the pile of weapons you got there," Dan said as way of appeasement.

"I know what I need to know," Halek said fast.

But the point had been made.

Dan looked at Raine.

"Think it's time you had a shot or two of what we like to call Hagar's Finest."

"Something to drink?"

Now both Dan and Halek started laughing, as if in on some private joke.

"Oh yeah—something to drink indeed."

• • •

Raine put down the glass of . . . whatever it was.

Dan looked at him. "Home-brewed stim juice. Packs a punch, so probably enough for now. You need a place to sleep. Food, maybe?"

He watched Halek shoot his brother a look. The reason for it then became clear.

"Halek—you got a place back in here that our friend from the past can sleep?"

"It's way too crowded here, I can't—"

"Just a cot, okay, brother? I know this isn't a hotel. I'll send over some food. We eat very simply. Things we can grow. Probably bland for you."

"Thanks," Raine said.

He looked around the room. It reeked of guns and oil and the man who worked on them. Raine wondered if he hadn't been better off sleeping inside the Ark.

Halek stayed focused on his brother.

"*Then* we talk about him?"

"Yeah. In the morning."

"Talk?" Raine said to Dan.

"Don't worry about it for now. It will be dark soon here. We'll be beefing up our security. You may hear some gunshots. Perfectly normal."

Halek took a big sniff, his last expression that he wasn't too happy with his guest. Then he stood up.

"Got a space over there. Get you a blanket of some kind. Don't know if I got any damn pillow."

"I'll be okay."

Dan also got up.

"I'll be back in the morning. Then"—another glance at Halek—"we'll talk."

Raine stuck out his hand. An off moment—Dan acted as though he didn't know what to do with it. Then a grin. "Right. Yeah, a handshake."

And he took Raine's hand.

Was there a reason people no longer shook hands here? New diseases? Or maybe that pledge of friendship, what a clasping of hands represented . . . didn't apply?

Raine couldn't guess. But for now he was eager for whatever space Halek had for him. Even a sip or two of the foul liquid they gave him had him wanting to shut his eyes. Or perhaps it was the ironic fatigue from waking up decades after doing nothing.

"Dan. Thanks. For saving me."

Dan released his hand. "Yeah. Well, we'll see."

And he walked out of the chaotic armory.

Raine turned back to where Halek was muttering as he pushed piles of metal around.

Raine stood there. Stranger in an ever stranger land.

And he felt that whatever the morning brought, it might be even stranger still.

He walked back, a bit unsteady, to where he hoped to lie down . . . and simply sleep.

TWELVE

TO SERVE SOMEBODY

He dreamt.

And even while Raine dreamed, he realized, in a lucid way, that for all those decades of deep sleep he hadn't dreamt at all.

Now, though, he dreamt of the Ark station, the scientists milling about, looking at him with sideways glances as if they were in on a practical joke.

That gave way to images of the bandits who attempted to kill him. They screamed at him, making threatening gestures. Waving knives. One shot a gun that echoed hollowly in the aural caverns of his sleeping mind. A muffled shot into the sky.

Where he could look *up*.

Something coming. Covering the sun.

The asteroid. I didn't miss it after all. It is coming right down on me.

Except he could see . . . this was far too small an asteroid. It was more like a hovering aircraft. Like a helicopter, but boxy, the engine sound roaring above the screaming bandits.

And the flying thing—whatever it was—started shooting at him.

He blinked. At the glare of the sun suddenly revealed. The gleaming metal of the strange chopper.

He blinked.

Awake.

And even before he took in the dingy light and foul smell of the place where he had slept, he saw something . . . within his eyes.

Like a screen.

First just wavy lines, as if fruitlessly chasing those floaters made by blood vessels crisscrossing the iris. But then resolving. Showing a thin red bar that rose and fell . . .

Rose and fell, he quickly realized, with his heartbeat. Then another bar. Immediately filling his point of view from the bottom of his eye to the top.

Green.

The nanotrites. The small biomechanical engines. One showing heart rate, the other . . . his body functions? His health? Could they show other things? Did the scientists who planted them know all they could do?

When he blinked again, their work done, they vanished.

He sat up on the wood plank covered with a thick blanket that had been his bed. On the floor, a plate with a roll-like thing that Dan had brought over. Cheese, or something like cheese. No meat.

Meat was rare, Dan had said. But there was soy.

He took a breath.

Day One, he thought. He cleared his voice, wondering if Halek was around. That sound brought a jumble of noises, as gun parts were pushed away and a chair scraped the floor.

Halek walked back to him.

They sat at the table again after Halek had gone to get Dan.

Dan's face seemed set. No repeat of the handshake. No smiles. They sat down facing Raine as if this was an important meeting.

Dan let Halek start.

"You've got to do a . . . *service.*"

Raine nodded. "Sure. Of course." He took a breath. "A service. Mind telling me what the hell a 'service' is?"

"Easy there Ark man," Halek growled. "This is the Hagar Settlement. You can be tossed out as easily as Dan dragged your ass in here."

Dan put a hand on his brother's beefy forearm. If they ran this place together, Raine thought, then Dan was the brains and restraint . . . and Halek got what was left over.

Though from the look of the guns all around, Halek did pretty well putting bits and pieces together to make weapons.

"It's the code here. Hell, not just here. All the outer settlements, and Wellspring—"

"Wellspring?"

"It's a city," Dan said. "Or, what we call a city. No one survives here without help. And without everyone *helping* each other, you might as well just let the muties have you."

"A *service* . . ." Halek repeated, getting Dan back on track.

"To stay, Raine, you have to do something that helps the settlement. And then to keep staying, there will be other things. It's either that—"

"Or leave?"

"Yeah. Pretty much."

"Tell him, Dan. Tell him what it is." Halek leaned close. "What *he's* got to do."

"So I talked with some of the others here. They got something for you. We lost someone on a patrol a few days ago. Never came back. He was on the road that runs northeast from here. It goes a way out, ultimately turning into a jumble of rock and rotting buildings. With the disappearance, we are down a man."

"So—what do you want me to do?"

"You go check out that road," Halek said, a gleam in his eyes. "Bandits are always trying to creep close to us, especially of late. It's like they're getting ready for a raid on us. We need to watch all the main roads here—so you check it out."

Raine saw Dan watching him. His easy manner—the smiles, the "welcome to the future" stuff—gone.

Is this why he rescued me?

"We'll set you up with a buggy. Won't be much."

"It'll run. That'll be enough," Halek said.

"Right. It will run," Dan said. "We have a radio. Not too reliable. But you can communicate. When the wind's right, at least. Keep your eyes peeled for deep ruts, stray boulders . . . you don't want to blow a tire out there or crack an axle. You go out there, and if you see signs of bandits, you radio it in. Then we'll come out and—"

"We'll rub the bastards out," Halek said.

"Weapons?"

Dan looked away. Raine guessed that he and his brother had discussed that issue as well. "You got that rifle I gave you."

"Maybe something else?"

Dan looked at Halek.

"Shit. Damn. Okay. I can give you a handgun. Think there's a piece of what you used to call a Glock in it. Fires .44s. Your people stockpiled a ton of them. God," he said, shaking his head. "What we could really use is some serious shell power against the bandits. RPGs, you know? Yeah, I'd give *anything* for a crate of them."

"Okay. And I call in if I see something?"

"Yes," Dan said. "And Raine—do this and you can, well . . . stay here."

"For a while," Halek added.

"For . . . a while." Dan's expression relaxed a bit. "Also, the buggy is yours. And the guns."

"If you come back," Halek muttered.

Dan ignored his brother. "We'll be—guess what you'd call them back in the pre-asteroid days—friends."

Halek spit on the ground. The future wasn't turning out too friendly.

"When do I leave?"

"Now. If there are some Wasties out there, we best find out sooner rather than later."

Raine stood up.

The sudden move made his head turn a bit dizzy. Fiery specks in his eyes. He didn't react, though. Didn't want to give Halek the satisfaction.

"Then—let's do it."

Raine sat down behind the wheel of the small buggy.

"Look familiar?" Dan asked.

"Yeah. Think you have pieces here of a Humvee mixed in with—God—could be a Mustang?"

"Cars? Lot we don't know. About your days, your stuff. Okay, the tires have been reinforced with an extra layer of steel cord. Takes a lot to puncture them. But I won't kid you, it's not much of a vehicle, even by our standards."

Raine could believe it.

Dan leaned into the buggy.

"Use that radio. See anything, let us the hell know."

"Don't worry. I will."

"We don't have a map to give you. It wouldn't be too accurate anyway. Just head northeast once you're through that end of the settlement. You'll see what looks like a road. Forty miles out, and then back. Maybe you'll see nothing." His eyes did nothing to convince Raine that he thought that was a possibility.

Dan reached behind his back to his belt buckle and pulled out a knife.

"Take this. You never know. I'd give you more . . ."

Raine took the knife, looking at the five-inch blade. Serrated. More of a fisherman's blade than anything else. But it looked nasty and sharp.

"Thanks. I appreciate it. My first road trip in the new world. Feels like, I dunno, a driving test."

Dan nodded and grinned. "Yeah. Well, guess it *is* a test."

He backed away from the vehicle.

"Time you're off."

No key. Just a switch to start the engine. Raine threw it. The unmuffled roar made hearing any other words from Dan impossible.

Though Raine could see that he mouthed something.

Good luck.

With that, Raine started pulling away from the collection of metal buildings, heading down one of the dirt roads to the way out of the settlement.

THIRTEEN

RADIO SILENCE

Raine took the smoky, coughing buggy slowly through the streets of the settlement. He noticed that people came out of their podlike buildings to gawk at him.

Drawn to the sound, or the fact that he was a stranger? Looking at his suit and knowing he was from the past?

No one smiled—though he saw a kid staring, his face smeared with what looked like oil. Raine wondered . . . did everyone here work at keeping the settlement's buggies running?

The boy's eyes widened. Then he smiled. Raine smiled back. His father pulled the boy close.

Guess it's not a good idea to get too close to me, Raine thought.

Though I'm still not sure why the hell not.

He followed the winding dirt street as it funneled to an entrance. The barrier—it was a stretch to call anything this crude a "gate"—was constructed of chunks of metal, girders, seemingly anything that could be piled together to make the settlement secure.

Two guards, gun barrels held high, waited at each side of the way out.

They didn't react as he went by.

Okay, he thought. He wasn't the most popular person in the Hagar Settlement. Maybe a few good "services" would change that.

But even if he could change their opinion of him, he couldn't help but wonder, Was this his life now? Was this where he'd stay?

If not, where do I go?

And more to the point: *What the hell do I do?*

He looked at his buggy's compass, a plastic sphere that might have been stolen from a kid's bike. He turned and it spun, showing northwest . . . north . . . northeast.

He kept his foot on the accelerator, trying to ignore the way the buggy bounced and jostled over the rubble.

This was no road. Barely a path through the hills ahead.

The buggy chewed up miles. Surprisingly, the odometer worked. Had they built it or simply ripped it out of some century-old vehicle? The last working item from an infamous Pinto that didn't explode into flames?

A Mercedes?

It was old school—nondigital.

Just like this bizarre future.

The landscape changed, turning flat, endless. But Raine still had to keep his eyes ahead for any deep pits and large rocks. How much abuse could this vehicle take?

The hills that surrounded the settlement area gave way to a broad empty plain. Could be called a desert but for the fact that it was dotted . . . not with the stone monoliths like you'd see in Monument Valley . . . but man-made monoliths.

Pieces of buildings.

Stray, curled chunks of rusted and burnt metal that could have been anything a hundred years ago. At one point he swore he saw what looked like the forward half of an oil tanker. It reminded him of videos he had seen way-back-when, of Robert Ballard diving down to the *Titanic* in a minisub to find just half a prow, looking like it had been sliced like so much cheese.

Could have been.

Who knew?

Looked like hell had taken place here. Or, perhaps more accurately, as if hell had simply been dumped here.

Thrown to this spot by . . . Apophis? By whatever Apophis did. Or was it all here already and this was merely what was left?

Eyes forward again, he narrowly missed a foot-tall boulder right in his path, a path that grew increasingly more vague.

He looked at the odometer as the number to the right kept rolling—too slowly by he thought.

Twenty miles so far.

Halfway.

He didn't think he ever felt so alone in his whole life.

And Raine thought that considering what he'd seen, what he'd done . . . that was saying something.

The handset of the radio clipped to the dash crackled.

He picked it up, amazingly grateful for its sound.

At first it was nothing intelligible—just the hiss. Some squawking noise. Until he heard words.

"—this? Come in, Raine."

He pressed the button. There must still be some towers out

there to get that much range. Amazing how good a bit of old-fashioned tech could feel.

A goddamn two-way radio.

"Yeah. I'm here."

More hisses. Not the most reliable form of communication, apparently. He looked around to see if the signal might be getting cut off by a nearby hill.

"—mileage? See anything?"

Raine pressed the Talk button again.

"I'm at about mile twenty . . . twenty-one." He looked around again. "And seen nothing yet."

"—again? Couldn't get—"

Raine repeated the message.

He thought it sounded like Dan Hagar—but he couldn't be sure.

"Good. Halfway there. Got a—"

The word dropped out. Then:

"—for you when you get back. Good—"

Raine waited. Then responded. "Thanks." And, remembering two-way radio protocol. "Over."

He had another thought then, one that actually came from his training, his background, his experience: *Are these people in over their head?*

Did he happen to get picked up by people whose days—out here, at least—were numbered?

One didn't get to choose his rescuers, that was for sure.

But he was starting to grow increasingly curious about the world beyond the Hagar Settlement. About the city. About the Authority.

Realizing that this was no tour of duty.

This was it.

This was life.

• • •

Driving became increasingly a matter of swerving left and right to avoid the boulders, still catching the stray rock that would send one half of the buggy flying up before it landed. Then it was apparently the other side's turn.

Another glance at the odometer: 34 . . . 35.

Five miles. At this speed . . . maybe twenty minutes.

With nothing seen. Nothing to report. He remembered the relief he felt as a young lieutenant leading his squad in the Pakistan mountains, hoping—without letting the men know—that they'd find absolutely nothing.

Except they often did. And he grew to squelch that thought. It jinxed the whole deal. Almost became a guarantee that you *would* see action.

Once you start wishing.

But that thought came now. It was natural.

And naturally, the jinx still worked.

Because ahead he saw . . . smoke.

Smoke. Fire. Humans.

He slowed his buggy.

Could be they had heard him already, this piece of chugging metal, kicking up its own cloud of dust and sand. But there was nothing he could do about that.

He threw the switch to kill the engine. He reached out and grabbed the handset again.

"Dan? Halek?"

He took his finger off the button. Nothing, not even the semi-reassuring hiss of static.

Could be . . . nothing and no one was ahead.

Maybe there could still be spontaneous brushfires in this world.

Except he hadn't seen much in the way of brush.

He looked at where the smoky plumes rose and then got carried away by a steady wind. He took another look around at the terrain, and suddenly, surprisingly, he was in reconnaissance mode.

It felt good to be thinking in a way that was familiar.

After all these years.

He grinned at that.

Something *familiar*.

Okay—he could get closer, see what was happening.

It occurred to him he could just turn around, too. After all, he had nearly reached the forty-mile mark. Say he saw nothing. At least retreat until he could radio back to the settlement.

But that wasn't how he was wired.

Slippery slope, he thought. Lying to those depending on you. Then lying to yourself.

Raine took the rifle and the handgun. When he got out, he put the knife at his back.

You never know.

And only then did he start moving toward the smoke, hugging close to the massive boulders, crouching as low as he could.

It didn't take long. Soon he was close enough to hear voices. Bits of English, though with an accent that years of living out here had shaped into a strange kind of Creole, a bandit patois. But the words—understandable.

"I got 'er. *I* decide."

Then laughter. Then a scream. Must be the prisoner's voice. High-pitched. Female. The voices sounded drunk—unless too much sun and throat-slitting made you sound that way.

"*We's* decide. Together. Our clan, our property."

Grunts. The sound of others agreeing. The word "property"

sounding way too complicated for the bandits in whatever state they were in.

Raine looked for a way to get closer. He'd have to climb, work his way through a jumble of rocks, where any pathway could easily turn into a dead end, and any false step easily turn into a signal.

But he needed to know how many were there. He needed to see what was what.

Then get back. Try the radio again, or get to a spot where he could use the radio.

He wasn't trying for any goddamn heroics here. Not his first day in futureland.

But he would do his duty.

He squeezed through a V-shaped opening in the rocks, moving sideways. Slowly, taking care not to trigger any scraping noises. He heard the scream again. They had a woman up there, and it sounded like party time in the Wasteland.

Then someone yelled after one loud shriek: "Maybe's we gonna eat you? You like that? We get hungry out—"

The bandit couldn't finish the rest of his threat since they all became convulsed with a mixture of laughing and coughing. It made Raine apprehensive. *How many of them are there?* Still, if he was going to report back, he'd have to see how many there were.

Doing his duty.

His goddamn duty.

He pressed on. The vee made by the boulders opened up, and he could see he was only meters away from the smoky plume, a bonfire. He paused. Slid out his handgun. Finger clenched on the rifle.

Raine licked his lips. The sun felt so incredibly warm. Beads of sweat formed on his brow and rolled down, stinging his eyes. He blinked. After time to adjust, he felt ready. He took a breath and leaned forward, hoping he could steal a look before anyone noticed he had crashed their party.

Just slightly forward . . . and this was where he knew he had to take his time. He'd seen too many grunts on street patrol take cover, then stick their whole head out too far, too fast.

And he had seen heads disappear.

Closed coffin for sure.

He would tell his squads, then later his squad leaders—the young second lieutenants who thought they could change the world: "Take your damn time."

At this point, at this . . . "juncture, gentlemen" . . . go slow.

One error would be an error too many.

He caught movement, the bandits standing, passing around a liquid. A few with rifles over their shoulders. One with a handgun.

Five.

They were gathered around something; the source of the screaming.

I should back away, Raine thought. He'd seen them here. What Dan wanted to know. *Yeah, you got bandits on this road. Armed. Drunk. With a prisoner.*

But there was the voice of the girl, the prisoner. Raine couldn't see her unless he leaned forward. Doing that, he'd be exposed if anyone turned.

In his world—his old world—there were times you backed away, and times you didn't.

Old Brooklyn street rules. Sometimes you had to stand up.

No matter how bad it looked.

He leaned forward again, taking care that his gun barrel didn't scrape the stone.

And he saw that the bandits had gathered around a wooden

cage. Makeshift. Just some sticks lashed together, enough room to stand up.

Something to transport someone, he thought.

The sun . . . a steady stream of sweat. He blinked.

Inside, a woman. Though almost of indeterminate sex in her own version of a Wasteland costume. Layers of cloth, a turban-like headgear. Her face smudged with dabs of color, black and red. Different from the bandits that held her.

Might that be the factor? Was she from some other bandit clan?

A prize? A hostage? Something to be bartered?

From the looks of things, they had other ideas for now.

The one with the handgun came close to the cage. He was bare to the chest, his face markings—wild swirls of color—stretched all the way down to his upper torso.

That bandit pointed his gun at the woman—no more than a girl, now that Raine looked closer. Couldn't be much more than a teen.

"You will die if'n they don't pay."

A few others gave out a bellowed, "Yeah, yeah. *Die!*"

They laughed.

So funny.

But the girl didn't blink. Instead, she leaned close to that bandit, her young face, still unburned, and unwrinkled features barely visible through her painted face—and she spat in his face.

Dead on target.

And the man didn't even pause to wipe the spit off.

He raised his gun at the girl, who, amazingly, didn't flinch. Her screams replaced with silence, her eyes wide, scanning her captors, as if she were trying to figure if there was any way out of this.

Now, Raine told himself.

Or never.

To help, he would have to come out of his hiding spot, this wedge of stone, and get his guns ready, all in one move. His body still didn't feel back to normal. It felt like parts were still sleeping.

Goddamn duty.

He pressed down, ready to spring out. Tightened his muscles. And he moved.

The first shot went wide of its target. He stumbled getting to the level ground of the enclosed area around the fire.

But that shot got the attention of the other bandits, and they turned away from the girl . . . and right toward him.

The four with rifles started leveling their weapons, as if Raine had turned himself into a shooting gallery.

But they moved slowly, stupidly, getting their guns in position.

Save for the girl's tormentor with his handgun. Drunk or not, he moved fast.

He fired a shot that Raine thought missed completely.

Until—delayed reaction—he felt a spear of pain on the side of his right leg. He didn't look down but he felt the wound. And even without looking down, he knew he was dripping blood onto the ground.

Couldn't let anything else distract him now.

Two guns. One in each hand. Like out of a movie. No aiming. Christ, no getting any cover.

He fired each gun simultaneously, doing his best to target the bandits without raising a gun site to his eyes.

He caught one bandit with a shot to the gut, sending him to

his knees. Then another blast took one down in what had to be an amazingly lucky shot to the chest.

Two down.

By then Raine heard bullets ricocheting around him. They, too, were firing quickly now.

The bandit by the cage stuck his arm out and actually took aim with his handgun. And despite the new pain in his right leg, Raine *rolled* forward. He felt bits of gravel and dirt dig into the wound. A flash of white light exploded in his eyes, only to clear just as his roll ended.

Down on his knees, closer to the bandits.

Raine fired his rifle at the handgun bandit, once, twice—both times hitting. The bandit's wide, wild eyes turned dull.

Then Raine quickly wheeled to the right, seeing the stupefied expression of another bandit trying to take aim at the moving target he had become.

It was no contest, and Raine fired a shot right between the dumb bastard's eyes.

Now the last bandit tried to take a bead on Raine as he moved through the dirt, rolling, smearing a blood trail on the sand. Until, popping up from one painful roll, he fired his handgun at the last bandit. A shoulder wound.

All his training helped.

That, and maybe the fact that, unlike the bandits, he hadn't drunk any of what was in the bottle.

That last bandit, wounded, bleeding, looked at the bodies and started scrambling away.

Always a mistake.

Though he was able to put some distance between him and the mayhem, it now gave Raine a chance to really aim. Too easy: a single shot in the back.

And the five were all dead.

Raine kept kneeling there.

Until he heard the voice. "C'mon. You there. Shooter man. Get me out. Now, now!"

He turned to the girl in the wooden cage, remembering why he had started this melee to begin with. She was urgently waving to him, imploring him to free her. "C'mon! Hurry!"

"You're welcome."

FOURTEEN

NO GOOD DEED

The girl kept her eyes locked on him. Was it from fear, or just the wild-eyed look that anyone living out here took on as their natural expression? It certainly didn't look as though she trusted him.

Suddenly, letting her out of the cage didn't seem like the best of ideas. But Raine checked the rusted lock. One of the bodies around him must have a key.

On the other hand—

He fired at the lock and it shattered into three pieces.

The girl pushed open the wooden poles that had kept her trapped and then stood there, as if expecting Raine to do something to her.

"You okay?"

She nodded.

"Good. Now, what are you doing here? How'd they capture—"

The girl pointed past him, gesturing over his shoulder. "Look—more of them!"

Raine turned and saw nothing. But he felt the girl touch his back, and in one sleek move she had grabbed his knife. When he turned around, he saw her running away, hugging close to boulders, running as fast as she could, her new prize held tight in her hand.

Could she be going for his buggy?

But she ran in the other direction, farther into the surreal landscape of the Wasteland.

Raine shook his head. If the knife could help her, maybe she should have it.

And then he went around to the dead bandits, relieving them of their weapons and ammo. It was the same grisly job no matter where it was done. No matter what an enemy wore. What they believed. The language they spoke or the color of their skin.

You took what they had.

After all, they were dead. They certainly didn't need it.

Still, unwrapping fingers frozen to a trigger never got to feel like a normal thing to do.

Driving back, he guessed that the radio was still totally useless.

The weapons—his prizes—rattled in the back of the buggy. He half expected to run into more members of whatever clan he had just killed, but—so far—the road was quiet.

Just the deep, throaty roar of the vehicle. The rattling sound of the chassis. It was starting to sound comforting.

He had wrapped a piece of one of the bandit's shirts around his wound. It stopped the blood, though it was definitely not sterile.

Raine thought about this world he found himself in.

He'd been here a mere two days, and already there was a new *normal.* He knew he shouldn't have been too surprised, though. Even a newbie arriving into an area with firefights, IEDs, and snipers learns very quickly: *This is the fucking way it is.*

Adaptable.

The species was goddamn adaptable.

Still, nothing told him what he was going to do. Strange to be in the future and not have a clue what your future held. So far it had been all about shooting people. Not that they didn't deserve it.

Not like they didn't have it coming.

But if that's what was ahead, he'd better get his head around that idea.

Too many questions—*why this, why the hell that*—could screw up reflexes. Play games with your decision-making.

So—a first bit of resolve.

Acceptance. This was the world. Forget the other one. That was long gone.

And then, as if to accentuate just that point, the radio came to life.

"Raine? Raine!"

It was Dan's voice—barely recognizable over the noise. Raine picked up the handset. "Yeah. Here. Where the hell—"

"Listen, we've been hit. Watch yourself coming back."

"Hit?"

Bits of gritty sand flew into Raine's face as he drove into a steady wind. He kept blinking to keep his eyes clear.

"The settlement—" Dan's voice broke up. "Big attack."

And he'd thought *he* would be the one to have the news. Five dead bandits. Some weapons.

"Watch it coming back. They're likely to be—"

Another drop-off.

"Okay. I will. About twenty . . . twenty-five klicks, shit . . . I'm about sixteen miles from the settlement."

Dan didn't even ask about his recon. Guess it didn't matter much.

"—careful, Raine."

"Got it."

He put the handset down and reached over to touch his rifle, making sure it was one quick grab away. The handgun was stuck awkwardly in a side pocket.

He drove fast, dodging the rubble where he could, scanning left and right, thinking what easy pickings he'd be out here.

He saw nothing.

Not another soul until he saw the settlement, the Hagar compound. Four smoky streams showed where they had been fighting fires, one a dark, sooty black. Raine guessed that maybe some fuel had been hit.

Guards by the entrance. He could see one with field glasses. The sun was behind them, nearly down, and they were shadowy figures.

Hope they can see me, he thought. Recognize me.

Friendly fire. It happened. Even here, he imagined.

Especially here.

He picked up the radio.

"Dan, almost there. Can you tell your guards . . . not to shoot?"

A female voice. Young. "They got you, stranger. Just slow it down a bit. No racing in. And watch your butt coming in. People are hurt here, shit."

"Thanks."

The last yellowish cusp of the sun slid behind a hill. Only

minutes more of daylight. Torches had already appeared on top of the razor ribbon that served as a wall around the settlement.

He slowed down.

And then something he felt in his gut, that he had indeed felt before, told him the attack here had been real bad.

Abreast of the two guards, one waved him in.

The smell of smoke and gunfire filled the air.

Then . . . slower still, past the gate, he heard the sound of moans, shouts.

Which was when someone—a woman—walked in front of his buggy, a hand up, stopping him. Raine hit the brakes, pulling himself out of the buggy. He looked around and was shocked to see what had happened.

FIFTEEN

MASSACRE

The woman's voice—clipped, to the point, an order—didn't offer any discussion.

"You have to leave this buggy here. Too much debris still in the streets. We're still looking for anyone missing."

"What happened?"

She hesitated. "You best ask my father about that. After all—he's the one who brought *you* here."

The disdain in her voice felt like a physical kick. *This was Dan's daughter?*

"Okay. Where is he?"

"We've set up an infirmary right over— Hey, Tomas! Keep your goddamn eyes peeled out there," she yelled at one of the guards who had been watching them. "Christ. They're tired and so am I. But we can't afford any more screwups."

"You were attacked?"

"How observant. You Ark guys are really, really smart."

"Okay." He wanted more information, but clearly she wasn't in the mood. "Dan. Where is he?"

"There's a garage area behind Halek's shop. Got the living and the dead in there."

"Thanks."

Which brought no reply.

He headed off in that direction.

Walking down the street as dusk took over, he saw signs of the battle.

Expended shells, bits of metal where something explosive ripped off a chunk from a nearby building. Even guns broken into pieces.

Some of Hagar's people fought a fire still streaming out of a metal shed, handing buckets of water through a line. A rubber smell in the air—tires, probably. The smoke was noxious, and the people were using the water carefully.

A rare commodity here.

He walked past Halek's shop to an alleyway leading in back, to see Dan, nodding as an elderly woman gestured at him, anxious. He spotted Raine. His face grim.

Raine walked up to him.

"They will die without it, Dan," she was saying. "We just don't have enough medicine." The woman's voice was surprisingly strong.

"Okay. I'll take care of it."

Raine stood by.

A voice came from behind. "Dan, the guards down by the gas tanks want some backup. Can't afford to lose—"

Raine watched Dan take a breath. As if inhaling that much air could somehow fortify him for all the hard shit still to come.

"No. Tell them they'll have to make do. Can't pull anyone off any other—"

He looked at Raine.

"—what do you call them? In the military. *Details*?"

"Yeah. Sometimes."

"Tell them to stay alert. Get them ammoed up. I'll get them another body or two when I can."

The messenger turned and ran out of the area.

Halek, who had been talking to a few settlers hunched over people lying on the ground, noticed Raine.

No smiles there, either.

Raine even hesitated asking the question.

"Dan, what . . . happened?"

"An attack. Like we've been expecting. But, God, not this soon. It's why we had the patrols out. Like you. Had a few out today. The bandits must have seen them leave, been watching." He shook his head. "Came damn close to taking the whole settlement."

Raine looked at the people attending the wounded. Then, just to the right of them, other bodies, covered. No one attending them.

"They stormed both gates. Vehicles crashed through. Barely had time to react." He looked at Raine, perhaps sensing that he hoped he'd understand. What it was like. What it felt like.

"Killed people. Just ordinary people trying to survive here. People trying to get by, out of the city, away from the Authority."

"How many you lose?"

"Five dead. That we've found so far. Good people. And the same number wounded."

"What can I do? Is there—"

Halek walked up.

"Did you say 'do'? What can *you* do? Look around this place, stranger. You've done enough."

Raine turned to Halek. He didn't like the brother's words. But he forced himself to listen.

"What do you mean?"

"Halek, forget it. What's done is—"

"They came here for *you*. They must have found the dead ones by your Ark. They came here for the Ark survivor." Halek spat at the ground. "This is because of you."

"Halek, ease the hell up. We don't know that. Get back to work. You've got things to do. Salvage any weapons, any ammo. And I've got to go to the Outriggers."

"You're leaving?" Halek said. "With all this going on?"

One of those people nursing the wounded came up. "We're good for medicine for maybe another twenty-four hours, Dan, tops. That's it. Then we're going to start losing them."

"And whose gonna check the gates?" Halek continued, seemingly not even hearing about the medicine. "They listen to you, Dan."

Raine had seen situations like this before: it was a lot of weight on Dan's shoulders.

How much weight before he snapped?

"I know," he sighed. "But we need the medical supplies. I have to go."

Raine noticed that Halek had his eyes on him. They might have to have a private talk soon.

I may be a guest, but I'm not going to be treated like garbage by that bag of wind.

He turned to Dan, and it was clear to Raine that the leader of this settlement's stress levels were off the chart.

"What happened to your leg?" Dan said, noticing the bloodied shirt bandaging his leg.

"Just a scratch. Found some bandits. Took them out."

"Did you try to call us?"

"Yeah. No signal out there."

Dan nodded. Apparently not an uncommon problem.

"They had a girl captured. I freed her—"

"And killed her, too?" Halek said.

"No. She got away, I mean."

Another step closer to Raine's face. "You let a goddamn bandit get away?"

"It was a *girl*."

"Doesn't matter—they're all the same, all scum, as bad as the Authority. Maybe worse."

Dan held up a hand. "I have to go first thing tomorrow, get these medical supplies. Maybe you can—"

"No."

Raine's voice cut through the room. As if bouncing off the metal walls. Did any of the people nursing look up? He couldn't tell—he just looked at the man who saved his life.

"I'll go. I made this happen."

"No, you didn't. You don't have to—"

"That's how I feel. But forget that—it doesn't matter what I feel. *You're* needed here. These people need you. If it's a goddamn supply run, I can do that."

"To the Outriggers? Not always so simple with them."

"Is anything simple here?"

For the first time Raine could remember, Halek was quiet.

"I can do it, Dan."

"Let him go," Halek finally said. "We need you here, brother."

Dan hesitated—Raine knew how Halek felt about him, the newcomer. But the truth in his words had penetrated his stressed brain.

"Okay. All right, you can leave at first light. Could still be dangerous out there—no, it *will* be dangerous out there." He shook his head, realizing it didn't matter. Taking another deep breath, he stood a little straighter. "Halek will get together a list of what we need from them. We'll have to offer something to barter. God . . . not sure what that will be. We'll think of something. You should be back here before noon."

"Sounds good."

"Now get some sleep. You're no good out there exhausted."

"If they come back—"

For the first time that day Dan grinned. "Don't worry. If they come back, you can be sure I'll wake you up. But do me a favor— get that leg checked out, will you?" He walked away, his brother behind him.

Raine got his wound cleaned out and a fresh bandage put on, then went to his small space at the back of Halek's. In minutes he fell dead asleep.

SIXTEEN

JOURNEY TO THE OUTRIGGERS

Someone kicked the wooden bench that Raine slept on. The dull vibration shook him awake.

To a totally dark room.

The person standing in front of him wore a headlamp, conveniently pointed right at him, rendering it impossible for him to see.

"Let's go, stranger. Time to get ready."

Raine recognized the voice. The young woman who met him on his return. Someone else who didn't like having him around.

"I thought . . . first light?"

"Give it ten minutes and the sun will be up."

The woman turned and pointed with the light at some type of bread and a drink.

"I put water in your buggy. Also fiddled with the engine a bit. Not my area, but I could see that your engine was lugging."

Raine sat up.

"Thanks. And—who are you?"

"Loosum Hagar. I do a lot of different things around here. Which apparently also includes getting your butt moving."

"You're doing a good job of that. Tell me—is everyone in this settlement named Hagar?"

"What's the matter? Don't like the name?"

"No. Fine name—just seems—"

"C'mon. You have five minutes less than you did when I woke you. Eat, drink, move, go. There are people hurting here."

Raine swung his legs to the side. His feet touched the ground and he felt his guns.

Funny, that's how he came to think of them.

My guns.

"Also got some extra ammo for you. Should be a clean trip. The bandits like to hit and run. Today will be a running day for the bastards."

"Thanks again."

"Don't worry—I'm not doing any of this for you. We need those medical supplies. You go, and my dad can stay here."

Raine walked over and bit into the bread. None too tasty, and the whitish liquid in the glass was a poor imitation of milk. He didn't even bother asking what it was.

Loosum handed him a sealed pouch. "And this—this is the deal Halek put together for the supplies. Just give it to Rikter. He's their boss."

"Says what you will do for them?"

"Right. Yeah. Okay, breakfast over. Let's go."

Light had started to color the clear night sky.

Now Raine could see Loosum. She was young—and with

the headgear and bulky outfit gone, was probably fairly attractive.

Too bad our chemistry is so off, he thought.

"There's a map in that compartment there."

"The glove compartment."

"The what? Gloves?"

"Forget it. Was already archaic when—"

"Like I said . . . should be quiet out there. If not, drive like crazy and shoot even crazier. If you're not back by nightfall with supplies, we'll know what happened."

Raine looked up.

Every minute, the deep purple of the sky shifted to a lighter shade, the sun still only looming. Time to go.

"Okay. And—I won't say, you know, thanks again."

He got in. Started the engine. The roar did sound cleaner, a deeper, tighter rumble. More than just tuned.

"Nice," he said.

Loosum came close, clicking off her headlamp now that it was no longer needed.

"Look, we deal with the Outriggers on occasion, but the Outriggers deal with everyone, including the Authority. Just be careful around them. They're not to be trusted."

"And the Hagars are?"

"I will forget you said that, *Ark man*. Just a warning. Take it—or don't."

Loosum backed away.

"Now get moving."

A hint of yellow on the horizon, the beginning of another day in the Wasteland. Was he keeping track of the days? Should he keep track?

It certainly didn't seem to matter.

He pulled away from Loosum and went past the guards to

the road and open expanse of the great desert that surrounded the settlement.

Though the buggy sounded and ran better, its suspension, or lack of one, still sent Raine flying out of his seat when it hit each rock and crevice.

The sun sat a full ten degrees above the horizon now, not quite in his eyes. Pair of sunglasses would be useful. He did have a hat that he found in the back of the buggy. Not much of a brim, but it might help a bit.

He opened . . . the compartment.

Gloves . . . as if!

He pulled out the map. Hand drawn, and rough; it had scribbled mounds indicating hills and mountains, arrows for passageways.

A jumble of lines crisscrossing was labeled "Outriggers."

He looked at the ball compass in his buggy. His course looked fine.

All he needed was some music.

Instead he was left with his thoughts, like maybe if he brought back the supplies, people would accept him. Let him just be.

But then again, maybe not. Because there was that catch.

I'm not a Hagar.

He stuffed the map back. If he stayed in this direction, he should be fine. Nothing but clear open space between here and the Outriggers' settlement.

He began to relax.

Which, if you had asked him, was always when things seemed to go . . . wrong.

• • •

It was the slightest of sounds.

Competing with the wind—that steady whistle near his ears—the shooting spray of rock and rubble, and the still-loud engine.

Another noise.

He turned his head left and right as if he could aim his ears.

The sound . . . he slowly, finally, identified it.

Another engine. Then, more clear, two engines.

Behind him.

He looked at his compass. The open space ahead. And only then did he risk a look back.

To see the two vehicles racing toward him.

They had taken flanking positions behind him, one on either side. Still too far away for a good shot. From his glance back—and the rate they were gaining on him—Raine guessed that their vehicles were faster than his.

One had a classic jeep front. He couldn't be sure, but it looked like a machine gun mounted on the hood.

So, maybe two bandits in there.

And then, on the other side, a Camaro from hell. The engine exposed, tinkered with so it couldn't even fit under any normal car hood, and a rear end raised up that gave the whole thing the look of a projectile.

Least it didn't have a gun mounted on its front.

And both were gaining on him.

How many seconds until they opened fire?

Raine looked ahead. Wide-open space to maneuver. Seemed to be their advantage, not his.

A crack. The first sound of gunfire.

No opportunity for a long debate.

He hit the brakes of the buggy hard.

The vehicle nearly went end over end with the force of the sudden stop.

Raine didn't waste any time. He picked up his rifle.

Another crack, and the ping of a shot that hit the roll bar ran over the buggy's seats.

He saw the bandits on the left—the ones in the jeep—edging closer to him. One of them was standing, aiming the mounted gun . . .

Raine watched a line of bullets begin racing across the sand, strafing its way toward his vehicle.

Shit.

But they were going so fast, and with their target no longer moving, the bandit at the mounted gun was turning the gun fast as well to try to compensate, his aim all over the place.

Not so for Raine. He was stopped.

And he'd had sniper training. Maybe the most useful thing he'd ever learned—at least at the moment. He fired and the bandit at the mounted gun kicked backward, right out of the car.

Raine turned hard to the other vehicle, the metal torpedo about to pass him. No front-mounted machine gun, but he still saw a passenger bandit taking aim with a rifle.

Raine noticed that his wound from yesterday didn't scream out in agony with his sudden turn. Sure, it had been cleaned out, but this was something different . . . almost like it was completely healed.

Almost like he had never taken a bullet there at all.

Nanotrites. Not sure he knew how they worked or even what they even were. But he was mighty glad to have them coursing through his system.

A shot from the killer Camaro brought him out of his reverie, and he ducked as the vehicle on the right flew past.

He slid back down, knowing that both vehicles would now turn, showing him their broadsides.

Time to gun it.

He sat up and hit the accelerator. Whatever Loosum had done made his underpowered buggy *leap* forward as if it had been kicked in the rear.

He didn't even bother holding the steering wheel. He let the car wobble left and right as he took aim at the two vehicles in front of him.

Where the hell are their gas tanks?

Finding it on the Camaro-type thing should be easy. He took his shot, just to the rear of the driver, and low.

Should have been just about where the tank was.

As if in answer, the bandit's vehicle exploded into flame. The flash created a heat he could feel from all the way back where he was.

And the other car? The one with the dead shooter?

He saw it heading in a circle, trying to turn back on him.

Go on, Raine thought. Give it a shot.

Suddenly this was personal for him.

Never a bad thing, despite what they tell you at officers' school. "Personal" used in a disciplined way could be terribly effective.

Better than adrenaline.

He saw the other driver curving around . . . and then begin to change direction again. He had probably changed his mind and decided that this was more fight than he wanted.

And that was a fatal mistake. Once you were in it, that was kind of *it*. No dodging, no running, no escape.

You had to finish it.

And now, as if it was an old-school dogfight, he was on the tail of the fleeing bandit. There was no remorse as he held the rifle and—while steering now—fired.

First shot—the guy kept going.

Then another, and the vehicle streamed off in a random direction, the driver hit. The car was slowing, heading nowhere until it came to a dead stop.

Raine wondered if he should stop, too, pick up anything useful from the surviving bandit car.

But that would take time. Time taken away from getting the supplies back to the settlement, and also time when more bandit friends might come around.

Seemed like in the Wasteland, bandits were like flies at a picnic. Leave something tempting around and they were all over it.

So, running at full speed, he checked his compass and left the dead bandits behind.

It took a few minutes of driving before he realized that—on some level—he had enjoyed that.

The Outrigger Settlement didn't appear out of nowhere, like the Hagar Settlement resolving itself from the desert haze.

No, he could see it from miles away.

Huge tanks sat on the sides of the road, built into rocky ledges on either side, all linked with pipes.

Raine stopped his buggy.

Best to take all this in from a distance before he just drove into unfamiliar territory.

Hate to be mistaken for a bandit.

No flags in this world, no uniforms. Life seemed cheap.

No, life *was* cheap.

Even from out here he could see people walking around. Hard to tell if they were armed. From the looks of things, the Outriggers had a big fuel-processing gig going on here, and they probably would do anything to protect it.

It made the Hagar Settlement look like a rest stop.

Had they spotted him yet? Raine wondered. They must have

radio signals so they could have been given advance notice if he had been spotted.

He decided to cruise on in, nice and slowly. Let them know he wasn't making any mad dash for one of their big tanks.

He put the car in gear, and the buggy started moving forward again.

SEVENTEEN

THE DEAL

To enter the settlement, Raine had to pass between two jutting cliffs. Armed men in Mohawk hairdos looked down at him, black smears under their eyes, their heavily muscled arms sporting swirling designs.

Stole a few tattoo tricks from the bandits, it would appear.

Or maybe they were ex-bandits? Recruited for security?

He passed under great pipes that crossed from tanks on one side of the dirt entrance road to the other. A girder let guards walk across, looking down as Raine cruised in slowly.

No one tried to stop him.

Not yet.

Then he saw a formal gate—not just a collection of twisted razor ribbon and abandoned car parts, but a real mesh gate.

There were more guards here, except these wore a brown outfit as if they worked for Shell.

Back when there was a Shell. And an Exxon and all the other fossil fuel companies now turned fossils themselves.

How'd the Outriggers get so lucky to have this franchise in the desert?

Maybe a question he'd get to ask the settlement's boss— Rikter.

That might take some doing, though, as the gate remained closed. A guard spoke to him from the other side.

"Your business, stranger?"

Stranger . . .

Seemed to be a powerful word here. You were either part of a settlement, connected to one group or the other—or you weren't. That left two options:

Bandit

or

Stranger.

Neither was a particularly welcoming label to be given.

Then there was the—so far—elusive Authority. Though Raine hadn't seen any sign of anything that one would call "Authority." Right now, the only thing that meant authority out here was a gun. There was a lot of "authority" pointed at him at the moment, so he chose his words carefully.

"I'm from the Hagar Settlement—"

The two guards looked at each other. A dismissive look, as if the Hagars weren't thought much of. Easy to see why, when looking at the refinery-sized proportions of this place.

"—and I have something for Rikter. From Dan Hagar."

Not much of a reaction to that, either. Raine held up the sealed pouch that he was to deliver. Then, to help their decision-making, he decided to put a bit of fear in them. After all, even rough, tough-ass guards didn't want to screw up. "It's for Rikter. I'm sure he doesn't like being kept waiting. Let him know I am here."

Another look—a lot less dismissive this time. One of the guards reached down and picked up a radio handset. After a few moments of hushed conversation, they looked back at Raine. Finally one guard said, "Okay." They started opening the gate. As Raine pulled through, the first guard said, "Head straight until you see that large dome, the main tank. Across from that is Rikter's compound. He'll be there."

Raine nodded.

And then he heard the gate close behind him.

Inside the fence, he passed the Outrigger Settlement's residents, all staring at him, some pointing at his vehicle.

It made him wonder about the other day, when he had driven out of Hagar for the first time. Was it him they had pointed at, or his car? He imagined your status was definitely connected to the level of wheels you drove.

He saw a big blackish-gray tank looming ahead, an oversized ball that dominated the compound. Ladders stretched up one side to a flat top, with an antenna rising meters above the whole settlement. Definitely some communication capabilities here . . .

Across from it, a square building. More guys with guns outside.

Raine stopped his buggy.

One of the guards smirked. As Raine walked up, they openly grinned and nudged each other as they looked past him at his ramshackle vehicle. "Not much to look at, hm?" Raine asked. "But you should ask the bandits out there"—he pointed—"what they think of it." The guards sobered up a bit at this.

"I'm here to see Rikter."

The guard nodded at the door, and Raine entered.

• • •

A man stood there looking at rolls of blue paper—like schematics or architectural drawings—that filled a long table.

Another man in a hard hat nodded, standing beside him.

For long seconds Raine stood there, the message from the Hagars in his hand.

"Get the damn pipe fixed. Right here." The first man jabbed a finger down at a spot on the drawing. "I don't care where you get the parts from, got it?"

The hard hat left, and Rikter finally looked up.

"Yeah. What they want now?"

Rikter was massive. Unlike a lot of the people Raine had met since his emergence, he looked well fed. Access to some private stock that only the fat cats got to munch on?

He also had two swirls on the side of his cheek, similar to the ones he had seen on the guards on the ride in. Tribal markings of some kind? The mark of the Outrigger boss?

Fuel equals power. Back before the asteroid, and apparently now. If you got some, no matter how little, it meant something. The Outriggers were clearly sitting on something.

Had to be a cache.

He wondered why the Authority, if they were as powerful as everyone made out, didn't simply take it from them.

Unless—the Outriggers ran this on behalf of the Authority.

How large was the Authority's spread?

So many questions . . .

Raine cleared his head—it was becoming a habit—and spoke. "The Hagar Settlement was attacked. People need medical supplies. It's probably all in here," he said, holding up the pouch.

"And who the hell are you?" Rikter came from behind his desk, sizing him up. "You're not a Hagar."

"No. I'm not."

A nod. "So? Where'd you come from?"

"Is that important?"

Riktcr grinned. A few missing teeth. Dentistry a lost art?
Lose a tooth and it remained lost.

Like limbs. Eyeballs.

That glimpse of the gaps in Rikter's mouth reminded Raine
of where exactly he was. This wasn't Earth. Not the Earth he
remembered. Might as well be on another planet.

What happened to the great plans to preserve civilization?
The great Ark Project?

Was this the result? He hadn't had a lot of time to think about
the situation, but it was becoming clearer:

There's something wrong with all this.

"Let me see," Rikter said, extending his hand and taking the
envelope. He unwrapped the cords holding it tight, then read it.
"Didn't peek, now did you?"

"No. You saw that it was sealed. I'm just here to pick up some
supplies."

"This the deal, hm? Could be we got something here. Let me
talk to some of my people. You wait here, 'kay?"

"Sure."

And Rikter left him standing in the office while he went out.

Raine didn't hesitate: he looked at the charts on the table.

No small operation, and the hand drawn plans showed ex-
pansion in the works. Business must be good. Financed by—

Rikter walked back in.

"Like our plans?"

Raine looked up. He had two men with him.

"Looks like things are going well in the fuel business."

"Always need fuel in the Wasteland. You know, if we can only
get up to speed, we could even get some planes back in the air.
Be helpful"—he took a few steps closer to Raine, the two men
with him following—"to have planes."

"No flying?"

Rikter looked at the two men with him, then back to Raine. "What? I mean, the Authority has a few hovercraft. And here and there you see a balloon vehicle, though they've been outlawed. But—jets?"

He laughed.

It occurred to Raine in that moment that Rikter somehow knew . . . *knew* where he came from. And that meant he was in trouble.

Gears started falling into place. But by the time they clicked, the two men had quietly moved to either side of him, each the equal of Rikter. Big guys, arms that turned giant valves on fuel pipes, hands that steered girders and metal into place—and now suddenly had a new job.

They latched onto his arms.

"As you can guess, I accept the Hagars' deal. I'm having the medical supplies sent on to their settlement now. And you, according to the deal, Ark survivor, are *mine*. To deal to the Authority, I suppose. And I thought today was going to be a nothing day."

"Hold on. *I'm* the deal?"

"Afraid so. Always the last to know, huh?" Then to the two goons, "Take him downstairs. Give him some water, that's it. Then"—he clapped a hand on Raine's back—"we simply wait for the Enforcers to show up. You're going to love them."

They dragged Raine away.

EIGHTEEN

NO GOOD DEED— PART TWO

They threw him into a cell, an eight-by-eight stone box.

No place to sit or lie down but the stone floor.

They don't plan on keeping me here long, he guessed.

He stood there, smelling the dankness of the underground jail, scant light sneaking in through barred windows on the wall outside.

As he would in any bad situation, Raine started to weigh options.

And it wasn't long before he realized that there didn't seem to be any.

Dan swapped him in a deal with the Outriggers for the supplies he needed. On some level it made sense. He had people hurting and dying; they needed help. And Dan's rescue of him *could* have brought the bandits sniffing around.

Still—he knew what he would do to Dan, or to anyone named Hagar, who crossed his path again.

He heard voices. Two men, down to the right. Talking and laughing.

The voices came closer, until finally the men stood in front of him, one barrel-chested, with eyes that seemed recessed in his nearly perfect spherical head.

Not much room in that skull for brain activity.

The other guy was as gaunt as the first one was fat. A comedy routine, the two of them. They stood there for a moment and just stared past him. Finally the fat one spoke.

"So, this is what the *past* looks like."

"Looks like a big piece of nothing," the skinny one replied.

Raine stood a few feet from the bars watching them. One held a stick. No, not a stick—a pole. Like Little John from Robin Hood. Except it was metal.

Nothing too merry about these men, though.

"Too bad we have to—"

The move from the fat one came quick, swinging the metal pole around and jamming it hard between the bars and into Raine's midsection. The end of the pole went into his stomach, and he gasped, unable to breathe as he doubled over.

The blow sent him to his knees.

When he looked up, the staff had been passed to the thin one, who was—as best he could in the confines of the space—bringing the pole down to smash on his head.

Raine didn't have time to get a hand up to catch or deflect it.

The smack sent sparks flying in front of his eyes.

As he reached up to touch his head—feeling the wetness there, the skin broken—his eyes suddenly flashed with iris readouts, showing them drop.

The nanotrites don't like what's happening. Hopefully they can repair it quickly.

The pole had been passed back to the fat guy, grinning, his mouth open, a watery cave of brown teeth and bloated tongue that worked slavishly to keep the jailer's lips wet.

He was going for another jab, this time at his exposed back.

Guess they're not going to kill me, Raine thought. Made sense, if he was to be traded. *Bruised, bloodied . . . imagine that's okay.*

And what would the Authority do with him? He wasn't optimistic.

The pole came jabbing through the bars, and Raine moved fast, rolling onto his back and grabbing it inches from his chest.

It became a battle of strength and leverage as the big guy tried to twist and turn it to yank the pole away. The other jailer joined in, wrapping his skeletal hands around it. But now Raine had both hands on it.

He could play this game. Basic martial-arts training, a bit of aikido. Twist, turn, use an opponent's overcompensation.

In seconds Raine had the bar free of their hands, sliding it into the cell.

He stood up and got off one sharp poke right into the side of the fat jailer, where even all his blubber couldn't keep the terrible pain from making him howl.

The other jailer had already backed away.

Until they both stood as far from the cell as possible.

When the fat jailer could finally talk again, he wheezed, "Don't worry, you'll get worse than that. We know what the Authority does. They know how to make survivors *beg.* You'll disappear—just like the trash from the past that you are."

Raine raised the pole as though he actually had a shot at the two of them.

They instinctively cringed and backed away.

"If you want more," Raine said, "you know where to find me."

And he didn't say that just as a show of bravado. If they came back, if they tried something more, if they wanted to appease their sense of having been beaten, they could screw up.

Screwups were good. They could be goddamn lifesaving opportunities.

For now, they just moved on.

The corridor outside the line of cells—with Raine as the only apparent guest—turned dark.

The air turned cool, and in the dankness felt clammy.

For once he was glad to still be wearing the Ark suit. As bad as it was in the heat of day, now it gave him some warmth.

He lay down on the floor.

In seconds he was asleep.

Still on the floor, cheek against the stone, his eyes popped open.

Noises—from down the corridor. A hacking, wet sound; a cough. Then a groan.

Raine sat up, then quickly stood. Maybe his two keepers were back to play some more.

He grabbed the pole from the floor and stood ready. Neither of them had the balls to try and retrieve it.

He heard steps. Light steps—not the jailers—and then . . .

There stood the girl he had rescued from the bandits.

She was barely visible in the dark shadows of the jail, but it was unmistakably her.

"You? What are you doing here?"

She didn't answer, but instead started to insert random keys into the cell lock, fiddling with them, the keys jangling. She did speak, though.

"C'mon, c'mon, c'mon—"

A click—the tumblers of the lock turning—and the cell door swung open.

She looked up at him.

"Are you saving me?" he asked.

He expected her to smile, but her face, as best he could make out, looked grim, determined.

"Yes." He realized she had an accent, almost like something from the sun-drenched islands of a century ago. Did those islands exist? Any of those people?

"You saved me, I save you. Now we"—she rubbed her hands together as if sanding one with the other—"clear!"

"Right. That's the way things work here, hm? Nobody does anything without some payback. Thanks anyway. But how do we get out of here? The guards? The fence?"

She looked left and right. Raine realized how small the girl was, not much more than a kid.

"The way I get in, you get out. That's how I saw you."

"You were here . . . to steal?"

A nod. "Outriggers. They easy to steal from. They stupid. I come here lots. For fuel. Weapons. I will get you out."

"My buggy? My guns?"

Now, finally a smile. Proud at her thoroughness.

"I got them. But hurry. Never know when new guards come."

She turned and started running down the corridor. Light on her feet, hugging walls, a feral thing.

That just saved my life.

When they got to the stairs leading up, Raine saw Thin and Fat. Both on the ground. Both surrounded by dark pools that Raine didn't need a light on to know were blood.

He saw his knife stuck on the side of the girl's cloak, held by a strap.

The knife she'd used to kill them.

She took the steps two at a time. Raine's midsection still felt the blow that they had rammed him with, but he hurried as best he could.

They were outside.

In the distance, twin flames snaked up from metal buildings, shedding a pale light over the Outrigger complex. Brighter lights dotted the outside of some of the buildings.

But not enough that anyone would see anything Raine and the girl were doing.

He followed her as she went ahead cautiously, looked, then went farther from the lights.

She knew what she was doing. Probably grew up doing this.

And probably was still growing up.

She turned to him and put a hand up. *Stop. Wait.*

He nodded.

Voices off to the left. Some workers standing there, just talking.

He and the girl had to remain crouched, waiting.

Eventually, Raine could hear the rhythmic sound of the people saying goodbye, or good night, or whatever the hell it was they said to end their middle-of-the-night conversation.

When they moved away . . .

"What's your name?"

She turned back to him, eyes narrow, face set, as if he had asked a bad thing.

"You do not need that. You don't need name." She looked around. "We go."

She led the way across a road, both of them in the light for a bit before hugging a building across the way.

He realized that he was completely in her hands.

• • •

He didn't have to worry—at least not at this time—for she led him to his buggy.

"I moved it," she said. "After everyone asleep. Your guns—they in there." She ran to the fence, which looked perfectly intact.

That is, until she pulled at a corner, and like rolling up a piece of paper, it made an opening. Big enough for the buggy to get through? Guess he'd find out soon enough.

"C'mon. You go. Now, hurry."

"You're not going to want to hear this again . . . but thanks."

Nothing. A world without thanks. Without helping people. The total land of tit for tat.

So much for preserving civilization.

He turned to the buggy, then stopped and turned back to his savior.

"My knife?"

She quickly shook her head. Different rules for that, for stealing.

But she smiled again.

Here's the lesson, Raine thought . . . not all bandits are the same. They are just existing in whatever way they can, with whatever code they have. Kill? Yes. Steal? Yes. But at least this one, from whatever group she came from, had some kind of rules.

Rules that saved his life.

But could probably just as easily end his life some other time.

He got into the buggy. Flipped the switch. It started, the roar seeming horribly loud.

Best to get the hell out of here fast, he thought.

He pulled close to the opening in the fence.

The buggy's front cleared the opening, but then the roll bar above the driver's seat got caught. He stopped. The girl wedged herself against the car and yanked the metal mesh up a bit higher. The roll bar popped free, and she jumped away, rolling in the dirt.

And he was outside the fence.

Still night, morning hours away. The old-fashioned luminescence of the compass showing a direction.

He turned to look back for the girl . . .

But she was gone. He should be, too.

And now, guest in this world or not, he had a score to settle.

NINETEEN

BETRAYAL

Raine rode back to Hagar, rifle in hand, waiting for either bandits to swoop down from nearby hills or Outriggers to come roaring from behind. Could they have found the two dead guards?

Chances were such things like killing guards and escaping didn't go down too well here.

He looked at the radio. Not that he was tempted to use it.

No, he figured a surprise return was in order.

Were there other options?

He could just head out, on his own. Find some other settlements, town, a city. But where? What direction? There was only one place he knew, and that was the Hagar Settlement.

And he wanted to look Dan in the eye when he confronted him.

A plan? Get some supplies. Get them to give him some idea

of where to go, what to do. Because he knew that the Hagar Settlement couldn't be safe. Not when the Outriggers discovered he was gone. Not when the Authority discovered they'd lost their prize.

And why the hell do *they* want me so much? Raine wondered. Just because he was a survivor?

None of it made too much sense.

Like the rest of this world.

I've gone down the rabbit hole, he thought.

Was there any way out?

The settlement took shape in the shimmering waves of the sun blazing down, half blurry illusion, half real. He kept driving toward it, wondering if the guards had been told not to expect his return.

But they lowered their weapons as he came close, and backed away, permitting him to enter.

Raine slowed his buggy, gave them a nod.

Just back from a little drive, gents.

Already he saw that much of the debris and destruction from the other day had been cleared. Life returning to normal.

He turned left, around to the makeshift infirmary, past Halek's weapons workshop.

And every few feet—much as he didn't want it too—he felt his anger growing.

He walked in. The wounded in the back, the dead bodies removed.

One of those attending the wounded looked up.

"Yeah, can we—"

"Where's Dan?"

"He's—I dunno—with his brother, I guess."

The person went back to looking at an IV drip. No meters hooked up to the wounded. This was medicine circa 1912. They probably had it better in the trenches. But this was the stuff his life had been traded for. If anything, that made him angrier.

He turned, walking past his buggy and heading toward where he hoped he'd find Dan.

He pushed open the door, a rattling piece of metal hanging lopsided off its hinges. The push was hard enough so that Dan, standing at a table, looked up, startled.

Nearly went for his gun, Raine thought.

Raine held his at a nice forty-five-degree angle, fingers wrapped around the trigger.

"Raine? You're here?" Dan stood up, noticing the gun. "Alive?"

"Funny, isn't it? Yeah. Guess your deal didn't take. Though I see that you got your medical supplies."

"They told Halek that . . . you had been wounded. Killed."

Raine took some steps forward. Clanking sounds from the back. He was experienced enough to be aware that Halek was back there with all his gun stocks and barrels.

"They said—wrong."

Now Raine released his gun and took a swing at Dan, fast and hard. A good old-fashioned crash to his lower jaw. And Dan Hagar went flying down to the ground. Raine leveled his gun . . .

And then put it down on the table.

This was how he saw it: he still—in some way—needed these bastards. So a bit of payback—and punching someone in the face always felt good—and then he'd get their help. If not, then someone would really get hurt.

Dan rubbed his chin.

"What the *hell* are you talking about?"

"C'mon, Dan. Get the hell up." Raine held his hands open. "See, gun down, no weapons. Stand—the fuck—up."

Dan did.

And Raine threw a left this time. But Dan—now aware—moved fast. He deflected that blow with his right forearm, while he threw a punch at Raine's head, a punch that fell short by a mere inch.

"What are you doing?" Dan yelled. "I saved your goddamn—"

Raine reached out and grabbed Dan by his jacket, pulling him close as he brought his head forward and smashed his forehead right into Dan's face.

Dan staggered back, blood now coming from his nose.

"You're crazy," he said.

"You dealt me to Outriggers! For medical supplies, remember? Is that what you were planning to do the whole time? Hold onto me until the opportunity was too good to pass up?"

Then he saw Dan freeze.

He turned, rubbing his bloody nose, and looked to the back—toward Halek. Dan didn't face him now, expecting the next punch.

When he turned back, he held his hand up. "Wait a second. We can keep doing this. As much as you want. But wait. You said . . . *I* dealt you?"

"Rikter told me. They got me, you got your supplies."

But Dan was shaking his head.

"No. No fucking way. Not even close, friend. Not even a chance."

Again a look back. A rattling of metal. Then steps.

Halek started moving. A back door opened, and Raine could see Halek about to flee into the darkness.

But Dan—blood still streaming from his nose—ran to his brother and grabbed him.

Dan's grip was so strong, the pull so hard, that he lifted Halek off his feet, yanking him backward and letting him fall to the ground.

Interesting, Raine thought. What was this about?

"Stand up, Halek," Dan said.

His brother's eyes looked terrified.

"Stand up, Halek! Or I will pull you up. By your fat neck."

The troll started to get up, getting to his knees, and—even before standing—started shaking his head.

"I don't know what you're thinking, Dan. I mean, you gotta—"

Dan shot a hand out and covered Halek's mouth. Then he turned to Raine.

"As I said, just a minute, Raine. Rikter told you we offered a deal? You for the supplies?"

"Yeah. It was in the pouch you sent."

Dan nodded.

He took his hand off Halek's mouth.

"Speak."

"Look, Dan—we needed those supplies bad. The wounded and all. And other stuff. We always need things from them. A prize like that, like *him*"—he pointed at Raine—"how often does something like that fall into our laps?"

Dan paused, then he did something that was worse than any punch—more humiliating, more disrespectful: he smashed the back of his hand into Halek's grizzly face in a viscious slap. Halek collapsed to the floor.

Then he turned back to Raine.

"Okay. I—guess you can see—I didn't know. Had nothing to do with it." He took a step toward Raine. "I would *never* have anything to do with that. Might as well be a bandit. Damn Outriggers, for all their fuel and buildings, pretty much are just that—bandits. You got out?"

Raine explained his rescue.

Dan laughed. "That is one hell of a bandit girl."

"They're not all bad."

"Bad? No, they have a code. Some do, at least. Still, let's just say you got lucky." Dan dabbed at his nose. "Shit."

"Hey, sorry." Then, with a head tilt to Halek, "Do you mind?"

"Be my guest."

And Raine sent a surprise fist into Halek's gut. The sound of wind being expelled was like the pop of an explosive.

When he went to the ground this time, no one cared whether he got up.

"I'll have to watch my brother."

"You know why I came back?"

"To work me over? Good punches, by the way."

"No." Raine looked around. "Not sure you get this . . . but this, here, your settlement. It's all I know. Where the hell would I go? What would I do? Can't go back to the Outriggers, that's for sure."

"Well, you're welcome. As long as you want."

Which is when Dan's daughter ran in, and in mere moments . . . Dan had to rescind his offer.

Loosum had news.

TWENTY

ON THE RUN

"**D**ad—they're looking for him," she said.

Dan turned to his daughter. "What?"

"Got a message from one of our traders. Enforcers showed up at the Outriggers, and now they're starting to search the area around the settlement."

Raine caught Loosum looking at him.

Like I'm a doomed man, he thought.

"Not good news?" Raine said, stating the obvious.

"Well, thanks to my stupid brother, they won't think you're here," Dan said. "Not at first. Not if they think that *we* dealt you to the Outriggers."

Loosum came up to Raine. "So you have some time."

Dan nodded. "Not much, though. They'll come here. Have to. They'll check everywhere. Once they know there's a survivor free, they won't stop."

Raine looked at them both. In that moment he realized that, like it or not, his only human connection to this world was this place, these people.

Now what?

He didn't have to ask.

"Okay. So here's—" Dan started, but then looked at his daughter. He obviously relied on her for support and ideas.

"You have to leave," she said bluntly. "We can get you stocked up. Some food. More ammo. Halek can get you a shotgun, which is the best thing if you run into muties."

"The mutants?"

Loosum nodded. "They don't exactly go down the way the bandits do."

Dan put a hand on his shoulder.

"But hit them enough and they do go down."

"So you get me . . . supplied. Then what?"

"Wellspring," Dan said.

"The city?"

"It's the only place you might disappear. I do some deals with their mayor. Guy named Clayton. As corrupt as they come, but he honors his deals. I know you can make yourself useful to him, and he, in turn, can buy you some time to disappear into Wellspring life. The Enforcers will still show up, but hopefully you can be invisible by then."

Loosum walked closer.

"But you've got to lose that suit," she said. "I'll get some clothes together. You can't show up looking like a survivor."

"Get to Wellspring," Raine said. "Meet the mayor." It seemed surreal.

Dan nodded. "And then what? Is that what you're thinking? Look, Raine, I'm guessing this isn't what you signed up for. This isn't the 'future' you thought you'd get. Well, unfortunately, this is all there is. Right now, you have only one job. Survive."

"I'm okay with that plan."

Dan smiled.

Loosum looked at her father. "The races. It's the only way."

Another nod, and Dan turned back to Raine. "You'll learn about them as soon as you get there. The races in the stadium. People come from all over the Wasteland to compete. You might easily pass as another one."

"Doesn't sound too healthy."

No smile this time. "It isn't. A lot of the racers don't last long. But—you don't have a lot of choices. Of course, Clayton may see another use for you, though I'm guessing it won't be until you have remade yourself as a racer."

Loosum tapped her father's arm. "In that buggy? God, they'll eat him alive."

Dan looked at Raine apologetically. "Can't give you anything else, friend. I *can* see that my people get it working as well as it can, though."

"Better tires, for starters," Loosum said. "Another layer of rubber might help."

"Yeah. We can do that. Look, I stay out of Wellspring. That's a world . . . I want to avoid. Too close to the Authority, and too close to people who don't care whether anyone lives or dies."

"On my own, then?" Raine said.

"'Fraid so." He shrugged. "And I can't tell you what to do. But it's an option—likely the best one you've got."

"I got something . . . an idea that might help."

Dan turned to his daughter, a question on his face.

Loosum smiled. "How about I teach him how to use a wing-stick?"

Now Dan grinned. "Right—good idea." He looked at Raine "You're going to *love* this."

"I'm guessing it's a good thing?"

"It can be." He turned back to Loosum. "A quick lesson, then you better get him the hell out of here." To Raine, he said, "Who knows? Our paths may cross again."

Loosum grabbed Raine's arm and started pulling him outside.

"C'mon. I don't have a lot of time to show you. And trust me—it isn't easy."

She held the stick, a Y-shaped piece of metal that looked like a boomerang.

Which apparently was the model.

"Okay. See here—I got the detonator shut off. Now it's just a stick. Flies pretty much with just your throwing power, but it does use some of its charge to gain velocity."

Loosum took a stance. Not for the first time, Raine thought that it would be good if he could stay here. Loosum had turned friendly now that he wasn't the enemy anymore—now that Halek had taken over that role—and he could see the appeal to being friends with her.

"Focus, okay?" she snapped. *So much for friendly.* "Arm all the way back, see? You have to gauge your throw to the distance. Practice is what you need. Unfortunately, you won't get much time to do that. When the stick begins to curve back, the small engines kick in, bringing it back to you as fast as it left."

"And then you have to catch it?"

"Watch."

She tossed the wingstick straight toward an open space behind the weapons shop. The stick spun around like an axle flying through the air, creating a shrill whistling noise.

"We could have cut the sound, but hey—let it shriek. Scares the hell out of the muties."

The spinning stick started to curve around, and then Raine saw that its small engine kicked in and the stick got a burst of speed right at the bottom of its trajectory.

"Okay. Here she comes."

The stick came flying back to Loosum, looking as if it might slice off her head.

"Will be just about . . . gliding . . . when it reaches me."

The stick came back precisely to the point where she threw it, her right hand—gloved—open, ready to pluck it.

"Got to catch it. That's the fun part."

"Fun? Looks damn—"

She had reached up and closed on the center of the axle, and the stick stopped.

"There. Got it. And it's ready to go again."

"My turn?"

"No. Not yet. A few more throws by me. Just try to see how to gauge distance, strength of the throw. First . . . over that barrel there."

Like a sports star, she made the stick swing perfectly around the barrel.

"Now a bit farther. Right up to the door to that supply shed . . . Hope no one comes out."

A stronger throw, Loosum's eyes locked on the target.

And again the stick started to loop around just as it reached the wooden porch. The stick came within inches of nicking the door, but safely curved around.

Another perfect catch.

"Okay, *now* your turn, Ark man. Start by aiming at something close."

Raine took the stick, a bit unsure. It's not as if he had ever thrown a boomerang. He imagined that the Aborigines would take months learning how to throw. He had just these minutes.

He tried to model what Loosum showed him.

"No." She grabbed his arm, lowering it. Then took his hand and gave it a small twist. "There. Nice and level. One smooth . . . *move*. But flat, like the horizon. Keep your arm nice and flat."

"Got it."

Raine tossed it. The stick immediately moved out of its nice and level spin. It wobbled upward, then began curving around, and then started to race back, not to Raine, but to the ground.

Loosum ran ahead and caught the stick before it would have hit.

When she turned she was laughing.

"Takes some time."

"I can see that. Don't think I have much time."

"C'mon, a few more. Show me how smart they were. Way back when."

Raine started throwing.

And each throw got better and better.

It wasn't long before he was sending the stick around the barrel, looking almost as smooth as Loosum's throws.

"Okay." She took the stick from him. "Here's the killer secret of the stick. You throw this switch . . . right here. Now it's set to send a targeted explosion shooting from each of its three arms. Like . . ."

"A pinwheel?"

She shook her head, confused.

Pinwheel. Fireworks, carnivals. Kids' toys.

All gone. Might as well be talking about dinosaurs.

"Can't do an explosion here. But when you use this . . . out there. You turn on the wing. And then send it flying around whatever you want—"

"To explode." Raine laughed.

"Right. See. Dad told you you'd love it. Now, we can—"

Dan's voice rang out from behind them.

"Raine. You're all set. Got to get going, friend. Enforcers could be here anytime."

And Raine gave Loosum a look, a smile. He almost said: *Hope to see you again . . .*

But somehow—in this world—such a thought seemed crazy.

Raine sat in the buggy, now riding a few inches higher.

"We put extra ply on the tires," Dan said. "We do it ourselves. Kind of our secret process. Got some food back here. The ammo. And I see my daughter has taught you the ways of the stick."

He caught Dan looking over at him, maybe gauging if he had any interest in Loosum. As beautiful as she was, no doubt she was also a handful.

And probably damn good in a fight.

But that's all he had time for at the moment.

"Nice little weapon."

"Yeah. Might just save your life."

Dan looked at the open gate, his people standing by to let him out.

"Look, there's a note to Clayton . . . in the—what did you call it?"

Raine laughed. "Glove compartment."

"Right. You can read it. It's the best we can do. Map, too. Once there, it will be up to you. It's not the Wasteland."

"You make it sound worse."

"Worse, better? Hard to say. I like it here. Wish you could stay."

"Thanks. And Dan . . ." he looked at Loosum at her father's side, "Loosum—thanks for everything. I think I'd be dead now without you."

"You may still be. But somehow, I don't think you go down that easy."

Raine stuck out his hand, the habit still ingrained in him.

Dan looked at the hand, grinned, and took it.

A firm shake, then a release. A custom from the past, reborn. Raine did the same to Loosum, who looked perplexed with the gesture.

But when she took his hand it was no girl's hand, but strong.

Not surprising.

"Okay, Raine, time to get moving."

Dan nodded to the guards, and they rolled away the metal gate.

"Travel safely. Or as safe as you can."

Raine nodded.

Time to go indeed.

The unknown ahead.

He began pulling out of the settlement, and he didn't look back until it was the merest outline on the horizon.

TWO

THE DEAD CITY

TWENTY-ONE

THE DESERT SEA

The rocky hills and jagged cliffs of the Wastelands changed into a flat plain of rubble and sun, with nothing on the horizon.

A few times Raine checked the map and tapped his globe compass—a far cry from GPS—to make sure he was heading in the right direction to the city of Wellspring.

And it seemed to be, though he would be reassured by seeing someone else heading this way—or anything at all on the horizon.

But the map showed that he still had a lot of ground to cover, especially if he was to reach the city by nightfall.

He imagined that you didn't want to be out here when the sun went down.

It didn't feel any too safe being out here now.

He was well beyond the radio range of Dan's settlement. It's not that he had anything to say, but another human voice would be comforting.

So thinking it might help, being out here all alone, he started talking to himself.

An hour later he stopped to pour more gas into the tank.

Dan had given him four large containers, nearly fifty gallons. Enough—he said—to get him to Wellspring.

He looked up, the brilliant sun overhead.

Raine had wrapped a cloth around his exposed neck and lower face, even though that made him sweat. The material was sodden where it touched him, but he guessed it was a good idea to keep the sun off his skin.

Did it feel different? Was the sun here, now . . . any different?

Clouds seemed scarce. Was there ever a rainy season?

Then he said it aloud. "Ever rain here?"

He laughed. "Rain, Raine."

Again, aloud. "Got some Raine now." He got back in the buggy and started once again toward Wellspring.

It didn't take him long before he resumed his conversation with himself.

"Damn sun is hot."

Dan had given him a hat with a big brim and a flap of material on the back. His hands, though, were exposed, and all he could hope was that whatever it was that helped his wound heal so quickly made him resistant to sunburn, too.

More words . . .

"C'mon, Wellspring. Pop up. Let me see you."

Had to be real, right? Couldn't be a made-up Oz? Fall asleep during the disaster and wake up in a fantastical land. Follow the yellow brick road.

Any wizards there?

He drove, letting his thoughts drift to the movie. The red shoes and the hidden magic they contained. The flying monkeys. They had given him nightmares as a kid. Real nasty monkeys that could *fly*.

And the four of them on that hunt for Oz? Good buddies. Allied in their mission. Loyal, true.

Strong values there, he thought.

Watching out for each other.

Good stuff.

And though he was no singer—even on the most drunken of karaoke nights—Raine began, quietly . . .

" 'We're off to see the wizard, the wonderful—' "

As if in response, he heard a noise from behind. A sputtering cough from the engine.

"C'mon, wasn't that bad. You've heard—"

The joke dying on his lips as his engine coughed again, now followed by a puff of smoke belched from the front.

And that one cough turned into more, until he felt the wheels halting, the drivetrain slipping. The engine clearly in trouble.

"Christ," he said.

And he couldn't do anything as the buggy jerked ahead a few more meters before the engine died and the vehicle rolled to a complete dead stop.

No manual. That was for sure. Not when you had a vehicle that had been cannibalized from a dozen other vehicles.

It was a massive Lego construction, with the only person who really knew how it all worked being the person who made it.

Raine bent over the engine.

The smoking had stopped, but the engine, when switched on, just produced more coughs.

Battery, he thought. They had to be using decades-old batteries, somehow their life prolonged. If he kept playing with the on/off switch, he'd be dead in the water.

Or the desert, as it were.

He had played with broken-down Humvees overseas. He knew the basics. But looking at this crazy quilt of belts and engine parts, with seemingly two carburetors and a handmade drivetrain—he was in way over his head.

He looked up.

Past midday.

He was losing time. And if sitting out here all day didn't kill him, what the night brought certainly could.

He leaned closer. The drips from his brow fell like rain on the hot engine block.

He saw two rows of spark plugs. Again, they looked handmade.

No Delco plugs here. Refurbished, remade, whatever.

"Okay," he said to himself. Another few drops of sweat. "Just take your time. It's an automobile engine. How hard can it be to figure out how it works?"

First thing, he thought, find the fuel line.

Yeah, let's begin with that.

Thankfully, the buggy did have a few tools in the back.

Nothing terribly useful except a tire iron, a screwdriver, and a chunky hammer better suited for driving two-inch nails into wood. But it was more than he thought he had.

Using the screwdriver, he was able to remove what appeared to be two fan belts. Did they both do the same thing? Why two? Then he saw the fuel line leading into the main engine, on its way up to the rows of handmade spark plugs.

If it was misfiring, it could be that the fuel line was clogged. Shouldn't be too hard to get that off. Suck out some of the gas. Clear the line.

He wondered if this happened because the fuel they used wasn't refined petroleum. That maybe it was some low-grade mixture, barely able to burn?

He also wondered if Dan knew that his trip to Wellspring itself could be a 50/50 proposition? Raine knew that staying at the settlement hadn't been an option . . . so maybe facing death in the desert was the only way, as bad as it was.

He pushed that thought away.

"Stay focused," he said.

He had worked on Humvees in the field, sure, but every engine was different. He reached down to the fuel line. It felt wet, slippery. A leak perhaps. Good. If he got that off, if *that* was the problem, he could get this thing going again.

For a moment he allowed no other possibilities, because this one at least gave him hope.

He heard a sound.

A voice.

Wasn't me, was his first thought. *I didn't say anything. Not just now.*

He looked up from his study of the engine. On the horizon, coming toward him and making a lot of noise, was *something*.

Wavy, blurry images of something. Noises like words.

Like words . . .

But clearly not.

He put down the screwdriver. Because he knew he might need both hands free.

Raine ran back to the buggy's interior. First he picked up the handgun. Stuck it under his belt. Then the rifle. For now, he let the shotgun stay in the back.

Could just be other travelers, he thought, immediately realizing how stupidly optimistic that was—and how this was *not* a world to be optimistic in.

All he could do was stand there and watch what was in the distance come closer, slowly clarifying into recognizable shapes.

Raine thinking:

Bandits.

Thinking:

Oh fuck.

But as he stood by his buggy, the sun baking him, it only took minutes for him to see that the figures racing toward him weren't bandits at all.

FUCK.

TWENTY-TWO

MUTANTS

They had no vehicles.

Instead, they loped along, a great bunch of them, almost as if they could gallop. And as they did, they made sounds, grunts mostly, and barking noises. Every now and then Raine saw one tilt its head up and give out a howling shriek . . . seemingly to the blazing sun.

They were still too far away for him to make out details.

But though they had a basic human shape, he could see that their heads looked oversized, eyes way too big in deep-set skulls. Mouths constantly open, grunting. Their arms were extra long, nearly simian.

A line of mutants racing right at him.

Guns, he thought, do these things have guns? Could they shoot?

Because there had to be . . . how many? Ten . . . fifteen of them? They were now spreading apart, fanning out into what appeared to be a tactic for them.

But a tactic for what? What did they want—the buggy, this dead buggy? The weapons?

As they came closer, though—to where he could see their mouths more clearly—he realized it wasn't his possessions they were after.

No. These mutants had moved along on the food chain.

Their interest would only be for the lone stranger stranded in the desert. A gift from above. For them to enjoy.

Raine licked his lips.

Not ever taking his eyes off the line of mutants racing toward him, he reached back inside the buggy without looking. He found one of the water bottles. Brought it to his lips. A big gulp of water. Another. Then, eyes away from the horde for a moment, he put the cap on.

If I survive, I'll need water.

It registered in his head that he had thought *if*.

He brought the gun up.

Still out of range, all he could do was wait.

As he kept them in his sights, he knew there was no way he would have enough time to take them all out before they overwhelmed him. His guns just weren't designed to take on this number of enemies at once.

And then he remembered.

The wingstick! He turned his back on the line of mutants, their sounds an animal braying that filled the air. He went to the back and picked up the stick.

He had barely practiced with it.

But, again, at the rate the mutants were running, even if he shot fast—even if he was amazingly accurate—there would be enough muties left alive to get to him.

And what? Rip me into pieces, most likely.

He looked at the stick. Loosum had done her best. It was up to him now.

He gave it a heft in his hand, remembering how to hold it. The stance. He saw the detonator switch, actually a two-switch system: throw one, then the other switch—and then give it a toss.

How good would he be in gauging how far away they were? Maybe he *was* better off with the rifle.

But no. Dan had mentioned that these things were hard to kill, and something about the way they came at him confirmed that these deformed creatures could probably take a lot of bullets.

He put down his rifle, feeling as if he had taken a step into some distant, ancient past—only a hundred years in the future.

He took the stance that Loosum had taught him. Wingstick behind him, held parallel with the ground. Sweat dripped in his eyes, stinging, making the attacking mutants turn blurry. He wiped it away as best he could.

"Okay, bastards," he said, used to the sound of his own voice, glad of it. He flipped the two switches. "Here we fucking *go* . . ."

And he threw it.

He watched the stick fly through the air in pinwheel fashion, and then—*God, too soon*—it started to arc around. In seconds it would shoot out its explosive charges.

"You get three . . . four throws . . . max," Loosum had told him.

It curved what looked like three meters in front of the mutants. Each arm of the wingstick shot off a low-grade explosive, enough to take a bunch of them out . . . if it had been better thrown.

In seconds the stick was winging its way back to him.

The mutants were closer. He'd get—at best—another throw or two if he was fast. He debated grabbing the rifle. Fight it out in a way that was comfortable to him.

The wingstick flew toward him. He reached up and caught it, those days being a wide receiver in Bay Ridge High School now seeming so incredibly valuable.

I wonder if they even have football now? For some reason, the thought made him grin briefly.

He blinked and took the stance, getting ready for another throw—wishing that the mutants were much farther away, instead of now so near that he could make out the features of the individual monstrosities coming at him.

He threw the stick again.

Raine watched it fly this time as though the wingstick had a mind of its own . . . once free of his hands, it started its journey.

I could have used so much more practice.

But as he watched, he saw that because either the mutants raced closer or he had adjusted properly, the stick started to curve just before the line of attackers.

And he watched the explosions go off, shooting out from each arm.

Two of the mutants got torn apart by the blast, puffy red clouds erupting from places where their heads once were, those severed heads blown backward. The carnage was gruesome. And yet there was a more disturbing thing: their bodies, though headless, kept moving a few more feet before pitching forward.

Two other mutants got hit by the blasts. But despite massive wounds on their sides—Raine could see the blood gushing out—they kept coming.

He looked up to see the wingstick flying back to him.

The line kept coming.

He had time for only one more throw. Then it would be down to guns.

Could he take enough out before it got to that?

He wasted no time resetting and throwing as soon as he caught the stick. His first two tosses had shown him better how to gauge distance. Now he aimed at the mutants to the left, unharmed by the first blasts.

Like goddamn bowling, he thought as he threw.

Need to pick up the spare . . .

The stick flew straight at the group to the left. They paid no attention to it, though they had to have seen its effect on their brother mutants.

Closer now, Raine could see what they had for weapons.

Jagged pieces of metal. Long blades that looked like chunks of steel sharpened into three-foot-long approximations of swords.

Like a butcher's convention. If the butchers worked in hell.

The stick flew at them, then past them.

Shit, he thought, wasted shot. But no, it curved behind the mutants, and at the apex of the curve it exploded, and the blast blew three mutants forward, facedown into the sand.

None of them got up.

The stick flew back.

C'mon, c'mon, c'mon, he thought. *Maybe one more shot, and I got a chance.*

He caught the stick, his fingers latching onto the center. He had to hurry now, no time to take a look or think about distance. Had to get it out.

And too close—he'd have to make this a short throw. Right down the middle.

He took his last throw, but he didn't wait to catch it.

Instead, he grabbed his rifle and—while waiting for the stick to curve around—rested the gun on the front of his buggy, next to the still nonfunctional engine. He barely set himself before he started shooting. Aiming right at their heads.

Had to have a brain, no matter what mutation had turned them into these creatures.

And as he shot, he saw the stick do its last curve and explode. A few of the mutants had pulled ahead, and they caught this last blast, great holes ripped into their midsections.

He kept firing with the rifle, sometimes catching one in the head, at other times a body shot that seemed to do little damage.

No question about it, they could take hits and keep coming . . .

He stopped his firing just a moment to see the wingstick fall to the ground a little ways past where he had originally thrown it. If he lived, it had made the difference.

Thanks, Loosum.

Now it was a last stand. In this desert, the buggy his fort. He kept firing, the line of mutants halved, and now they were close enough that he swore he could even smell them.

And that smell triggered something primal.

Definitely higher on the food chain . . .

If he needed any more motivation, he had it.

He targeted one, then another, mixing up the wounds, trying for the kill.

But they moved in such a strange, crab-clawing way that it was difficult to get a steady bead on their heads, between those egg-sized eyes that clearly weren't human.

A memory flashed through his mind: diving off Belize. Facing a fourteen foot blue shark. Dark, black, ancient eyes focused on only one thing.

To strike, to kill, to eat.

He pulled out the handgun.

With a half dozen of them close now, unfazed by the dead mutants they left behind, Raine was past the point or use of aiming.

They had raised their odd assortment of jagged and sharp weapons, their homemade devices for cutting and tearing.

And just when he wished he heard another human voice—always so important when in battle, having a guy chattering next to you; the little bit of bravado that helps you go on—he found that he couldn't say anything now. No words to cut across the desert silence.

Just the endless chatter of the guns firing, one in each hand like some psychotic character out of a spaghetti western. The grunting bellows of the mutants, so close. He kept firing.

Until—

He was out of ammo.

Out of ammo. And no chance to reload.

How many left? There were two nearly on him. A third, wounded, was still shambling toward him, but then stopped, finally dead.

The last two—one mutant with a curved piece of shining metal that caught the sun, the other with what looked like a medieval weapon, a club with nails and spikes stuck at the end.

They seemed to realize in some insane, brainless way that he couldn't shoot anymore.

They slowed. Barking at him, nearly like grizzlies, testing him before they made their final attack.

Up close, Raine could see the way their bodies were different from a human's. The torso thick, barrel-shaped. The mouths deformed, more like an open chute that had to be filled.

Looking at that mouth, he thought: *No fucking way.*

Not happening.

Not after a hundred years.

Doesn't end here. Not like this.

The two mutants had gone to either side of him, as if deciding which one of them was going to be the first to make the move.

A feast for two.

Raine still held the guns out, though they had both turned useless.

He slowly moved away from the buggy. Should he survive, he didn't want them screwing up the engine any more. They followed his steps.

With an instinct born of a hundred firefights, he knew they were seconds away from making their attack.

He looked—for the quickest moment—at the back of the buggy. A long piece of pipe.

A tire iron. Homemade by the Hagars probably.

A good piece of hard metal.

A last bellow. Their attack about to come.

Raine dropped his guns, spun to the left and grabbed the iron.

And of course, they had started moving.

He swung the pipe like a baseball bat, trying to clear some space before they landed on him. Their smell—now that they were so close—made his stomach churn.

The iron caught the mutant with the curved piece of metal—which Raine realized was a crude sword—in the side . . . to apparently little effect, as it merely staggered backward.

The other mutant, with the club, quickly raised it over his head to smash down at him.

Raine recovered from his first useless hit and—locking two hands on the pipe—jabbed at the club mutant's throat, just under its simian chin.

It reeled back, its intended blow forgotten.

But that gave the mutant with the makeshift sword a chance to hack at him—and hit.

The blade dug into his left shoulder, hitting bone. With a little more force, the arm would have gone flying off.

With all his adrenaline pumping, Raine ignored the blasts of pain, the screaming agony the wound created.

He also ignored the immense amount of blood that started gushing out.

His eyes filled with red lines, the nanotrites feeding back to his brain the information on the calamity that had just overtaken his body.

Absolutely of no use to him now. He blinked it off.

In time to see to the mutant with the club, still gasping for air, but also readying a second chance to plant the club into his head. Its mouth was open, hacking from the throat blow.

A perfect—ugly and smelly—opening.

Raine leapt at the thing as best he could, jamming the pipe right into that hole.

The dark, soulless egg-eyes of the thing went even wider.

Raine pressed harder, all the push coming from his one good arm, the other now useless, hanging at his side.

He heard words.

Curses. Over and over. A litany of death.

His words, as he jammed the rod deeper, like digging in dirt, harder, past the mouth cavity, deeper, cracking bone, penetrating to where there had to be a brain.

Sometimes it's not such a good thing to have a brain.

The thing toppled backward, the dull eyes lifeless.

Without even looking, Raine rolled to the right, shaking free of the dead mutant. He couldn't see it, but he could *hear* the other mutant's blade strike down to where it thought he would be.

Missing by inches, hitting its dead partner.

Raine noticed that the pipe in his hand had a narrow end, where the metal tapered. It wasn't that sharp, but then again, this wasn't a real weapon.

It would have to do.

The last mutant was trying to remove its blade from where it got stuck in its now lifeless partner. The blow had been so strong it lodged the blade deep in the bloated body. From the grinding sounds, it must have caught bone.

Raine took the tapered end of the iron and used it as a blade, slamming it hard against the side of the mutant's head.

The mutant turned at the last minute, eyes trying to comprehend how things went so wrong.

Raine rammed it hard. At first he thought it would just slide away, a useless blow against an obviously stronger skull than what mere humans had.

But then the telltale *crack*.

Not a death blow.

But the skull cracked. The thing's blood, not red but a near blackish-purple, seeped out.

It had its blade free, standing up. Ready to use on its intended target.

But Raine had a way in.

Despite the agony from his arm and the fireworks display behind his eyes, he used the tire iron like an oversized dagger, right at the same spot.

And with the crack open, the iron slid *in*.

Raine left it there. Staggered backward.

He had nothing more to give.

One way or the other, the battle was over for him.

But he saw that for that last surviving mutant, the battle had indeed ended first.

Raine fell back onto the sand.

TWENTY-THREE

KVASIR

He came to, his head bumping up and down, banging against metal.

He opened his eyes, expecting to be looking straight up at the sun.

But the sky had deepened in color, and the sun had to be behind him, low. It felt cool.

He looked left.

Someone was sitting next to him, two gnarled hands on an oversized wheel. A man. He nodded as he steered, as if having some kind of internal discussion.

Then the man happened to casually look over at him.

"Oh! Oh, well. You're up. *Up* is good. Eyes open. Sorry for the—" He slapped the wheel of whatever he was steering.

Wasn't a buggy. Or a car.

More like . . . a tractor.

Raine started to sit up, and the move made his wounded arm ache. He groaned.

"Take it easy there. Just have that arm wrapped for now. Gonna need some real attention once we get to my place."

Raine continued to sit up, taking care not to pull on his arm. Something wasn't adding up. Wait . . .

"Where is . . . ?" he asked, shooting his head around, looking.

"Your buggy? Towing it behind us. That will need some looking into as well. That the best they could give you? Come a hundred years—a hundred years into the future—and you're driving a piece of garbage like that? No respect."

The man laughed. A cackle. Sounded like something he would do whether he had an audience or not.

"No respect for their elders." Another cackle.

Raine saw his buggy being towed by this . . . thing. Not completely a tractor, but most of it was. High seats. Big wheels. Moving so slowly.

"Thanks for—"

"Saving you? Seemed like you did a pretty good job of that yourself. Never saw so many muties just scattered around. Quite a mess. Though I imagine if I hadn't seen you, others would have come."

"Thanks, anyway."

The man shot him a look and grinned through his bristly, wiry beard. "Yeah, well you might have held out. But—sooner or later—you'd be just another body in the desert. Be a shame, after you made such a hash of them." The man went back to nodding, analyzing whatever it was going on inside his head. After a long spell of that, the old man finally said, "What's your name?"

"Raine." He remembered something the man initially said, which had been bothering him. "You said 'a hundred years.' You know—" He hesitated, not sure of the term. "—that I'm an Ark survivor?"

Another cackle. "Word gets around . . . word gets around, my friend. How many days you been here? Amazed you're still alive." The old man's eyes narrowed. "Most don't last long." He sniffed the air. "I'm Kvasir."

"Thanks, Kvasir." A bump jostled Raine, and he winced. He looked at his shoulder. "How's my arm?"

"Seen worse. Will have to unwrap it at my place. Got a real lab there. Be able to take a good look then. But you got those nanotrites. Probably why you're still alive. Damn things can be useful. Sometimes."

"You know about . . . nanotrites?"

The man laughed loudly, head back, a bark up at the desert sky.

"Know about 'em?" Another laugh. "You might say that."

Kvasir shook his head at the private joke.

"I was headed to Wellspring." Raine took a breath. "Or maybe you knew that, too?"

Kvasir took the sarcastic question in earnest. "No. Can't say that I did. Not surprised, though. Out here, where else would you go?" The tractor hit another bump, moving through a ravine. On either side Raine saw a jumble of random chunks of metal that seemed to stretch the length of the pass.

"Not sure how long you would have lasted there. Still, I guess you're thinking about what options you actually got." He looked at Raine again. "Let me tell you, that's the right thing to be thinking about: *options,* my friend."

"If you say so. Where is . . . *what* is your place?"

"You'll see, Raine. For now"—another grin—"just enjoy the ride. Getting dark. Don't want to be out here in the dark."

Raine got as comfortable as he could in the seat as Kvasir took him wherever he was taking him.

• • •

The ravine opened up to a huge, craterlike gash in the ground ahead. The sun was down, but the sky still had enough light for Raine to see . . .

A bridge with a gate at one end, leading across the massive hole in the ground, up to a stony hummock with a building on it. Like everything he'd seen in this world, the building seemed made of three or four different structures slapped together.

Kvasir stopped at the gate, pulling up to a device Raine hadn't thought he'd ever see again. Out of a small speaker—like those from a fast-food drive-thru—a voice.

Kvasir's own.

"Who's there? Go away! Don't want to see anybody."

The old man calmly ignored his recorded self and said his name: "Kvasir."

The metal barrier opened up, pulled by a rickety gear and pulley system. Raine noticed it wouldn't be too hard to ram right through it, so he wasn't sure how much security it gave Kvasir.

"That sounded like your voice."

"It was. Works even when I'm not home. I call it 'voice recognition.'"

Raine grinned. "Never catch on," he said.

Kvasir caught the sarcasm.

"Oh you think that because *you* had everything in the past, that what we do—what we *make*—all means nothing?"

"No. I just meant—"

"You may have had all that. So much. And when you weren't wasting it, you were using it to kill yourselves. And in the end, when the rock fell, what the hell good did any of it do for you?"

"Apparently not much."

The bridge swayed with the weight and movement of the tractor.

Neither spoke for a moment.

Kvasir might have saved his life, but he also was pretty damn prickly. Raine wished the old man would start cackling again.

Then, like a cloud passing, Kvasir said, "Ah . . . who can blame you? It's what makes us humans and not muties, hm?"

Finally they got off the swaying bridge, leaving the disturbing creaking of the metal braces behind, and Kvasir pulled up to his "place."

Raine walked in, and immediately saw that Kvasir's home was more like a science lab: tables with microscopes, a row of computer screens, a mechanical arm suspended from the ceiling ending in a series of pointed tools—something out of an operating room or a nuclear lab. Shelves with jars. The smell was of chemicals and machine oil.

Off to the side, in a smaller room, a cot-sized bed was just visible.

Kvasir threw a switch, and Raine heard the sound of an engine from outside.

"Gets cold up here. At night, at least. Got a heater. Uses my 'special blend' of fuel. Burns like gas, but I can stretch farther than I could with petrol. Even runs my tractor, but it's useless for anything like regular buggies. I'm working on it, though." He nodded to the sound outside. "The generator charges my batteries. And that's the five-cent tour. Okay—lie down."

"Hm?"

Kavsir pointed to a metal table. He went to it and cleared a microscope and metal trays.

"Go on. Lie down here. Can't leave your arm like that, nano-trites or no nanotrites. Got to get something on it. Maybe sew it up a bit."

"You're a doctor?"

The cackle came back. "Not exactly. Research is what I do. But I have some of the Mendicants' herbs. And I know how to sew."

"Mendicants?"

"They grow the herbs. Sometimes they work. Sometimes they don't. We'll see. Now come on, you've had that wound just wrapped up for way too long."

Options, Raine thought. None now but to let this crazy guy look at his wound.

He lay down on the table.

"Well well," Kvasir said, unwrapping the wound. "Yessir . . . the nanotrites are definitely doing their work. Almost hard to tell how deep the wound went. Pretty incredible things." He spread a cream-colored paste on the wound.

It felt cool, and stung when it hit the wound. Other than that, Raine felt nothing.

Kvasir continued. "Those little bastard are good at rebuilding tissue and killing an infection. And I do mean *kill*."

"In my eyes"—Raine wondered whether Kvasir knew that he could see his recovery appear in front of his eyes—"they show that they've still got work to do."

Kvasir didn't look up—so no surprise at that, either.

"Oh, sure. You need more time. And I do think you should let me sew it up. Take a long time for them to seal you up. Make new skin, and all that. Couple of days at least. The stitches will help that process—that's the ticket."

"Okay. Go ahead."

Kvasir leaned close. His hands still unwashed from their trip, wrinkled, covered with the dust of the desert.

"You know, I don't really have a local anesthetic. Got something from the Medicants . . . takes you away a bit. But that's all." He sniffed. "It will hurt."

"I'm okay. Go on."

Kvasir nodded. He turned and put on plastic gloves, not a pristine pair but a pair he took from a nearby wall.

Then pieces of thread. A needle that looked too big.

Raine looked away.

More steps, and Kvasir was back with some leaves.

"Chew 'em. Chew, turn them into mush. Then swallow."

Raine took the leaves with his good hand and put them in his mouth.

He started chewing.

In seconds, he seemed to be aware of more things: the sound of Kvasir moving things; the engine outside; the chemical smells, more intense. Then for a moment, he thought he wasn't really there at all, but back on the desert floor, bleeding out.

Hallucinating that he had been rescued.

He felt the needle go in, except the needle was miles away.

The device with the long arm was above him, now holding a massive magnifying glass above his wound.

The needle began going in and under, then out, pulling its thread, weaving a line to lace the wound tight.

It hurt, but there were so many other sensations to pay attention to.

He barely heard Kvasir say, "Okay, it's done. Ain't pretty. But sealed up. The 'trites should have you in good shape by tomorrow."

The words addressed to someone else. The room suddenly a

warm, sheltering place. His eyes heavy. Sleep seemed irresistible.

He didn't resist.

He woke up on the same metal table. The room was dark save for a light coming from the other room, the small bedroom he had noticed on his way in. He leaned up, the surreal feel of the room gone, now back to its reality. The pungent smells, but not so intense. The puttering of the generator, but not quite so loud.

He had no idea what time it was.

"Hello? Kvasir?"

Raine looked down at his arm. Definitely not pretty, but the wound was closed. And amazingly, it already had a scab forming down the line of the stitches. He touched it with his other hand.

A bit of a sting, but not bad at all.

He heard feet hit the ground. Kvasir getting off his bed.

Raine used his good arm to sit up.

Kvasir threw a switch, and the room lit up, painfully bright. The scientist frowned and blinked in the light.

"Thought you would sleep till morning."

"Sorry. Feeling okay. It's kinda—" He gestured at the table— "hard."

Kvasir moved his head from side to side. "Yeah, well couldn't exactly lift you, now could I?" He sniffed again. "I put a cot over there." He turned away and started shuffling back to his room.

"Thanks, Kvasir. I owe you."

Without turning around, Kvasir grunted.

"I know."

As he disappeared into his room, he muttered as to himself, "Doesn't everybody in this world?"

Nothing for a second.

Then: "Raine. Listen. I'll tell you things. In the morning."

Raine wondered what that meant. Things? His debt to him? Or something else.

"I'll be here."

Kvasir made one last barking laugh, and Raine went over to the cot to sleep.

TWENTY-FOUR

SECRETS AND LIES

Kvasir hovered over Raine.

"There's a hot drink for you. Over there," he said, pointing to a nearby table. "And some food. I guess you're used to eating the synthetics by now."

Raine nodded. He took a breath and sat up, rubbing his eyes. How long had he been sleeping?

Not much light got in here.

"Thanks."

Kvasir was already walking back to his worktable, filled with instruments and trays, his workday—whatever that was— already begun.

The old man sat on a metal stool and peered down at one tray.

"Took a look at your buggy. It's fine now."

"The problem?"

Kvasir shook his head. "Fuel line clogged. You can only burn that crap they use for fuel for so long before you have to go in and clean it out." He looked up from his work. "Didn't they tell you anything?"

"Not much."

"Well, you better learn how to repair your buggy yourself or you won't last long." A snort. "Not that you'll last long anyway."

Raine walked over to a side table. A chipped mug with a hot liquid. Tiny cloud vapors rose from it. Next to it, a chunk of something to eat. Cheese, bread, soy, chemicals? All of the above?

He picked up the warm mug and took it over to Kvasir's table.

"How long did I sleep?"

"Through the night and most of the day. Guess your 'trites needed time to do the repairs." He looked up again, eyes narrowed. No cackles yet today. Definitely in a more serious mood. "How's it feel?"

"Good. I think." Raine raised his injured arm above his head. "Yeah, almost like nothing happened. Even after the stitches. Guess the nanotrites are one bit of tech from the past . . . that's turned out well."

The laugh. Directed right at Raine. "Oh, really?"

Kvasir dropped the two metal scalpels that he held and they clattered onto a tray. Raine saw that he had been doing something to a rock, a clunky analog microscope nearby.

"You think so?"

Then again the grin.

"Think *again*."

Kvasir paced as he spoke.

"Sure, the nanotrites are wonderful biomachines. They'd do incredible things for you. Lifesaving things. Or so it seemed.

Then something happened." He stopped by Raine and looked him right in the eye. "Those miracle machines could turn bad."

"I don't get it."

"Not with everyone, not all at once, but they can take over in a way that nobody saw coming. Instead of healing, the 'trites started changing. Some people just died from them. They were the lucky ones."

Kvasir's laughs had vanished. His face was set now, grim.

"You think the asteroid, that radiation, made *all* the muties? Think again, stranger.

"Sure, the asteroid may have made some of them, the subsequent radiation and all that. But when the Authority began experimenting with mutants and the 'trites, suddenly those savages were everywhere."

"What? The Authority *made* muties?"

Kvasir shrugged. "Word is they took people, prisoners, and regular mutants, too . . . and let the nanotrites take over. Maybe like those things you left dead on the desert floor." He sniffed the air. "Bottom line, they turned people into muties using the nanotrites, and also made the mutants *worse*." He took a breath. "Nice folk, huh?"

"And they just let them out, let them escape?"

Kvasir grew quiet. Not saying anything, as if he had something secret and debated telling Raine. "I don't know."

Not true, Raine thought.

"Who knows? In the end, who cares? They got out. They spread. The fact is that these new mutants loaded with 'trites became like a plague, a disease. Something that could be passed on. You're already infected, so at least you don't have to worry about any muties taking a bite out of you!"

Another barking laugh from the old man.

Raine reached out and grabbed Kvasir's arm. "You mean to say I'm going to turn into a mutant?"

"Are you listening? Hell, doesn't seem like your ears are working too well. Something can trigger the change. Doesn't hit everyone. You could be one of the safe ones. He paused, then:

"I wouldn't bet on it, though."

"When will this happen?"

"You're new. The 'trites inside you have been sleeping as well. Could be months from now. Years. Maybe never. The Authority spent years trying to find out what triggered it and how to control it. In the end, any of the Ark survivors left opted to have the nanotrites removed. Your best option, too, friend." Another laugh. "Kind of an exclusive club."

"I should get them removed, then," Raine said.

"In good time. Don't think anyone ever had them turn this early. For now they help you, work for you. Eventually, you'll have to get them out."

"And then . . . the mutants will become even more dangerous to me."

"Yeah—just like the rest of us . . . Gotta say, though . . . most people don't know much about this. Most think it's just the asteroid. And that was part of it. Strange type of rock, I tell you. It's why I'm working here." He nodded, then picked up the chunk of rock on the table. "Something unknown, something strange inside that rock. And I want to find out what it is."

Kvasir put it back down on the table in front of Raine.

Raine's eyes moved to the table. The chunk of rock on a tray. Thin slivers of a strange material on smaller trays.

"Wait. You mean—*that's* part of the asteroid?"

"It's called feltrite. The core material of Apophis. The rock that changed everything." He started laughing, degenerating into a cough, his mad humor probably the only thing that kept him sane.

If indeed he was sane.

"I promised you secrets. And you know what, Ark man . . . I keep my promises."

He started walking to the door.

"Come outside. You have some decisions to make. Some *options.*"

They sat on a metal chest, like a footlocker.

From this porch—itself a piece of wavy metal that bounced if they shifted their weight—Raine could look out at the nearby hills and the metal bridge.

For the first time, he got a sense of the world here.

"Sun's going down." Kvasir looked over at him. "Gets even more dangerous out there in the dark."

"Guess I won't leave today. First thing tomorrow."

Kvasir spit, sending it flying past the porch. Though it looked clear, Raine could taste a salty grit, the fine dust and sand from the desert, filling the air and coating his lips.

"And where do you think you're going?"

"Wellspring. Only place I know to go. Been told I can disappear there."

"Disappear," he snorted. "You know, you are a *prize*, Raine. An Ark survivor. You know things. You could be useful. Though not based on your buggy-fixing abilities." A cackle.

Raine ignored the laugh. "You mean for the Authority?"

"They won't stop looking for you. They *will* find you. At best, you will be their prisoner. At worst, they will kill you. They have killed so many others. And some end up as prisoners—the scientists, the researchers—trapped in Capital Prime working for the Visionary."

"And who the hell is that?"

"Leader of the Authority. Don't know much about him. There

are theories. Point is, they have all the power. The guns. The science. Everywhere you see, and beyond—it's all *their* world."

"And you're saying they won't let me be?"

"That's for sure."

"So I go somewhere else?"

Kvasir turned and looked at him.

"Yes—and no. Okay, Ark man. Now I gotta just take a chance I can trust you. Can I trust you, Raine?"

"What do you think?"

"Anyone ever talk to you about the Resistance?"

"Resistance? Dan Hagar mentioned that some people were against the Authority. But he didn't say anything about—"

"Good. Best people like him not know too much or tell too much. They might leave him alone, and his settlement. The Authority needs the settlements. For supplies, to keep people in check. But there is a resistance; there are people who fight back."

Kvasir gestured at the open spaces of the Wasteland that lay before them.

"They have a 'vision,' too. Free people. Sharing the science, all the goods from the past. Sharing what was found after Apophis. Instead of it all going to Capital Prime." He took a breath. "That's where I think you belong, my friend. With the Resistance."

For a few moments Raine didn't say anything. "I was sent here on orders. You know. A mission."

"Yeah. To protect people. The survivors. Right?"

"Yes."

"Then that's how the hell you'll do it, friend."

Another pause. Raine felt that this strange world just grew a bit stranger . . . and even more dangerous.

"I guess I could talk to them."

Kvasir raised an arm.

"Look. See over on that hill there? Some muties. Just about

dusk they gather. Always want to get here. But my little traps on the bridge stop them." Another spit at the rock. The gesture belied the confidence of Kvasir's words. He took a breath.

"Fuck you!" he yelled at them.

"How do I find them. This Resistance?"

Kvasir turned back to Raine. He reached out and gave his arm a squeeze exactly where the arm had been wounded. No pain.

Incredible.

But frightening now, too, since Raine knew the nanotrites were like time bombs ready to explode his humanity.

"Your arm's good. You can travel. But not to Wellspring. No. You're going to another city, my friend. Best you give the Resistance a reason to want to contact you. A reason to trust you. Time for the last secret."

Kvasir stood up and headed for the door. The light and color was seeping from the sky.

"Let me show you something . . ."

Kvasir spread out a large roll of paper. Like an architect's blueprint, it showed buildings, streets, a city plan.

"This is the Dead City. The Authority used their scientists to carry out experiments—on the nanotrites, on the mutants themselves—while also trying to understand this . . ." He put his hand on the piece of asteroid, the feltrite. "There are secrets in here, and they're not even close to understanding them."

"Who's there now?" Raine said, pointing at the layout.

"No one. Dead, you know? Things started to go wrong. Things went so bad in the city." Kvasir grinned. "The mutants escaped. They don't know how that happened." He snorted again. "I do, though."

Raine looked at the old man's grin.

"Wait—you did it, you worked for them?"

"Not in the end. I escaped. And I messed up things for them before I left. That's another story. For another time, hm?" He paused. "I didn't tell them what my suspicions were. Where they *should* be researching. Here, I'm just a crazy old man in the wilderness. They leave me alone. Occasional Enforcers will drop by once in a while to see if I have found anything. I give them crumbs. They leave me alone."

"And this city is . . ."

"Deserted. Abandoned, save for the mutants. A half day's journey from here. A city of mutants, my friend. And not just like the ones outside. The Authority carried out experiments. Those 'experiments' still walk around."

"I'm guessing you're showing this to me for a reason."

"What were they trying to do? I never found that out. And what are they doing now? What was the Authority's ultimate goal in experimenting with mutants? Whatever they were, they've taken those experiments into Capital Prime. But they started here, in this city. The clues are here."

Raine looked at the layout, the streets, the buildings.

"Raine—what they were doing there, it got out of hand in a hurry. Bad enough for them to run without even packing up. Bad enough to not want to go back. They took their main hard drives and left, the city swarming with mutants. The experiments . . . out of control."

Kvasir gestured at the city plan.

"Mutants . . . all over. So—some of the backup drives got left behind. It was just backup data. Not too important for them. But with that information, the Resistance might have something it could use to grow stronger. It could have—the truth."

"So why don't they go there, get the damn drives—"

"Not a chance they could get close. To expose themselves there—the Authority could find them. People speak. But you—" Kvasir jabbed a finger at Raine. "Who knows you? No one yet."

Kvasir walked over to a tray, his pieces of the killer asteroid sitting harmlessly in it.

"You go there. Get the drives. Then, you go to Wellspring. I will let my contacts know you will be coming. There's a woman. I used to work with her. If she's interested, don't worry—she'll find you. It's the only way it can work."

Kvasir picked up his scalpels and scraped at the rock. "Something here," he muttered, not really talking to Raine. "Some kind of force. Subatomic. Chemical. A new kind of force. If only I had better equipment."

"And the mutants?" Raine prompted. "You said they are still in the Dead City."

Kvasir didn't look up. "Yeah. It won't be easy." A snort. "No. It will be hard. Deadly. But you are trained. Hell, after what I've seen you can do, it might actually be possible. Sometimes one man is better suited for a mission than a whole army." He shook his head. "Either way, it's safer than the stadium—"

"You mean the races."

Another scrape. "Death traps, they are. A stranger trying to make his way in the Wellspring? Drive, kill, or be killed."

Raine stood still, the repetitive scraping of Kvasir signaling the time passing.

Options.

What options?

He could just ignore him, this crazy old scientist. Could just go to Wellspring.

But then . . . if he were to do what he was sent here to do—if he were to carry out the mission, his *duty*—that wasn't the answer.

After what seemed like long minutes of silence, Raine spoke.

"Okay, Kvasir. I'll go get the drive. Or try. I'll bring it here, and then I'll go to the city."

Kvasir nodded. "Good. I will let them know. And Raine?" He looked up at the survivor. "I do have a few other weapons, things that might be useful. You can take what you want."

Raine nodded but said nothing. Instead, he watched Kvasir take a flake of rock and slide it under the microscope.

"Yes . . . something . . . *here* . . ."

Raine went back to the schematics for the Dead City.

He spent the next hours looking at them, preparing . . . before he finally rolled them up, carried them to his cot, and lay down.

TWENTY-FIVE

THE ENFORCERS VISIT

The commander, his helmet off, took steps forward. With armored gloves covering his hands, he whipped the back of one across Dan Hagar's face, sending him flying to the floor.

Two Enforcers—their protective face masks covering their faces, making them look more like robots than men—stood to the side, each one locked on an arm of Loosum, holding her tight.

Dan saw his daughter pull against the grip of the two Enforcers.

"Bastard," she spat.

"Loosum!" Dan said.

"The Visionary cautions against such disrespect of his emissaries. The rules of the Authority, in fact, make it a crime."

His daughter—always a quick temper.

And this commander, someone of rank, his face marked by scars. Someone who had seen a lot of fighting, whether with mutants, bandits, or settlers.

Someone who knew exactly what he was doing.

"Get up."

Dan stood up.

"Now—I will ask you *again*. The survivor. Where is he?"

Halek stood to the side, cringing. Dan knew if he had any hope of coming out of this, it would depend on Halek keeping his damn mouth shut.

"I *told* you. He was sent to the Outriggers and—"

The commander's hand went up. "Yes, same story. You dealt him for supplies. Yet—somehow he escaped. Resourceful, wouldn't you say?"

"He's military. Trained."

"We'll see how trained he is. When we find him. But that's the future. Let's focus on the past a little while longer." The commander started walking around the weapons shop, picking up odd pieces, looking at gun bores, stocks, bullet chambers. He stopped and turned. "So after he escaped . . . he came back here, yes?"

Dan shook his head. "Of course not! Why would he do that? If he escaped, if he knew we tried to deal him for the supplies we needed? Makes no sense."

The commander walked over to Loosum. "You know, the Authority can always use new blood. Smart people, male, female, who know how to live out here. Who know the ways of the bandits, the settlers." He raised a hand to Loosum's cheek. Gave it a caress.

She whipped her head back.

"And as you know, the Authority doesn't have to ask for volunteers. We take them." He took a deep breath. "All for the good of the people."

Dan's eyes had locked on Loosum's. She didn't look scared. But she did look ready to explode. The wrong move, the wrong words, and she could get both of them in trouble.

"You there. In the shadows. Come here, into the light."

Halek came forward, his face showing his fear.

"Tell me about this . . . 'deal.' "

"This deal. Yes, it was . . . medical help for a survivor. That is what the Outriggers sent to us."

"The deal went wrong?"

Dan watched Halek nod, lick his lips. So damn nervous. "Y-Yes . . . Commander."

"Look," Dan said, "my brother—"

The commander removed a control stick from his side, and smashed it into Dan's midsection, doubling him up. The blow left Dan gasping, looking down at the ground, trying to get air into his lungs.

"You will wait for questions," the commander said nonchalantly. "Next time, I'll turn this on." He directed his attention back to Halek. "Where do *you* think the survivor, this Raine, is?"

Dan looked at Halek, his brother's eyes darting back and forth. If anyone looked like they were ready to lie, it was Halek.

Finally, Dan caught Halek's eyes. Trying to project the message:

Shut the hell up.

"I—I, er, don't really know. N-Not here. Of course not here—"

Said too damn fast.

The commander nodded. "Really. Then—where?"

"To Wellspring. The city. Has to be there."

"Hasn't shown up yet. Least as far as we can tell. Though with all the human cattle who come into the city, he could easily disappear. But sooner or later, everyone gets found."

An Enforcer came up and whispered something in the commander's ear.

He paused and turned back to Dan. "Oh, good news. A real prize has just been captured. A much bigger fish. I'm afraid . . . we'll have to go."

Maybe we're off the hook, thought Dan.

"These settlements. You know, the Visionary tolerates them, as long as they are of use to the Authority and Capital Prime. That tolerance can end, Hagar. I'm sure you haven't told me everything."

"We have," Dan said.

The commander dismissed that with a wave of his hand. "So here's what we are going to do, in case the survivor comes here. Just in case this Raine shows up in your settlement . . . or you hear about him." He leaned down, getting right in Dan's face. "Or you get *any* damn information at all. A bit of encouragement for you to come forward and do your duty."

He turned to the two Enforcers holding Loosum.

"Take her."

"No!"

Two other Enforcers by the door, their guns ready, came and stood by the commander.

"It's called the Authority for a reason, Dan—no matter what you think out here, *we're* in control. The sooner you grasp that, the sooner you can see this pretty young girl. You might even want to do some digging yourself. Until that time . . . your daughter will be a guest in Capital Prime."

"Sick bastards," Loosum said as she was dragged away.

The Capital, Dan knew, was usually a one-way destination. Ostensibly anyone who went into its prison never came out. What did they do with the inmates? Kill them? Let them rot? Use them for experiments?

"Don't," Dan said. "Please. We've cooperated—"

He could still hear his daughter yelling as they dragged her into one of the Predators waiting outside. Just the appearance of the armored vehicles had been enough to clear the streets of the settlement when they arrived earlier that day.

One of the armed vehicles could obliterate the settlement in minutes.

"Listen to me, Hagar. Your daughter will be safe. My word, and the word of the Visionary. Just remember your part of the deal . . . let us know anything you hear about this survivor."

"And if I hear nothing?"

The commander looked at the two faceless Enforcers, signaling them that it was time to leave. "Let's just hope that somehow—for *her* sake—you do hear something."

The commander reattached his control stick to the side of his uniform. He put on his own helmet, shaped like an Enforcer's protective face mask, but with silvery insignia to indicate his status.

"I look forward to your news of the survivor."

The commander turned and walked out of the shop.

The Enforcers stood a second longer, the necessary moments until they knew their officer was in the Predator. Then they, too, turned and left.

When the two Authority vehicles pulled away, roaring out of the settlement like avenging animals, Dan sat down. Loosum taken away, a price set for her freedom.

And Dan kept thinking, wondering . . . what was he going to do?

For now, he didn't know at all.

TWENTY-SIX

INSIDE THE DEAD CITY

When Raine left, loaded with a box of small incendiaries that Kvasir had bartered from someone, he looked back and watched the old man study his progress across the bridge.

The early light colored the hills in brilliant morning shades of yellow, orange, and—in the rocky shadows—a deep purple.

Kvasir had shown him on the drawings the main Dead City building used by the Authority for its experiments, which was once a hospital.

He had also warned him about what he would face.

"Muties. God. Lots of them. Hiding. Waiting. People still try to get into the city to get things. Most don't get out."

Then about the things that were there that Kvasir knew nothing about.

"What they did after I escaped—the experiments; what's there *now*—I can't tell you."

So, as Raine drove, he couldn't even imagine what lay ahead.

And there was nothing he could do about that.

The journey was free of any bandit or mutant attacks.

Almost too free, Raine thought. He spotted a few burned-out vehicles, buggies that maybe had been attacked on their way to the Dead City. As he passed one, he saw the charred skeleton of its driver, still grimly holding onto the wheel. All black bone, flesh long gone.

The flesh. Just burnt away or stripped away? Raine wondered.

He came to what remained of a highway. For a while he tried to drive on the road, but the cracks and jumbled sheets of up-turned pavement made it worse than the rocky desert floor, and he quickly got off it.

It had barely looked like a highway anyway.

Kvasir had said it would be about a half day's journey. Raine wanted to get there fast, hopefully returning to the old man's before dark.

Then on to Wellspring.

And is that what I should be doing? He had been sent here with a mission. Did that mission now include joining the Resistance?

He remembered reading by flashlight in a cave in Tora Bora. A history of the French Resistance. How *Le Résistance* might have done little to deter the Nazi's plans. And worse—it made life hell for the people of France. A hundred people executed for any Nazi or *Pétainiste* killed.

Heavy price to fight back.

Raine's philosophy was that, in a war or a battle, you best

have a chance of winning. Otherwise the struggle and the loss of life just wasn't worth it.

So he told himself, at that moment, he'd decide where he stood—and what he'd do—when the time came.

The broken road by his side, even more gaping pieces without any pavement, curved right. He followed alongside it.

And then—around a small hill, just ahead—he saw a city.

Raine tried to match what he now saw and what he had studied on the charts. A few towering buildings had obviously been broken in half, like branches stuck in the ground during a hurricane and roughly snapped in two.

He saw a few glimmers of reflected light, windows that still had glass. But most of the buildings had dark, gaping holes. Other buildings missed a wall or had no top. It looked as if some force had pried the roofs off like the pull tabs on a can.

The hospital, he thought. Near the center of the devastated city. He'd have to go deep into this destroyed city, the Dead City, to get there.

Did they use this place because it was well away from the cities and settlements . . . so they could keep their work secret?

Or was what they were doing so dangerous that this "dead city" was the only place they could do it? Suddenly he wished he had a convoy with him. A few squadrons of well-armed grunts following in his tracks. Because—sitting here in his buggy, a few sidearms and grenades his entire arsenal—it seemed absolutely insane to be going into the place alone.

He went slowly.

Crevasses mixed with chunks of broken street. Towering buildings had fallen across what were once avenues, forcing him to stop, turn around, and find another way forward.

Once, he nearly drove over what looked like merely another oversized pothole but in fact turned out to be an opening that could have eaten his buggy, a giant pit sliding down to . . . what?

Sewers? A subway? Underground tunnels?

And all the time, while he navigated the streets, he kept looking left and right.

He heard a sound.

At first he took it to be the wind sighing through the open structures, creating weird whistling and groaning noises that cut through the skeletons of the buildings. And some of what he heard was definitely that.

But then he heard other noises. Sporadic. Sudden. Like barks. Quick. Sharp. No wind was making that particular sound.

It was made by something *alive*.

He had the shotgun across his lap. His automatic rifle and handgun sat on the seat next to him.

Each few yards deeper into this city made him feel more edgy. It got to the point where he had to remind himself to be steady. *Keep your eyes open.* Finally saying those words aloud, as he might to a squad trailing along with him.

"Steady. Eyes open. Don't rush."

No, rushing could be the worst. Wanting to get in and out without proper scouting, you made mistakes.

He passed two cars, one a cab, the other an SUV. Both with their hoods open, their innards removed, paint vanished. He wondered if whoever came for the parts got out of the city.

Then, barely recognizable . . . a store.

God, he thought, a bodega. A few letters were still visible, and the faded sign advertised fruit, a few faint bananas sitting next to a faded apple.

He stopped and, from the buggy, looked inside the hollowed-out inside of the building. Whatever it carried had long ago vanished. Now only the ancient signs remained, a reminder of what life used to be.

He took a drink of water from the canteen Kvasir gave him. Then he ripped off a piece of the "bread," its doughy texture a poor excuse for what he remembered.

"Loaded with good stuff," Kvasir had said.

He thought: *Will I ever taste real, fresh food again?* He looked longingly at the pictures of fruit. He imagined that all those tastes, the smells, were gone forever.

All gone.

Raine started the buggy again.

The way to the hospital was blocked, as though someone had piled up a line of smashed cars and trucks, half a bus, and a container car from a train to create a wall of metal.

Odd, that they all just ended up here, cutting off the street.

He'd have to leave his buggy, climb over, make his way to the entrance of the building.

Raine looked up.

Three stories tall, and Kvasir said the data room of the hospital was at the top. The Authority had run their experiments out of this building until they couldn't anymore.

He had heard sounds. Were there mutants here? And if so, where were they?

It was an edgy feeling that he'd had before, patrolling dark city streets in Iraq.

But never this bad.

He killed the buggy's engine and grabbed the pack from the back. The hard drive Kvasir described would be compact and not have much weight—the pack Kvasir had given him should be perfect for the job. And, despite how quiet it was, he put a few incendiaries into the pack.

He got out, stuck the handgun behind his back and filled his pockets with shells.

He'd like a free hand, but it would be wisest to bring *both* the automatic rifle and the shotgun. He looked into the buggy, seeing if he'd forgotten anything.

He grabbed the tools from the back. The screwdriver. The hammer.

The tire iron.

You never know . . .

Quiet wasn't always a good thing, he told himself. He slid the iron into his pack, the handle sticking out over his shoulder.

He started climbing over the wreckage that blocked the way to the abandoned hospital.

The revolving door had been smashed, the rotating blades devoid of glass.

A sign in the lobby said: BE PREPARED TO SHOW PROPER AUTHORITY IDENTIFICATION.

The place smelled. A sharp metallic stench mixed with something like oil, as if pipes had burst here. To the right he saw stairs. They were behind two security doors, both now hanging off their hinges.

Whatever—whoever—went through this building didn't like doors.

A sea of shattered glass glistened on the floor. A reception desk had been smashed in two.

Would anything be left of their computers?

Seemed unlikely.

Holding the rifles at hip level, he took a breath, the smell still horrible, and started up the stairs.

On the second-floor stairwell—in the darkness, with scant light coming from the corridor outside—he stopped.

He heard sounds now. Nothing too loud. But there was definitely movement. A sound of steps. He tried to place it. On this floor, or below? Or maybe just above him?

Fuck, he thought.

He just knew one thing now: he definitely wasn't alone. How many incendiaries, the handmade grenades Kvasir had given him, did he throw into the pack. Four? Had he taken enough?

And though his pockets were filled with ammo, if there were muties here, you could go through bullets so sickeningly fast with them.

You never had enough.

The sounds stopped.

He started up the stairs again.

He walked past laboratories, the once gleaming metal tables turned over, cabinets with empty shelves ripped off the walls.

And past the labs, what might have been patient rooms—save for the fact that the bed frames had leather straps all around. Whatever was put into these rooms . . . no one wanted them to get up.

In one room, he saw walls covered with a dark, purplish crust. Like blood spatters, the type of thing you'd find after a firefight in close quarters. Except here the color was wrong. He thought back to his fight in the desert with the mutants and remembered something.

They didn't have the same deep red of human hemoglobin.

He squeezed his guns tightly. His companions.

Where the hell was the data center? So far he just saw rooms with echoes of whatever mayhem had taken place here.

Finally, at the end of the corridor, he came to a room without any glass. Two heavy doors lay flat in the hallway.

Something wanted in, and had ripped them off.

He looked into the room. Without electricity, it was dark. But there were two high, narrow openings, the glass shattered long ago, sending in thin shafts of light.

It would have to be enough.

He had a moment's hesitation at the entrance. The sounds seemed to have faded.

Rats, he thought. *Mice.*

Except he imagined that the rats and mice of this world were long gone.

He walked into the room anyway.

Raine ran his hand along the flat metal face of the hospital computer. Kvasir had shown him which section held the hard drive. And as he touched the metal, he felt indentations in the panel.

Someone had tried smashing into this metal wall, denting it but unable to get inside.

If it had been mutants, they probably wondered what might be inside that they could eat or use as a weapon. If it had been humans, maybe their thinking was that the stuff inside would be of use in trading. No matter who, they had moved on, never getting at the guts of the computer.

He came to the third section of the machine's casing, his hand still sliding over more indentations.

Then he crouched down.

Shit—hardly any light at all. At the bottom, the front face of the panel ended in a lip. And below that lip, three different holes with a hexagonal shape.

He put down both his guns and dug out the screwdriver from the pack.

Raine worked it into one hole—not a perfect fit, but tight enough so he could wedge the iron into the hexagonal hole, twist it to the left, and then begin to loosen the bolts holding the bottom of the panel.

He worked on each bolt.

And when the last one came loose, the metal panel popped open a few inches from the bottom.

More bolts probably on the top. But now, with that opening at the bottom, he could use the tire iron as a wedge. He slid it into the open bottom, and began to pry the metal panel open.

He kept prying it until he could slide his arm in and up.

The interior felt pristine.

Undamaged.

He felt along inside, running his fingers over the wires and chips that made up the machine's brain.

He felt for the hard drive—a flat, book-sized rectangle, Kvasir had said. One of many backups and redundancies.

His arm buried awkwardly in the thing, Raine weighed getting something to stand on so he could get up to undo the other bolts on top.

Just get the damn thing open.

But then he felt it. Smooth. Firmly planted in a rectangular bay.

The drive. Had to be.

All the data from whatever they did here. Whatever the hell the Authority had been doing with the mutants.

He grabbed it, his fingers barely able to close around the shape, because of the bad angle. He was hurrying. He told himself to slow down.

He pulled on the drive. Nothing.

And he didn't want to pull so hard that it snapped. Or popped out so fast that it flew up and out of his hand, smashing to the floor. Useless.

He gave it another controlled pull up, measuring the amount of strength he used.

And then he felt *movement*. He adjusted the pull, and the drive popped free.

Now, like removing a living creature, something being born from its mother, he withdrew his hand.

He had it. For a second he looked at the prize.

His gift to the Resistance. His ticket, too. Maybe.

Now to get out and away.

But in those seconds of looking at the drive, at the thin black brick in the shadows of the room . . . Raine heard the noises again.

Louder now. On this floor. Steps.

Mice, he thought. *Nice try, Raine.*

Something was stumbling over debris. The sound of shattered glass being stepped on.

Not too much stealth going on.

He was deep in this hospital from hell—and he was trapped.

He put the drive, the screwdriver, and tire iron into his backpack, slipped the pack on, and picked up his rifles.

There was no point waiting here for them to arrive.

Time to see what's still alive in this "dead" city.

TWENTY-SEVEN

A BIG PROBLEM

Raine got to the doorway to see exactly what was coming.
At both ends of the corridor was a line of shadowy figures, outlined enough so Raine could see the way they walked.

The stumbling gait.

He thought he even saw a few down on all fours. Crawling?

Haven't seen that before . . .

A result of the Authority's work here?

As soon as he stepped into the hallway, the mutants started making their barking noises, some sending out high-pitched screeches.

He wasted no time taking both guns in one hand and reaching into his pack for one of the grenades. Antiques. Handmade grenades. Would they even work?

He pulled a clip on one, tossed it to the line of mutants to his left, and then quickly grabbed another. After wedging the second grenade under his arm to get the pin out, he sent that one down to the right end of the corridor.

The blasts went off within seconds of each other, cacophonous in the closed hallway.

The mutants responded with screams and shrieks. If this place had been bedlam when the Authority was doing its experiments, well . . . bedlam had returned.

Now what? he wondered.

He had three more grenades.

It took seconds for him to see that they had done little damage. A scattering of dead and mutilated muties at either end, while a seemingly endless supply of mutants crawled over the bodies.

Raine started to think of other possibilities. One thing was clear: standing here was pointless.

He started moving left, since ultimately that was the direction of the hospital exit and his buggy.

Light-years away.

As he did, the smoke from the explosion faded, and now the horde of mutants, their heads tilted like a line of attacking bears, all holding things to smash, cut, or chop him up . . . kept coming.

He grabbed another grenade and sent it flying ahead, then tossed another back behind him as far as it could go.

One grenade left . . .

He passed a room on the left. No windows. A box to die in.

Move on.

He was getting closer to the mutants at that end, an insane move, he knew, but he had no other choice.

He now started firing his rifles, holding both at his sides. The automatic rifle sent out a spray of bullets. Moving, shooting, but without taking the time to aim at the dozens of them . . . his shots didn't do much.

The damned mutants could take hits.

The shotgun was a bit better, hard for even them to move with a basketball-sized crater in their torsos. But after two shots it was useless. No time to reload it. He stuck the shotgun through the strap of his backpack, barrel down.

He passed another room on the right.

He stopped. A patients' room. It had a barred window.

Third floor.

What was the building's facade like? he wondered.

If he went in there, he knew one thing—he wouldn't ever come out the way he went in.

Not in one piece.

He raised his automatic and started taking aim. He brought down a few of the mutants in front.

Give the others something to climb over.

He spun around to the other end. They were getting close, too, racing their monster brothers to see which would get to him first.

Raine could feel his own heart racing, adrenaline pumping, but also fighting an insane anxiety that screamed at him:

It's all over. This is how it fucking ends.

He was out of options. He ducked into the room and moved quickly over to the glassless window. He pushed against the bars, still firmly in place. He looked down.

The window below had a ledge, and if he could lower himself to it, he might be able to get to the ground safely. If he missed . . .

Anything like a jump from this height would leave his legs broken.

Again, though—no options. He pushed against the bars again. The mutants had to be only steps away.

He aimed the rifle at the window ledge and fired. The shot made the stone around the bar blast away. A quick kick and the bar went flying. He shot out another, but it was still not enough room for him to get out.

The mutant shrieks were now just behind him, tempting him to turn and fire at them.

But his training kicked in, and all that experience that made him able to lead men into the hell of battle—the ability to stay cool under so much goddamn pressure, to stay on task—took over. He fired another quick blast, and he kicked a third bar away.

He had room now.

He lowered his rifles out the window and let them fall. Then he quickly climbed out, turned around, and—fingers holding onto the lip of the windowpane—slowly lowered himself out of the window, legs dangling.

His upper body strength . . . not what it was. Not after a hundred years, no matter how good the cryo program.

The pull of hanging made his clawlike fingers ache.

He looked up.

The first mutant face peered into his, eyes wide at the dangling prize before it.

His feet *had* to land on the ledge below, on the second floor.

And he had to do that *now*.

The fall was only a few feet. But doing it blindly, knowing what he was in for if he missed—it wasn't a good feeling. He struggled to slide straight down, feet flat, knowing he'd have only a few inches of purchase to catch his fall.

He landed . . . but the weight of the pack and the way his feet hit gave him just enough of an angle so he tilted away from the face of the building.

And suddenly, after that moment of arrested fall, he was sliding down again, the bars of a second-floor window passing him.

He had one chance to stop this too-fast descent—and he made a quick grab at the bars of that window.

One hand missed completely, grabbing air.

But the other locked onto a metal bar. And after that hand slid down to the window base—despite aching fingers—it held.

Raine quickly brought his other hand around and grabbed a second bar.

He had stopped his race to the ground. But he knew he couldn't risk moving his hands, one at a time, to the ledge.

No, he'd have to fall from this height, and hope he could land well enough so he didn't break bones . . . and more important, not fall backward and smash the hard drive.

He counted down . . . three . . . two . . . one . . .

And then he let go, mentally willing his legs to be as flexible as possible.

He hit the ground, a good landing, the shock to his knees and upper legs not mind-numbingly painful; but he did stagger backward, about to roll onto his back. He quickly moved his legs—not the most graceful move, but it prevented the backward roll.

The judge from Romania gave it a 6.7 . . .

He hurried over to his guns. He picked up the pump-action shotgun and quickly reloaded it. He slid it back into its makeshift holster across his back.

Time to get the hell out of here.

It was quiet on the street—probably since it appeared that most of the Dead City's good citizens were in the hospital trying to get to him.

He took a step.

And that step was matched.

By a vibration.

The ground shook. Then again. Until standing there, his eyes wide as he tried to figure out what the hell was going on, he realized that the thundering noise, this shaking . . . were *steps*.

He broke out into a run toward his buggy. At the same time, something came from behind a nearby building, right near his buggy, stepping over the neat barrier of destroyed vehicles that Raine had scrambled over to reach the hospital.

Stepping over it all so easily.

A mutant. Thirty feet tall. Holding a sharpened piece of metal girder in its hands.

Raine went to his knees.

He took aim at the thing as it came stomping and roaring toward him, so fast for something so big. He fired at its head, its eyes. But he could see that this thing—this monster that outdid all the other mutated monsters—bore the results of a *lot* of wounds.

Others had tried to stop it—and failed. Burnt, blistered areas of skin. Additional holes near its eye sockets and skull.

None of it seemed to matter.

It was doing just fine.

Raine sent one bullet into an eye socket. But the giant bobbed and weaved as it moved, maybe a strategy learned . . . or simply its natural style. If he had damaged the thing's sight, there was no sign of it.

He kept firing the shotgun, the blasts echoing, even as he looked . . . seeing what was behind the creature.

A few "normal" mutants trailed it, like lampreys sticking close to a shark.

The creature brushed at its eye where he had hit it. Then it bellowed.

Raine could swear the nearby buildings vibrated from the horrific sound.

The creature picked up one of the smaller mutants at its feet. And threw it—

Like a toy. A doll. The crazed mutant kicking and flailing as it flew toward him.

Bad aim, though—as the mutant went harmlessly *splat* behind him.

He fired his shotgun at the giant's head. The blast left its cheek with a blackish hole.

Did it do anything other than change the cratered landscape of that thing's face? Because, Raine thought, if it did nothing . . . then he was truly fucked.

He stood up. This taking time to stand and deliver, taking aim at the thing . . . didn't seem to do any good.

Options. He imagined the other mutants streaming down. Soon they'd join this party.

Raine pumped the shotgun, aimed and fired again . . . and again, feeling more and more that the shells were mere pinpricks to the monster.

When now, the giant only meters away, he noticed something in the creature's repetitive bobbing and weaving.

At the tip of its skull—an *opening*.

Something had wounded it there, and blew off a piece of skull.

And, glistening on the top of its domelike head, what sufficed for its brain.

Raine turned away and dug out the last grenade, ignoring the hissing, howling shrieks behind him.

The thing had started swinging its girder at him. It wasn't close enough to hit him—not yet—but he could feel the force of the wind as the steel flew in front of his face.

Raine pulled the pin.

His fingers shook, whether from sheer fear or the residual ache of getting out of the hospital.

Twenty-second timer. Could be an eternity.

He attempted to count. Another thumping step from the thing, and it reared its head back as it roared.

A totally unpredictable move.

Counting . . .

Had to be time, he thought. *Now.*

And he lobbed the grenade upward. Thinking he had not gotten it high enough.

He had always been a football guy. Needed better skills on the basketball court. Never could sink the big ones. The grunts from East New York and Bed-Stuy always whipped his ass.

But then the thing lowered its head as if curious what this small thing flying toward it could be.

The open pit on the skull a good-sized target. But now—it was all a matter of luck.

And then Raine—thanking a God he didn't believe in— watched the grenade bounce into the open pit, hit the thing's brain material, start to roll out of the pit—when it exploded.

Stuff went *flying* from the thing's head.

It dropped its girder, pinning a group of mutants at its feet.

The thing's hands went to its head, thoughts of a human lunch replaced with a message of pain, and probably a loss of functioning as its brain material flew into the sky, spraying this closed-off street.

Raine didn't waste any time watching the thing tumbling to the street. He raced past it, taking care to watch which way the tree-sized monster would fall. He ran fast, knowing that the mutant horde couldn't be far behind. He reached the piles of cars and scurried over.

He heard the crash of the mutant falling behind him but didn't stop to look back.

Jack had his beanstalk . . . I have a pile of burnt-out cars.

As he came down the other side, he half expected his buggy to be smashed. But when he reached the ground, it sat there.

Looking perfectly fine.

One of the best damn things he had ever seen in his life.

Raine jumped in, taking care to stow the backpack securely in the rear.

He started it up and then hit the accelerator with a near maniacal fury as he raced away from the hospital. The buggy barreled down streets, past the eerie remnants of this place, this now dead city.

And when he was finally out of the city, he thought . . .

Dead City.

Yes . . . but I'm still alive.

TWENTY-EIGHT

SEEING KVASIR

The first hint Raine got that something was wrong was when he stopped at the entrance to the rickety bridge to Kvasir's place.

The gate was up—and considering how paranoid Kvasir was about keeping his place safe, it triggered an immediate alarm.

He pulled up to the order-box intercom.

"Kvasir?" Then again louder. "Kvasir. You there?"

But the automated response failed to come on. Was Kvasir's security system down? No booby traps ready to explode?

He looked at the squat building on the hill ahead, just across the bridge.

Couldn't see anything wrong.

Raine ached from his time in the Dead City. Some quiet and some security for the night would be good.

In fact—he wasn't even sure he could do anything more than get into Kvasir's place and collapse.

Now—he was immediately on guard.

He started across the bridge, traveling slowly, waiting for something to stop him . . .

But nothing did.

He stopped, and saw what now girded the building. Surrounding the building, overlapping, covering the doors and window, were banner-sized bills.

NO ENTRANCE PERMITTED BY THE ORDER OF THE AUTHORITY, UNDER PAIN OF IMPRISONMENT.

They'd been here.

Looking for me?

And where was Kvasir?

He grabbed his pack, the guns, and walked up to the forbidden door.

A board had been nailed across it.

Raine grabbed the wooden board and started pulling. The nails were driven in deep, but he yanked hard at one end and it finally sprang away. He then twisted the board back and forth until it popped free.

He took the stock of the shotgun, slammed it down on the handle, and the door kicked free of the jamb.

He paused a second, then walked in.

The place had been ransacked. The shelves, once filled with vials and containers and trays . . . now all empty.

The old-school microscopes—also gone. Nothing here at all.

But one sense told him that wasn't exactly true, and for a moment his intense fatigue was dispelled.

Something *smelled* wrong.

He walked back to where Kvasir slept, the dark room behind the lab. The smell stronger.

And he saw the old man.

Tied to a chair, head down. Blood spatters around the room. He saw . . . what had to be a terminal wound in the man's chest. Kvasir looked down at the floor as if wondering: *How did this happen?*

The pigs—they didn't even take time to bury him.

Just took everything, and left the body there to rot.

Raine could imagine the scene. The Authority blasting their way up here, past Kvasir's gate. Was there a firefight with the old man, or did Kvasir somehow hope he could talk to them?

He had been able to do his work and deal with them *and* the Resistance, for years.

What changed?

Raine guessed the answer.

They wanted me. They followed me here.

Did they then go to the Dead City? Did Kvasir tell them anything?

He hadn't seen them on the return trip. That, and the scene in the room, seemed to say no.

Kvasir said nothing and paid the ultimate price for it.

Raine walked around to see if there was anything left in this room. But aside from the man's clothes, it had been picked clean, too.

He turned and walked out to the lab area again, now as empty as the examination room in the Dead City's hospital.

Soon it would be dark.

The bridge was still there, but the gate wasn't functional.

He knew he couldn't go anywhere, not with night close. And besides, before he left—there was something he had to do.

• • •

He found a spot behind the building, flat dirt that ran flush to a sheer wall of rock.

Dirt that he could dig.

A small shed behind the house contained a few tools: a hand rake, clunky sheers. And a small shovel. Not really up to the job, but it would have to do.

So Raine dug, occasionally hitting stones that he had to pull out with his bare hands.

Until he had a hole he felt could hold the old man's body.

He went back into the house, the light fading more each minute, and cut Kvasir's body free. He picked him up. Some of Kvasir's blood stained Raine's clothes as he carried the body. It seemed a small price compared to the old man's.

Outside, he lowered the body down.

A different person might have said something more, Raine knew. But all he said was, "Rest in peace, Kvasir."

And he started covering the body with the dirt, eventually filling the hole, pounding the dirt mound flat with the back end of the shovel.

Then he went back inside.

Night was beginning.

And so, too—Raine guessed—his problems.

He sat on the porch, the generator—still some fuel inside, thankfully—humming away. Lighting the place up. He sat on the makeshift bench on the porch, the rifle across his lap.

Would anything come? Bandits, mutants, or maybe . . . for some reason . . . Authority Enforcers?

His eyes would shut and he'd quickly force them open.

And so, like that, eyes locked on the entrance to the bridge, he passed the next few hours.

Until he woke with a start and realized he had fallen asleep. He was still sitting out in the now cool desert night air.

Not good, he thought. Easy pickings to be out on the porch, exposed.

The generator still hummed away.

He got up and walked inside the building, the smell of death still in the air.

Raine shut the door, wedging a chair under the knob. He knew it wouldn't stop anyone who really wanted to get in, but at least he'd hear if someone tried.

He walked over to the cot Kvasir had put out for him only days before.

He lay down.

For a few seconds he cocked his head, listening to the sounds of the place, as if making an imprint of what the sound of safe and quiet was . . . so he'd know the difference.

If things changed.

Then he allowed himself, gun still in hand, to fall asleep.

He woke with a start. Light outside. Morning. He felt immediately that he held nothing in his hands. He turned to the side and saw the gun on the floor. He sat up, taking a breath.

He had been—as the expression went—dead to the world.

In a way, I am kind of dead to the world. Does anybody know that I'm here?

He stood up. He knew a few things. Staying here wasn't an option. There was no future in hiding at Kvasir's hut until something came for him.

No, Wellspring, and whatever surprises it held, was where he had to go. He had something the Resistance could use, if Kvasir had been able to tell them.

Otherwise, he would be on his own, having to find them somehow.

And how long before he encountered the Authority in Well-spring?

Maybe that was something that—now—he looked forward to.

This wasn't the first time he had seen an innocent person trussed up, tortured, brutally killed. And if he ever asked himself why he did his job—why the hell he was a solider in a strange land—seeing something like that answered the question.

Just as it did now.

Time might have passed, but the vicious, bloody battle of good and evil didn't look all that much different.

Raine always knew what side he was on.

That's all he ever needed. He might have to be careful, he might have to bide his time, but in his own mind he knew why the hell he was here.

And with his body still aching, he walked out of Kvasir's lab, taking his things out to his buggy for the journey to Wellspring.

THREE

WELLSPRING

TWENTY-NINE

THE MAYOR'S SUGGESTION

The walls that surrounded the city towered two stories high, each metal plane ending in a giant, toothlike serrated edge, as if to discourage oversized pigeons from landing on them.

Raine saw people streaming in and out of an entrance, guards milling about. By the time he got closer, he had joined a line.

He saw other buggies. Some were as small as his, while others were more like trucks, loaded with material in the back. Each driver had to stop and talk to the guards before being waved in.

Might need my passport, he thought, only half joking.

He pulled closer, and the guards held up a hand, stopping him, while they walked around his buggy. Finally one guard came closer.

"Don't see a travel tag."

Raine took a breath. He knew it was dangerous to expose how much he didn't know about this future.

"Travel tag?"

The guard looked at his compatriot. A small shake of the head. As in, *Maybe we gotta watch this one.*

"Anyone coming into the city needs a tag to do business. And if you're staying, you need to have a garage and place to stay. No buggies, armed or not, allowed sitting on the streets of the city." Another shake of the head. "Where the hell you from, anyway?"

"Right now? Came from the Hagar Settlement. Before that, did some work for other settlements."

Raine guessed that lie sounded okay, since the guard nodded.

He also knew it was best to anticipate the questions and problems in a situation like this.

"Dan Hagar said I should speak to the mayor."

"Looking for work? Ain't much here, stranger. Unless"—now guard one looked at guard two, this time with a grin—"you like to *drive.*"

"I drive okay."

"In this? Piece of—" The guard looked up. More vehicles had lined up behind Raine. This chat was slowing the operation down. "We'll let Mayor Clayton know you're coming right over. He can decide whether you stay or go."

Raine nodded. "Right."

The guard gave him a few directions to get to the mayor's compound. Then the two guards stood back and let him into the city of Wellspring.

And it was a city, with buildings looking almost normal—except where a wall had peeled away, replaced by random metal sheeting. Or the brick structures that turned into wood halfway up.

And everywhere there were signs. Some advertised things Raine didn't understand, such as a fat grinning face—a jowly man with poached-egg eyes—saying in a speech balloon, "Watch and Win! Mutant Bash TV, every Friday!"

Don't want to miss that, he thought.

Then there were signs from who called the shots here, messages from the Authority.

One sign: REPORT ANY ILLEGAL TRADING TO THE ENFORCERS.

And: THE VISIONARY AND THE AUTHORITY *ARE* THE FUTURE.

There were even bars, and Raine was reminded about how this started for him, being picked up at that Red Hook dive near his apartment.

People looked at his buggy as he drove down the streets, a few of the roads with rough, near-cobblestone pavement, but most just dry, packed dirt surfaces.

He drove past what looked like a sports stadium. A sign: RALLY TOMORROW—THE WHITE RABBIT!

This was where they race, he realized. The place was dark now, quiet.

Ahead he saw a building that looked like it had once been a museum or library—a few pillars left standing outside—save that half the building was gone.

Guess repairs and renovation don't get done around here.

There were more guards on the steps, standing casually, dressed like Wild West characters who'd had too much of the local brew. Long coats, big hats, vests, and guns in holsters, rifles slung over their shoulders.

He pulled his buggy alongside the building entrance.

"Can't leave *that* here," one guard said.

"Got a meeting with the mayor," Raine said.

"Best be back in fifteen minutes. Never know what can happen to a vehicle left on the street."

The guard laughed at that, and his partner joined in.

Raine walked past them. "Sure hope nothing happens to it," he said as he passed the guard who spoke to him. "That would be unfortunate." He held the guard's eye, unflinching. "All around."

The guard looked away.

Raine went into the building—a sign pointed to a stairwell, MAYOR'S OFFICE—and he went up the stairs to meet the mayor of this not-so-fair city.

Clayton had his feet up on a desk and smoked something. Not quite tobacco, yet it didn't smell like anything more powerful, at least anything Raine had ever smelled. He blew a smoke ring into the air.

"Son, come on in. Pull up a chair."

"Mayor, thanks for seeing me."

Another puff, another ring. Raine remembered a favorite film from his childhood. A videotape—God, VHS—of *Alice in Wonderland*. Of the caterpillar sitting above Alice, puffing away.

Talking in riddles.

He looked around and pulled a wooden chair close to Clayton's desk.

"Looks like you've had some bad times out there." Clayton gestured with a hand, pointing at the obvious smears on Raine's clothes. "Best get some new clothes, son. Stuff like that unsettles the good citizens. They're nice and safe here. Don't need any reminders of what's out there." A big smile. "Beyond our *walls*."

Clayton wore a hat as well, a leathery fedora of some kind. And what appeared to be a monocle that he could flip up and down. Added to his carefully crafted beard and mustache with tapered points and a perfect V shape, the mayor of this city was . . . something to see.

His long jacket had to be miserable to wear in the heat.

Part of the effect.

"I was hoping—" Raine began.

"Now hold on, son. Just wait a bit. See, I got this here note from Dan Hagar. Saying you would be coming. Needing some"—bushy eyebrows went up on cue—"help?"

"Just trying to get by, Mayor."

Those same eyebrows narrowed now. "That what you were trying to do out there?" A hand waved at Raine, as if his torn and spattered clothes clearly told the story of everything he had been through. "Get by?"

"Got some dangerous things in the Wasteland."

"Ha. Tell me about it. You know what?" Clayton took his feet off the desk and leaned close. "It's damned hard to keep the trade routes open. To the settlements, to Capital Prime, to the other regions. Hard to find someone with enough . . ." He paused, as if savoring the word. ". . . *balls* to make those trips. That something you might be interested in?"

"Yeah. Thought I could find some kind of work here."

Clayton took another drag of his cigar, the noxious smell and smoke filling the room. If he kept it up, Raine thought he might have to retch. He kept his cool, though.

Clayton nodded. He picked up a note. "Hagar doesn't tell me your name here. Got a name, son?"

Raine hesitated. He thought of creating something. Steve. Joe. But he didn't know what Dan had sent along. And if Clayton was the big kahuna of this city, best not to start off getting caught in a lie.

"Raine."

"Raine. Interesting name. Just . . . Raine?"

"Nicholas Raine."

Did the Authority, who had to still be looking for him, have that name? Or did they just know there was a survivor somewhere out there?

If the latter, a nameless survivor could have been easily killed in this world in a dozen different ways.

"Good name. Let's talk turkey, son."

"Let's."

"See, I don't know much about you. Not much at all. And Dan, well we deal with him. Hell, in my city we deal with *everyone*." He laughed. "Except muties. They're kinda hard to deal with, if you know what I mean."

Raine nodded.

"Even the Authority. They come here, we do some trading. I let them know that I am a big supporter . . . a *big* supporter of the Visionary. They tend to leave us alone."

A knock on the door, and a young man came in and handed the mayor a sheet of paper . . . and walked out again without a word.

And Raine wondered: *Did this guy get elected? Appointed? Who or what made Clayton mayor?*

"So," Clayton continued, "my motto is simple: 'No trouble.' With anyone. Now son, you might be trouble. That is, unless you fit in."

"That would be the goal."

The words made Clayton smile. "Good. Just what I hoped to hear. 'Cause you see, though Dan spoke well of you, seems he has his own problems."

"What happened?"

"Seems the Authority came looking for . . . somebody. They took his daughter. In case Dan learned anything."

At that moment Raine wondered if he might have to shoot himself out of this office, then out of this damn city.

He wouldn't have given much for his chances of success.

"The Authority will keep looking. Trust me on that one. They'll find . . . whoever they are looking for."

Bastard's enjoying this, Raine knew.

My life in his hands.

Or in Clayton's words . . . my "balls."

Still, someone who was willing to deal with everyone from bandits to the Enforcers might be looking for what worked best for him in his city. The fact that they were still speaking meant it wasn't time for him to pull out his gun and start making his goodbyes.

Clayton stood up and walked over to the window.

He looked out and tapped it.

"All the good people out there," he said with a look back at Raine, "and some of the not so good—they need what I get them. The food, the water, the fuel. More important—the reason to live."

He turned away from the window.

"And I think . . . you might help me with that reason, Mr. Raine. Seems you can fight. Seems like you can drive. Some people come here from all over, from all the settlements, from small shit-ass towns that barely hang on. They even come from the Capital. Know why? They come here to race. To race and to live."

Clayton had walked around to the front of the desk. He sat down on the edge, looking down at Raine. So close now. He stubbed out the ersatz stogie in a glass ashtray.

"The races keep people happy. Lets people fit in here, too. You race, why you'd be just like anyone else who came here seeking . . . fame and fortune."

The bastard knows, Raine thought. But he's willing to risk using me.

"So you're saying you'll let me stay if—"

Clayton put up a hand. "Son, I can find you real work. On the routes. But you're going to need to work up to a better buggy."

He thought for a moment—or at least was putting on a show of thinking. "The races," Clayton said, snapping his fingers. "*That's the ticket.*"

In just moments the job, a real job, had vanished.

"You see, Wellspring is an open city. You can come and go as you like. That is, if you got a place to stay. Place to keep your buggy. If you got work. Then, it's an open city. I'm just . . . *suggesting* . . . that if you want to stay. If you want to get yourself some better wheels . . ."

Clayton sent another ring of smoke up toward the ceiling. "If you want to avoid any *problems* . . . you'll race. Maybe then, after a while, I can get you some work keeping the routes open."

Again Raine thought about Dan talking about the races. He had seen the stadium as he drove here. Big place. Hold a lot of good citizens.

The racing car fans.

Thinking: *The bastard has me.*

If I have to race, then I'll race.

After all—how bad could it be?

"Okay. I'll race, then."

Clayton leaned forward and slapped him on the shoulder, a big smile showing his teeth freshly covered with the brownish goo from his smoke.

"Welcome to Wellspring, Raine."

THIRTY

THE RULES OF
THE ROAD

Clayton led Raine out of his office and down to the street. The two guards at the entrance nodded.

"That your buggy? God—not much, is she?"

"Does what it has to."

"Well, if you're gonna race, you'll have to get some tweaking done to it. And you'll need a sponsor."

"What is that?"

"Sponsor, son. Someone who pays your way into the race in exchange for getting their name promoted. Advertising. Not my area of . . . expertise. Go see Jackie Weeks, the race promoter; he can get you set up. Tell him I sent you. Race is tomorrow. I'll be there. So will everyone else in town."

Clayton again shook his head at Raine's buggy. "Didn't know you were driving something so . . . small, so beat-up. But hell, got you here, didn't it?"

"Yes, it did."

Clayton flipped his monocle device up, like a jeweler looking away from his examination of a rare stone.

"I can't make you any promises, Raine. About anything. But you just remember that today, here, now . . . I did you . . ." He leaned close ". . . a fucking favor."

Raine nodded. This was a world of fear. You never knew when you would need something, from somebody. A place where favors could be very, very valuable.

Is that why Clayton didn't deal him to the Authority?

Or did that deal lay ahead?

One day at a time.

Clayton told him how to find Weeks—in his office at the back entrance to the stadium—and Raine got into his buggy. As he drove, he thought of Dan . . . and Loosum.

If there was a way he could do anything about that, he would. And Kvasir, too.

He felt a growing need for payback, a need to change things. But for now he had a race to worry about.

Jackie Weeks walked around Raine's buggy.

"Yeah, yeah, yeah—Clayton called me . . . told me you'd be coming over. Christ, *look* at this thing." Weeks looked up, his round face disgusted. "You want to take this into the stadium?"

"If you have something better . . ."

"Right, right right— sure, we just *give* away Cuprinos."

"Cuprino?"

Another shake of Weeks's head, followed by no explanation. "Look, Mick in the shop handles all the prerace checkouts. Could be he can do something with this. Engine may not be too bad. But where the hell are your defenses?"

"Defenses? It's a race, isn't it?"

Weeks smiled now, followed by the condescending groan of one who knew something about talking to a total newbie.

"Yeah. Just a race." He shook his head. "You need to protect your buggy. Accidents happen out there. Got it?"

Raine wasn't too sure.

"Accidents? What the hell kind of accidents?"

Weeks leaned close, as if passing on a secret. "The cars, they bump into each other. Sometimes they crash. It's a race, but . . . it's also something else."

Raine thought: *Right. It's a goddamn demolition derby.*

"So, Mick might be able to do something for you. But Clayton said you got no sponsor? Key-rist. You can't drive—can't pay the tab—without a sponsor."

"Any ideas?"

"Been to Sally's yet?"

"What is that?"

"Keep forgetting . . . you're new here. You know *nothing*. Sally's is a bar, run by Sally LePrine. She used to be a regular sponsor at the races. Lets everyone know where to go for a drink, to hang and talk buggies. But she lost her driver."

"He quit?"

"Er—no. He lost a race."

"So?"

"Starky beat him. And when Starky wins, usually the other driver doesn't do so well. Trip to the Wellspring hospital at the least. Not a place I'd recommend visiting. Sally's driver avoided that fate, though."

Raine waited for Weeks to finish his tale. He didn't wait long.

"He didn't make it out of the stadium alive. Great fucking race, man. Great one. Just what the crowds love."

Rome, Raine thought. This place was ancient fucking Rome.

And I'm getting thrown to the lions.

But his face didn't betray anything. Instead, he simply said, "You think she wants to be a sponsor again?"

"Don't know. But worth a shot. Worth a shot. Meanwhile, I'll have Mick take a look at this piece . . . of automotive wonder, 'kay? Sally's is down that alley there. Don't stop at any of the cafés. They're not real cafés, if you understand my meaning. New blood like you wouldn't last a Wasteland minute in one of them. Oh—and get some new damn clothes. This is fucking entertainment after all."

Raine nodded and, leaving his buggy, started on foot for Sally's bar.

Sally LePrine looked around at the usual suspects sitting at the bar.

When a Mutant Bash show was on, the place would be filled, barely room for anyone to get to the bar for a drink as they watched the blood and death in the MB Arena.

But now, midday . . . her bar harbored only those who had given up any hope of anything, nursing their stim drinks, eyes bleary. Every now and then she'd have to call for Sheriff Black to send a few burly deputies to toss the guys out. But for now the place was quiet.

And that wasn't what she needed.

No, not after being on her own for the past two months. And despite the fact that she'd been assured it was an accident—that she had lost Jack to a bad move during a race—she didn't believe it.

The races could be fixed.

Everyone said that.

And the best racer in Wellspring, Starky, could make anything happen that he wanted to.

When Starky came into the bar, to pay his respects—
"Sorry . . . Jack was a good driver . . . He went down like a good
driver"—Sally didn't believe that's all Starky had come for. Because since then, Starky made a point of stopping by, moments
when she would make herself busy behind the bar, run into the
back, do anything so she didn't have to look into his black eyes
or hear his words.

Circling me, she thought.

Does he think I'm the goddamn prize as well?

Beat my man and you get me?

There were things Sally would do before it ever got to that.

For now, she just tried to pass every day with running the
bar, because it was all she knew, even if she didn't know how
long she could keep it up.

Wandering the Wasteland might be better than this, she
thought.

One of the regulars raised his head. No table service; if he
wanted another stim drink, he'd have to get himself to the bar.

The customer got up, making himself stand steady, and then
began his wobbling course to the bar. When he got there, he
looked left and right for someone to hear his order.

"Be right there, JT. Just hang on."

JT could maybe have one more drink before she'd have
to eject him. Or maybe he'd fall asleep in a dark corner of the
place.

Sally wished today was a Bash day. The quiet here, so deadly.

But then—as she ducked under the fold-down railing of the
bar and popped up in front of a bleary-eyed JT—someone new
walked into the place.

And even in those first few seconds, seeing the stranger back-
lit by the bright sunlight outside, she thought, *Who the hell is
he . . .*

. . . and what kind of trouble was he bringing with him?

230 • MATTHEW COSTELLO

• • •

The man walked up to the bar, positioning himself well away from JT, who hadn't attempted a tricky return to his seat. He stood there, scanning the row of drinks in the back.

Sally walked over to him.

"What can I get you?"

"Not sure," the man said. She looked at his clothes. Stained. She noticed the deep reddish-brown of the stains.

Blood. The guy had been into something.

Should I be nervous?

The man smiled at her. "Never seen those . . . things before. These drinks."

"Yeah? Never drank stim?"

He shook his head. "Where I come from—"

"No need to explain, mister. You want to try one, I'd recommend something light . . . here. This —"

She poured a half glass of one of the sweet stims. Good for dates. Or so some of the more experienced drinkers said.

She watched as the man took a sip.

His face registered that he didn't love it.

"Kinda sweet."

"Grows on you," she said.

She turned away and walked back to JT, who had picked up his glass and was about to find his way back to his table.

"You okay, JT?"

He nodded, then began the perilous journey, glass in hand.

Definitely cut off, Sally thought. Last call.

Later she'd get some of the Salvage Factory workers streaming in for after-work stories and drinks, their hands nicked by all the pieces of random metal, wood, and junk they handled.

Big deal in Wellspring.

Taking stuff found in the Wasteland and turning it into something useful. A door, a window, building material, car parts, *anything*.

Worse things than running a bar, she thought.

She wiped a spot on the bar where JT had dribbled some of his drink.

A glance at the stranger.

Looking right at her.

He didn't come in here for a drink, she thought. As if on cue, he spoke again.

"Excuse me, can I ask you something?"

And she walked down to the stranger, with his stains and air of someone from very far away.

He leaned close, taking a look at the near-empty bar. For now, it was just the two of them there.

"You're Sally LePrine?"

"Place is called Sally's, so that's a good guess."

He nodded. Something in his eyes drew her. A haunted look. Driven.

Guy's either on the run from something or is thinking about something that would soon have him on the run.

"I'm Raine."

"Like," she grinned, "the weather?"

"If you like."

"Okay, Raine—you had a question?"

He rubbed his chin. "I want to enter tomorrow's race."

Sally lost interest. *The goddamn races.* "Yeah. So enter it. Look, I got things—"

She turned to move away, but then she felt his hand shoot out. Not a tight grip, but he stopped her by the wrist, then released her.

"I need a sponsor."

"Right. Can't race without one. Unless you sponsor yourself."

"I heard that you sponsor drivers."

"Used to. Not anymore, Raine. Look, I said I have—"

"I know. Things to do. In a near-empty bar."

"Gets busy later."

"Can I be honest with you?" He took a breath. "Can I trust you?"

"That would be your decision. People come into my bar all the time. Lot of them tell me things. Is it trust or the stim speaking? Who the hell knows?"

"If I don't race, I can't stay here. Clayton as much as told me that. Said I could blend in. Someone from the Wasteland trying to make some money. And, well—I got to stay here for a while."

"Got business here?" she said, doing nothing to mask the sarcasm in her voice.

"Can you help?"

"I *told* you. I used to sponsor drivers. I don't anymore."

That seemed to silence the stranger. He looked away, as if thinking.

"Guess, well—thanks. Maybe I can find someone else, right?"

Except Sally knew that anyone who wanted to sponsor a driver would already have one. Raine would find no one.

Again she was drawn to his eyes. Something different about this man.

"Tell me why you have to stay. Tell me why you can't just wander around Wellspring."

For a second he just kept looking at her, as if debating telling her.

Finally, he spoke. "My guess is eventually Enforcers will come looking for me. They will ask questions. Clayton says—"

"You can't believe everything that liar says. In fact, I wouldn't believe much of it. Especially when it comes to the damn Authority."

Careful there, she told herself. She looked around the bar. One had to watch to whom one expressed anything other than perfect loyalty in regards to the Authority.

"But he's not lying about the races, right?" Raine said. "Lots of strangers come into the city to race, no?"

"Yeah. He has that right. You'd stick out less as a hungry racer than wandering around the city looking for work and a place to sleep."

"Do—" he said, now with a smile—"you see my problem?"

And she did. Though she wasn't sure how that made it *her* problem. She wanted no more to do with the Authority than she did with the races. She had enough trouble. Yet, something made her want to help this man. Instinct, she thought. Bartenders had to have good instincts.

She wanted to trust this man. So she did.

What did she have to lose?

"Sit down with me," she said. "I have something to tell you. And then—we'll see."

And she ducked under the bar and led Raine to a table near the back of her dimly lit place.

Before she could even begin, two more customers came in. Somebody from Mick's shop, all greased up from working under a buggy, and one of Black's deputies.

She hurried back to the bar to get them drinks, and then returned to Raine.

She kept her voice low.

"People are starting to come in. So, we'll talk quietly. Got it?"

He nodded.

"I sponsored someone. Named Jack. Good driver. Had a custom Cup."

The man's eyes narrowed, confused.

"A Cuprino. Fast, best armor, great steering system—most of it made by Jack himself. Sometimes he won, sometimes he came real close." She looked away, then back. "We were together. Y'know."

"Got it."

"But I guess he started to win too much. Most of it went into his vehicle . . . but he also bought me things. We even talked of getting away from Wellspring."

"That even possible?"

"People talk of places. Beyond the Wasteland. But because *he* was winning a lot, someone who was used to winning started to come in second. Someone named Starky."

The man took a last sip of his drink, killing it.

"Want another?"

He shook his head.

"Starky had been the champ. Everyone loved him. Had a fleet of Cuprinos. Trained other drivers. King of the goddamned races. Then, about two months ago, they announced a Dusty 8."

"Dusty 8?"

"Part road rally, part lap race. Part of the circuit in the city, part of it outside. Kind of race where anything can happen. Some action took place in the stadium, but most of it was out on the road. Things could happen out there that people couldn't see."

She stopped. She'd never told anyone what she felt, what she really believed about that race. *No,* she told herself, *it's not about belief.* She *knew* what had happened.

"After a run outside, and when the cars came back into the stadium, it was just Starky and Jack, nearly neck and neck. I was in the stadium, watching them roar in . . ."

"Go on."

She tilted her head and looked right at the man. "I could see that something was wrong. Jack looked hurt. I mean, there are no real weapons in the races —but everything else goes. And his Cuprino had a big gash on the right side. Smoke coming out, black oil hitting the track."

"You think Starky did something?"

"Yeah. I think he did something when they were out on the dirt. The damn hole looked like someone had shot it. But Jack, he had been hurt, too. He was fighting to keep the car rolling forward, to sit up. He had only a few laps to go."

"No one stopped the race?"

Sally laughed. *Where the hell* did *this guy come from?*

"They don't *stop* races. And as they hit those last laps, I watched Starky begin to maneuver his Cuprino so that one of its extenders—"

"And that is—"

"Something that sticks out and damages another vehicle. Jesus, and you want to race?" She shook her head, but he just sat there, determined. So she went on. "I saw then he was positioning it to cut right into the smoky opening of Jack's car. Jack was too hurt, too unsteady to see it. Just holding onto the wheel was about all he could do."

Now Sally stopped. She felt the tears. She hated the goddamn tears. This was no place for tears. Not when it was anger she wanted to hold on to. Anger. Even hate.

Raine didn't push her to go on.

They sat in silence for what felt like a long time but was only a few seconds. She wiped away the unwanted tears and looked back.

"Starky made his Cup slide into Jack's, just at the right point. I saw Jack turn, his face bloody, his eyes probably barely able to take in what was happening, The jagged metal of Starky's cutter sliced open that hole more, and then pulled away. In seconds it was over."

"What happened?"

"The engine must have seized. Everyone in the stadium could hear the noise, most of these bastards hoping something like this would happen. Jack's car seemed to stop dead even as its momentum made it fly end over end. I closed my eyes. I didn't watch. God, I couldn't watch."

The tears came this time. *Shit.* She didn't give a damn.

"But I heard it, Raine. I *heard* it as Jack's car spun around and smashed on the stadium track. The fuel erupting. An explosion. When I opened my eyes, all I could see was the fire, the great black clouds of smoke streaming up. The only good thing for Jack . . . it had been fast."

She stopped. Had she kept her voice down enough? People would talk. Word would get out that she had bad-mouthed the races. Not supposed to do that, nosiree, not in the good city of Wellspring. She wasn't sure she cared anymore.

"Starky had done that. They *let* him do that." A deep breath. "That's why—I don't sponsor racers."

"I understand," Raine said. But he didn't make a move toward the door. Instead, he waited as if knowing she had one more thing to say.

A smart guy, this Raine.

"But I see you need help. And I'm . . . willing to help. A deal. I will sponsor you—for one race. That's it. But only if you promise to take out Starky."

Now it was the man's turn to look around the room, keeping his voice to a whisper.

"Kill him?"

"If that happens, fine. But make sure that it's a long time before Starky and his car ever race again."

"My car is a piece of—"

"That's the deal, Raine. You want it?"

Now he hesitated. But only for a second.

He nodded. "Okay. You got a driver."

The door to the bar opened. Getting closer to quitting time for the workers. It would get busy now.

"Good. Tell Jackie Weeks. He'll get you set up and put the bar's name on your buggy. And look—you got no place to stay?"

"Yeah. There is that problem, too."

"When I close, later tonight, come by, help clean up. There's a storeroom in back. As long as no one comes around asking questions about you . . . you can stay there."

"Thanks."

"Okay, Raine. Now I got a bar to run."

And Sally got up and left the table.

THIRTY-ONE

THE DRIVERS

Raine awoke at midday, the darkness of the storeroom hiding the afternoon light.

He had helped pick up when the bar closed last night, pulling chairs back into place, cleaning the floor, taking out the trash.

Sally didn't have much to say after he came out of his room. They both watched the hours run down and race time draw close, lost in their own thoughts.

Eventually, though, she looked at him. "You better go," she said.

"Yeah," he said, and he walked out of the bar and headed back to where he left his buggy.

• • •

Except it wasn't there.

"Where's my buggy?"

Jackie Weeks looked up from the innards of an engine sitting on an open frame. Guess that's how they put these things together, Raine thought. Grab an engine, a frame, find some seats, get a fuel tank.

"No one told ya? Once you got your sponsor, Mick had to get Sally's name painted on. Of course, not much space for that on what you're driving. Still, you got a sponsor."

"So—Mick has it?"

"You really don't know how it goes, do you? See, the cars are put in position in the stadium. Yours is probably there already. Then at race time, I announce all the drivers as they come out one by one. Showmanship, got it?"

"Right. So I head in here?" Raine pointed to a corridor that led into the back of the stadium.

"Yeah. I'll walk you down later. Being that you're new and all. But hold on. Mick did some things to your buggy. Don't you want to learn about them?"

"Sure."

"First, that engine of yours? Not the most efficient or powerful. Not sure you'd even be able to keep up if I didn't have Mick tinker. What he did was . . . well, these engines don't burn the fuel that we cook up too good. Most engines have to be modified. Yours—no time to really do that. Know anything about engines?"

"I've had some die on me."

"Funny. I like that. A real *jokester*. 'Kay, so Mick figured out something—when you burn the fuel, the engine shoots out the exhaust, laced with fuel. But if the carburetors can reuse some of that exhaust, you can get a second quick burn. Just a little extra *push*. Like getting a double shot. Pretty nifty, if I do say so myself."

"An afterburner."

"Hm? An after-what? I dunno. Anyway, you will see, more speed, more power. You'll need it. And then there's your defenses, as in . . . you didn't have any." He laughed at that.

Everyone seems really *concerned about my buggy's defenses.*

"It's amazing you've stayed alive without them. So he put in some ramming hooks, front and back. Nothing fancy. But also, you'll see by the driver's seat, Mick put in a lever. Lowers a side panel on both sides of your vehicle . . . about forty-five degrees. Got a nasty edge to it. Good for taking a slice out of another buggy."

"Can I bring my guns?"

"You do like to make with the jokes, eh? So that's about it. I got to get to the booth. Showtime, you know. You can go find Mick if you got any more questions."

Then a smile that Raine took to be not a good thing.

"Oh—and you can meet . . . the competition."

Raine walked into a large room filled with smoke and loud chatter. The feeling in the room felt familiar.

Before a mission, grunts milling about, waiting for the order to hit their Humvees or get into choppers. Jokes, nervous excitement, stuff that would all dissipate once they made a move.

"You, Raine . . . Raine, get over here."

He turned and saw a scrawny guy wearing a belt of tools that looked heavy enough to drag him down to the ground.

"You must be Mick."

"Got it. Mr. Weeks tell you about the mods to your buggy?"

"Yeah. Thanks."

Mick looked around at the room of people. "Couldn't let you race against these guys in what you had. Goddamn, no. People would think it's a fix. Not that you, a newbie, will be able to do anything in today's race. Just stay alive. But you gotta pop your cherry somewhere."

Interesting, Raine thought, how some phrases survived. Probably all those connected to the most basic human functions. They lived on.

As Mick spoke he looked around the room. A few other drivers seemed to have taken note of him; others went on talking, laughing.

No one talking to me, Raine thought.

A newcomer must be bad luck.

He spotted someone tall wearing a broad-brimmed hat. Even from across the room, Raine could see the shiny glow of a badge.

"Mick—who's that guy?"

"Him? Sheriff Black. Likes to come back here, talk with the drivers."

"He works for Clayton?"

Now Mick laughed. "If you say so. Could be the other way around." Mick looked around, then back to Raine. "Black always comes in when Starky's racing." Now Raine looked at the man that the tall sheriff, this Wellspring lawman, was talking to.

He was dressed in brown leather, like what in the last century would have been a motorcycle outfit. Guy had a gut, a few extra pounds from spending his prize money on rarities, no doubt. The man nodded as Black spoke.

Then, just as Raine was looking at him, the man looked over.

That, Raine thought, has got to be Starky.

"Hey, gotta go, man," Mick said. "Enjoy your new wheels . . . long as they last." Mick wandered over to some other drivers, leaving Raine alone . . . and under the scrutiny of Starky. The race champ grinned, nodding as Black spoke to him.

Then a laugh.

Fresh meat, Raine thought. That's probably what they think I am.

Suddenly he wondered what he had agreed to—to Clayton, to do this race, to Sally—to get payback against what was obviously one nasty piece of work. A racing star.

Raine looked away.

Then, echoing from outside, he could hear the magnified voice of Jackie Weeks.

"Ladies and gentlemen of Wellspring, honored guests from Capital Prime, representatives of all the settlements who have joined us today . . . welcome to . . . The White Rabbit!"

The White Rabbit.

Chasing the rabbit didn't turn out so well for Alice . . .

What are my chances?

But Mick had gone, and now the drivers began gathering near a door to the back, getting ready to be introduced to the fans in the stadium.

No one looked at Raine as he moved into place.

It was as though he wasn't there at all.

And that can't be a good thing, he thought.

Jackie Weeks introduced the first driver, and Raine saw a kid—couldn't have been more than seventeen—push his way past the other drivers, out to the stadium.

A smattering of applause.

Like Clayton said, people came here from all over to try their luck. Must need a steady stream of new drivers, with their battered vehicles and dreams of success.

Then someone up front told Raine to get close, get ready; he was next.

Another newbie, he thought.

He had to push his way past the other drivers, down the narrow corridor, then out—

To the stadium.

The place was filled—but the sound that greeted him wasn't deafening. No, just a few whistles, some applause. But he could see the people of Wellspring filling every seat.

"And direct from the Wasteland, Nicholas . . . Raine!"

Raine walked out. Twilight here, but no lights on yet—though he could see big lights that must have once lit Friday night football games.

Bet they had to conserve those babies.

He looked around for his buggy, and saw it farthest to the left. Down the long line of a dozen cars or so, where the first announced driver—the kid—also waited.

Guess the pros got the center slots.

Jackie Weeks went on calling the other names. But Raine took the time to look at the course laid out on the track.

The White Rabbit.

He had expected a NASCAR-style track: a big loop, mile markers, pits where you could get a quick repair.

No pits here. A high wall around the sides made the arena look sunken. And while the stadium might have been a loop, it was dotted with odd structures as though someone forgot to clear it for the race.

Dead ahead—a trio of metal tubes. In between them Raine could see wavy chunks of metal with hooks sticking up.

Nice.

What the hell were they?

Past that barrier, at the far end of the stadium, he saw a ramp leading up two, three stories high. No telling what was on the other side, as the loop curved around.

Another name, and a driver appeared beside him.

Raine hadn't even checked out his own vehicle.

"Done this before?" Raine asked.

The driver to his right shook his head.

So the setup was—a bunch of new drivers to provide the

show, while a handful of regulars did the real driving for the prizes.

Except Sally's friend, her Jack, had been a real driver until Starky took him out.

And even though the other driver didn't seem interested in talking, Raine went on. "Why the 'White Rabbit'? Why is it called that?"

The guy barely looked at him, just a glance as if he wanted him to go away.

"Some story. About holes. Falling. Got to get into the holes and out again. Jeez, I don't fucking *know*. Wished it was anything but a White Rabbit."

Suddenly—so did Raine.

The roll call continued, leading up to—apparently—the real drivers.

Now the crowd roared, a sound he felt in his gut. Raine saw that some of their vehicles were nearly twice as big as his.

Others were more like sleek tanks. These had the armor plating of a prehistoric monster.

No engines had started yet, but Raine could imagine that the beastlike nature of the cars would be matched by the deep roar of their engines.

More roars and applause from the crowd.

Until the last name—

"Ladies and gentleman, three-time Dusty 8 winner, undefeated in the White Rabbit, creator of the Blue Sky Rally, Wellspring's own master driver, the one . . . the only—"

Jackie Weeks didn't finish it.

Because the crowd did.

"Starkyyyyyyyy!"

Popular guy. And his car, a sleek black thing that didn't look quite as dangerous as the others, bore the logo of something called SALVAGE EMPIRE. Yeah, salvage was big here. Sally had mentioned that.

Raine looked up at the crowd. He saw a special box and spotted Clayton, his monocle catching the fading light. But Raine wasn't interested in him. Rather, he was looking at who sat near him.

Men in uniform. Talking to Clayton and to each other. People brought them drinks.

Authority brass?

The people I'm supposed to avoid.

Then Weeks came back.

"Drivers . . . time to get in . . . and . . . start your engines."

THIRTY-TWO

THE WHITE RABBIT

As if choreographed, the line of drivers hopped into their vehicles, Raine the last one in.

Engines were switched on, and the combined roar filled the stadium—met with an equally loud roar back from the fans.

The air felt electric.

Raine could hear the difference in his buggy, the engine deeper. He saw a lever to the right. The panels Jackie had told him about. *Defensive panels.* He had noticed the hooks protruding from the front and rear of the buggy before he got in.

He looked ahead. Three tubes—each tube a quick shot forward on the track—while to the side, the road turned into a bumpy obstacle course, with metal pylons to be avoided.

Getting into a tube would be the difference between winning and losing.

Maybe living or dying.

Jackie Weeks's voice filled the stadium . . .

"Are we ready for racing action?"

The crowd cheered.

"Are we ready to run . . . the White Rabbit?"

Another great roar.

"Then . . . three . . . two . . . one . . . go!"

Raine hit the pedal as the line of vehicles zoomed forward.

He immediately saw the experienced drivers in their Cuprinos pull ahead, all jockeying for a good position to get into one of the tube openings.

No way he could outrun them, not with their initial burst of speed. So he planned on laying back a bit and hitting one of the express tubes second.

But he noticed a driver who had appeared on his right, apparently with the same idea.

The guy's car had a ring of metal spikes all around the perimeter, sharpened to a point.

The guy swerved toward him.

This is no goddamn race, Raine thought, not for the first time. It's a demolition derby . . .

As if in confirmation, an explosion came from behind him. Two cars jostling for position. He didn't look back—but he could hear the sound.

Meanwhile, the guy next to him gave his car another swerve to the left.

The three tubes were just ahead, but Raine was on target for the one on the left. No time for him to readjust and target one of the other two. It wouldn't have helped anyway, since each one had cars scrambling to be the next into these holes of the White Rabbit.

The driver to his right managed to jostle into Raine's buggy, a quick side ram with his spikes.

Raine's car punctured. A warning tap perhaps.

Get the hell out of my way.

But next time, that car could easily slice deeper into his buggy and this race would be over before it began.

The tube opening directly ahead looked like a funhouse ride.

Raine eased up a bit on the accelerator. The driver battling him ended up slightly ahead. And now Raine aimed to the right and floored the accelerator again.

Whatever the hell Mick had done to his engine worked, as his buggy rammed the right rear of the car that had just passed in front.

The driver reacted slowly, then overcorrected, wasting speed and getting off target for the tube.

By the time the guy corrected his path, Raine was now ahead, the opening just there—

And in!

Dark, the tube seemed round from the outside, but with a flat bottom, it was an expressway past and over the corrugated race-track on either side, the rolling bumps and pylons designed to slow or even disable a vehicle.

Raine flew out the other end.

Three cars ahead, with one on his left now.

I'm in the front five, he thought.

Not too fucking bad.

But then as they came to the big curve ahead, he saw the second part of this White Rabbit.

He muttered:

"Fucking *bad.*"

•   •   •

Most of the next obstacle was hidden by the bend in the track. But what Raine could see as he got closer looked nasty.

The track turned into a massive ramp leading upward. At its peak, an open space . . . to be *leapt* over. As if that wasn't enough, there was a bigger problem: only the driver in the dead center would have the shortest jump. The more to the side you were, the more you had a chance of not making that jump, and having your vehicle smash into the wall of the opposite down ramp.

He studied how Starky and the other two drivers handled it.

Starky had taken a center position, and then—as jagged metal spears popped out from his side—Starky slid left, first slowing down, then speeding up. The other car didn't have a chance as Starky literally chewed it up.

That driver's car started to spin around, out of control just as it hit the up ramp.

Spinning with enough force to keep it flying up the ramp.

And as Starky commanded the center, the third driver wisely settled for a position to the side. The out-of-control car cartwheeled into the gap at the top, and then plummeted off the edge.

You lost drivers fast in this race.

No wonder Clayton wanted him to drive. If this was the bread and circuses for Wellspring, well, they needed a lot of clowns. Men willing to take their chances on getting hurt or even killed out here.

Men with nothing to lose.

Just like me.

He was now in a race on the ramp with the driver to the side. Both held a portion of the dead center of the up ramp.

Probably, with this position, they could both make it across. With a goddamned compromise, they both could do it.

But that wasn't good enough for the other guy.

His car didn't have hooks. Instead, gleaming blades like giant knife points jutted out from the front and back of the vehicle, as if it was a razor blade on wheels.

With such nice sharp edges, they could probably slice a car right down to the engine block.

Raine considered backing away, ceding the spot to him. But then he'd be so far behind Starky, he certainly couldn't make good on his deal with Sally.

You could live to drive again, he thought.

But a deal's a deal.

Besides, amusingly, now that he was into it, he didn't feel like losing. He reached to his side and threw the lever that Mick had built into his car. Panels on either side of his buggy came down. Nothing fancy, nothing as shiny and gleaming as what he saw on the other vehicles. But the panels—each flying at a forty-five-degree angle and with a long, rough serrated edge that ran from the front of the car to the back—looked . . .

What was the word Jackie used?

Defensive.

Right. Just defensive. *Sure.*

The other driver took note of the panels and hesitated.

Raine made a small swerve left, then another. The other driver backed away . . .

Ceding the center of the ramp. In seconds Raine hit the gap and went flying over, his engine still roaring, wheels spinning madly, but *flying* through the air. He hadn't thought of this before, but a question popped into his head: *Could his buggy take it?* It was a battered heap before. What would this do?

But then his buggy landed hard on the down ramp, bumping up and down; it didn't explode into a hundred pieces, and Raine flew down the ramp, gravity kicking him forward.

He now was number four behind the front runners.

But was it possible to catch them, to catch Starky? It didn't seem that way. He had other things to worry about, though.

He had come to the third part of the Rabbit.

And it was a goddamn maze. Metal walls in the track at staggered intervals. But he also saw that there were a few panels with wires.

Could they be raised and lowered?

For a little surprise . . . ?

Driving through this maze, he'd have to guess how fast he could go, hoping that his steering and the response of the buggy were up to the weaving in and out.

Now—just behind Starky and two other drivers—he got a chance to watch and see how they did it.

Drivers two and three got into a battle just before hitting the metal walls. Something large and bulky jutted out of one driver's car, like a battering ram. It smacked the other driver hard just as they were about to enter the maze of walls, pushing him so there was no way he could avoid smashing into the first wall.

Which is what he did, his car exploding.

Even with the noise of that explosion, Raine could hear the cheering of the crowd.

Loving the mayhem. The fire. The death.

Are you not entertained?

Raine had to take that first opening with the flaming vehicle still shooting gusts of fire and black smoke.

He closed his mouth. The stench was practically overwhelming.

As soon as he entered the maze, he cut the car left. In this last part of the Rabbit there were multiple ways to go. He saw a panel pop up, and swerved at the last minute.

So now he knew he'd have to watch for that as well.

Did Jackie Weeks do that? If he wanted to amp the action,

could he raise a panel and make the race all the more interesting, all the more deadly?

Raine cut left, then right, alternately hitting the brakes, then the accelerator.

His brakes seemed feeble, and one time he nicked the side of a wall. Then, as he got a clear shot for a hundred meters or so, another wall rose from the floor right in front of him, and at the last moment he had to cut his buggy left again.

And then he discovered he had an advantage in this section:

The buggy was small, maneuverable. The steering responsive. And what he lost with bad brake action he gained with the improved engine performance, kicking the small vehicle ahead.

He heard cheers.

It dawned on him.

They're cheering for me.

To win? Or to catch up to Starky so he can take me out, like he did to Sally's last driver?

Caution, he told himself.

Four more laps.

He had a good position. And now he knew the traps on the track.

Caution. Take his time.

And see if he could get a shot.

He had made it to the last lap, and over the roar of the crowd, Jackie Weeks yelled, stirring them to a more insane burst of approval.

"Here they come . . . your final four. The homestretch for the big *prize."*

Starky ran neck and neck with a driver. Another driver lagged behind Raine, seemingly no threat.

But in the previous lap, especially when he hit the maze, Raine had pulled up close and tight behind the front two.

He let those two battle it out over the tubes, then the three moved onto the jump, keeping their positions.

And he got to see Starky in action.

Not merely battling for position, Starky moved like a shark over to the other driver and, with a quick flick of his steering wheel, cut into his opponent for the lead. His spikes slid into the side of that driver's car. Then Starky played with the accelerator and the brake.

The other driver tried to pull away but discovered he was trapped, hooked and pinned by Starky's spikes as they chewed back and forth, until finally the car did spin free, tilting forward.

And in a moment that had to have the crowd with their mouths open, that car nose-dived forward, just before the gap. It began cartwheeling, end over end, then disappeared, rolling into the gap before the jump.

Starky commanded the lead for himself.

Except—and this made Raine grab his steering wheel even harder—that brutal attack by Starky had eaten up some of that lead.

He was just behind him.

Two parts of the Rabbit ahead.

And Raine knew exactly where he could get neck and neck with Starky.

He thought: *I could just take second. A respectable finish for a newbie.*

But that wasn't the deal he'd made. And if he knew anything about this world, you were only as good as the deals you made and the deals you kept.

• • •

Just meters behind, Raine got on Starky's tale, as if tempting him.

He weaved past the first walls, closing the distance. Starky's Cuprino was way more powerful. But it was bigger, too, less maneuverable.

Then they hit an open stretch midway in the maze, and they both ran side by side, with the last few metal walls ahead.

When one popped up right in front of Raine.

Guess it paid to be the star of the show.

Whoever the hell worked the panels was trying to make sure that anyone betting on Starky made out fine.

Raine cut left, losing some ground. Now he and Starky both headed to the next opening, into the last mazelike row of walls, Raine trailing.

In minutes it would be over.

Which is when Starky looked over. He probably could have gunned it, beat Raine to that opening. With no more mayhem, no more carnage.

He was that close to winning.

But Raine guessed that wasn't Starky's style.

So Starky slid right, trying to hook his buggy and chew it up the way he did the last driver he battled.

But Raine had seen that battle, so at nearly the same time Starky made his attack, he jigged his buggy to the right, barely missing getting nailed by Starky's spikes.

No time to get cocky, though, because with some distance still left before the last walls, Starky would get another chance. Raine's side panels, with their jagged razor teeth, looked pretty ineffective.

Unless . . .

As he imagined Starky getting ready for another attack, Raine raised the lever, seemingly removing his defenses. This prompted Starky to move fast—Raine's buggy had become even easier pickings.

Raine glanced ahead.

Not much time.

Starky slid right, and as he did, Raine hit the lever again.

A miscalculation by the track's champ.

Raine's panels came down, digging into Starky's vehicle even as his spikes made contact with Raine's car.

The sheer weight of the panel, not terribly sharp, but cheap, heavy scrap metal, pushed Starky to the side.

An unexpected push.

And yet Starky's spikes had also nudged Raine. They were both heading into the last metal walls at a bad angle.

It might be the lagging driver's lucky day.

Starky, with the loss of control, slid to the side of the track, hitting the side of the stadium. Sparks flew up from the grinding as the side of his Cuprino slid along the stadium wall.

Raine—on the other hand—heading too fast at one wall, cut right.

Not quick enough. He smacked the side of the wall, his forward momentum turning into a sideways slide, wheels spinning, shooting up dirt and dust from the track.

He turned left as hard as possible, feeling like he had no control, no chance to avoid the last wall . . . the finish line just after it. He gave a quick look back, since this wasn't really racing or battling anymore.

It was down to luck. And momentum . . .

He saw Starky's car sparking, and then, though it had no wall in front of it, it turned over, spinning, a cloud of dust and metal, rolling only feet behind him.

Raine still had some traction, as ineffective as it was.

He felt the left front wheel fly off. The rim and axle fell to the ground. Three wheels, but the car kept moving.

Both vehicles slid toward the finish line, Starky's bigger car rolling *behind* him.

Raine crossed the line first, and only then could he finally take his foot off the accelerator, an effort, since it felt as though it had been madly strapped there.

Starky rolled over the line after him—over and over—until the Cuprino came to rest inches behind him, right side up. The wheels were on the ground, but the engine was on fire and the car looked like a dented can.

A crew raced out and yanked Starky free of his smoking vehicle.

No one came to Raine. He stood up.

Was the crowd in shock? The place had gone quiet.

Then Jackie Weeks got the show back . . . on track.

"We have a winner *of the White Rabbit, ladies and gentlemen! Raaaaaaine!"*

And then, properly cued—some probably still thinking of money wagered and lost, others taking in the incredible finish—they cheered.

He had won.

And from the look of things, it didn't seem that Starky would be driving anytime soon.

THIRTY-THREE

A STAR IS BORN

Raine ached in so many different places from the last insane minutes of the race. His car was totaled, but so was Starky's. And Starky would need a lot of downtime before the sweetheart of this rodeo was ready to ride again.

Yet, as Raine walked away from what was now a wreck, no one came up to congratulate him. If anything, people turned away from him as though he had a disease you did not want to catch.

There was one exception.

As he made his way back to the driver's prep room, Sheriff Black was there, standing in the center of the room, leather jacket open, hat tilted forward so that Raine just got the dead-on glare of his eyes.

Clearly waiting for him.

Raine walked up to the sheriff.

"You waiting for me?"

The sheriff nodded. "Let's take a walk."

It wasn't an invitation. Raine followed Black out of the room, down the corridor that led to the back.

Raine half expected to see Jackie Weeks there, basking in the success of what his mechanic Mick did, but Weeks was nowhere in sight.

Instead, when they got down the hallway, Black reached out and stopped Raine with an arm on his shoulder. Not a gesture that Raine particularly welcomed. Not here, not back in Brooklyn, not ever. There were things that you just didn't let go.

He shrugged the hand off his shoulder.

"You think you did good in there, eh, stranger?"

"I won. Isn't that what it's all—"

Black shook his head and interrupted.

"It's about the *show*, Raine. The good people of Wellspring having their favorites. You were to be *part* of that show. Not wreck it. Who the hell knew you could get that damn buggy . . . to win."

"But I did win. What do you care?" He knew he was on dangerous ground. Jackie had all but hinted that Black really ran the show in Wellspring. But the way he felt now, if this guy kept pushing at him, there was a point not too far away where he would push back.

Raine took in the man standing there, confronting him. The sheriff was taller than he was, lean, and had two handguns worn western style.

This guy's right out of Dodge City.

He took a step closer to Raine, in his face.

Raine took a breath. *Steady,* he told himself. *Nice and easy. He is the goddamned sheriff after all.*

"You took out *Starky.* People lost money. Worse, they lost their star. And what'd they get in its stead? You."

"I *won* the damn race."

Another shake from Black. "There's only one thing for you to do now. And I'm going to tell you what that one thing is."

"Clayton said if I raced—"

Black smiled. "*If* you raced. Right. Let me ask you something: what you gonna race in now? 'Fraid you didn't win enough to go buy a Cuprino. No fucking way."

"I'll do something else."

Raine didn't like the feeling that Black had an agenda here, that they were going somewhere in this conversation and he didn't know where.

"You took something away from the people of Wellspring. Now, you're gonna give back. The winner of the goddamned White Rabbit is going right onto Mutant Bash TV."

Raine remembered the ads he saw, thinking more bread and circuses. The porcine face of the host, his head looking like a wad of human-shaped dough. The leering faces of mutants.

"I don't watch TV."

"A wiseass?"

Another phrase that survived. A good one, too.

"Well, wiseass, you won't be *watching*. You will be *on* Mutant Bash. Tomorrow, it's the big Friday Free-for-All." His voice got low and conspiratorial, as if he was letting Raine in on a secret. "You see, people like their race night, and then they like heading home with containers of stim and getting drunk the next night watching Bash. They'll *love* seeing you in there."

"No thanks. I'll pass."

Black raised a finger and jabbed it at Raine.

It was one push too many, and Raine reached up. He twisted Black's wrist, quickly turning, making Black spin around from the pain as he bent the arm up.

In a moment he could break the guy's arm.

He saw Black go for his gun with his free hand, and Raine

reached down and grabbed that wrist. Now, right up to Black's ear, he whispered.

"I wouldn't do that"—he gave the trapped arm a slight pull up for emphasis—"if you know what I mean."

"You're fucked."

"Could be. I've heard that before. Now if you can talk in a civil manner, I will let your arm go. Just keep those hands away from those six-shooters, *pardner*. Deal?"

Black hesitated, perhaps weighing if he had another shot to get Raine off him.

Then: "Deal."

Raine let Black's trapped arm slide free. "You'd be a dead man. If Clayton didn't want something from you."

"I've been a dead man before. There we are. So—we were talking about TV?"

"You—" Black adjusted his tone a bit.

Good. Lesson learned. Though Raine guessed if Black didn't need him to do the show, he might indeed be in big trouble.

"You will go on the show tomorrow night. The audience will love it. Win there, and you just might have enough for a new buggy."

"Sounds like a dangerous show."

"Oh, it is. You can consider what happened out there"—he gestured at the stadium—"as a warm-up. The Bash Arena is not a happy place."

"Then why the hell would I do it? I'll go back to Clayton and—"

"Clayton sent me."

Raine stopped. He remembered seeing Clayton with the men from the Authority, their black uniforms standing out from the ragtag clothing worn by the people of Wellspring.

"He sent me. With this offer."

"And if I pass?"

"The mayor gets a lot of pressure. Ark survivors are a highly valued commodity out here." Black smiled. "Yeah, we know. We're not fools. You'd be a nice prize to turn over. But the mayor's a man of his word. He'll keep quiet. For now."

"*If* I do Mutant Bash." *Man of his word? His word seemed to change daily.*

Black nodded. "And I'll be quiet as well. Though the day will come, stranger, when you and I will deal with each other."

Raine heard a noise from down the hall. One of the other drivers limping his way down. He and Black stood there, quietly, as he passed. The man was not so quiet as he passed Raine.

"Fucker."

He kept limping down the hallway.

"Another new friend," Black said.

"I see."

"You show up at the studio on the east side of the city, near the mutant pens. About seven tomorrow night, an hour before the show. You do that, and the Authority will just see you as some other lucky guy who wandered in from the Wasteland . . ."

"And about to die in the arena."

"That," he said, adjusting his hat, "will be up to you. I know one damn thing, Raine—I'll sure as hell be watching."

And with that the sheriff walked away.

Raine went to a table in the back of the bar and sat down. His aches now mixed with a numbing fatigue as his body screamed for rest. Despite that, the race and the move he pulled off to win—and then the threat from Black—had his mind in overdrive.

Sally had a full bar. A skinny guy with a domelike head and jittery moves helped her. When she got a break, she walked back to him, two drinks in hand.

"You won."

"Isn't that what I was supposed to do?"

"Not that anyone expected it."

"Not even you?"

"Can I sit?"

"Your bar, right?"

Sally sat down, the place full enough that she had to lean close to speak to Raine.

"Heard Starky took a nasty spill."

"About as nasty as they get when the person's still able to walk away from it. Except he didn't walk away." Raine took a sip of the drink Sally had brought over. "He got carried."

"Thanks."

"Well, you know, the funny thing is that when I was in there, I kind of forgot what you said he did to your driver. But I could see how he operated. Taking drivers out right and left, even if he didn't need to in order to win. And suddenly *I* wanted to take him out. I wanted to win."

"So—more races?"

Raine shook his head. "The buggy's a wreck. Besides, Clayton has other plans for me."

"What does he want you to do?"

Raine nodded toward the tube television suspended over the bar. Had to be over a hundred years old and still working. Pretty amazing.

"Going on Mutant Bash TV."

Without thinking, Sally's hand covered his as she said, "No. You can't."

"Why's that?"

"You ever see a Bash?"

He shook his head.

"You have to fight and kill mutants, or at least get past them. Each setup is different, like a puzzle, only you have mutants coming out from all over. If I could, I wouldn't even let it be shown in the bar. But they'd tear the joint apart. I don't even look. You *can't* do it, Raine."

"I wasn't given an option. It's this or the Authority. Guess you figured out that they're looking for me, hm? And since Wellspring is my only option for now, especially without wheels . . ."

Sally leaned even closer.

"*They* know about you. Someone will be coming. Not sure when."

Raine raised his eyes. "You mean Enforcers?"

"No." She lowered her voice even more. "The Resistance."

"You're with—" He looked around. "Okay. Good to know that. I got something for them. And maybe I can find out what I'm supposed to be doing in this world. Other than races and bashes."

"I don't want to know too much, but I was told you will be contacted. Won't help, though, if you're dead."

Raine drained his glass. He noticed some of the men closer to the table looking over, perhaps flashing on the fact he was the out-of-the-blue newcomer who'd won today's race. No one smiled.

Cost them money, he imagined.

"Don't have much choice, Sally. Tomorrow night at eight." He laughed. "A star is born."

She didn't laugh back.

"If you do it, win, Raine. Do whatever you have to . . . to stay alive."

"Always do."

She looked around.

"Like I said, I don't know much about the Resistance. Don't *want* to know much—not healthy. But I do what I can, and I'm sure of one thing: they sure as hell can use someone like you."

He nodded.

"Another drink?"

He shook his head. "No. That bed in the storeroom still free?"

She hesitated, and he wondered whether another offer might be on the table. Then the moment passed as she smiled.

"Sure. Rest up."

The possible offer . . . vanishing with the idea that he might be a dead man.

And as Sally walked away he thought . . .

Not if I have anything to do about it.

THIRTY-FOUR

INTERROGATION

Captain John Marshall, his vision blurry from blood and sweat dripping down his face, looked up at the man standing in front of him.

He had been drugged for his transfer here, but he now knew where he was.

That much, at least, was clear.

Inside Capital Prime, inside its prison—with who knows how many other political prisoners. The ones still alive.

Or had they all been killed?

The man before him, dressed in a black officer's uniform and flanked by two Enforcers, waited until he felt Marshall's eyes on him.

"Tomorrow you will meet the Visionary. Quite an exciting moment for you."

Marshall looked right into the man's eyes. "The Visionary can kiss my—"

Before the word was out, an Enforcer smacked him with the back of his hand and sent him flying to the ground. Another Enforcer put his boot on Marshall's back, keeping him pinned there.

"You think this is a joke, Marshall? You think that we, the Authority, can permit scum like you to create problems in this world? There is much work to be done, and we've just started. You, and whatever is left of your Resistance, will not stand in our way."

"Fuck you."

Now the other Enforcer's boot was kicked into Marshall's side, knocking the wind out of him. Marshall gasped, choking to get air back in his lungs, still with a heavy boot stepping on his back.

"Y'know, it's too bad you won't cooperate. The Visionary could have use for someone like you. We have . . . openings." The man paused. "Let him up."

The boot came off, and now the only thing holding Marshall to the ground were the spears of pain he felt all over his body. He guessed the plan was to leave him in such battered shape that in the morning he'd just stand—if he could—in front of the Visionary, listen while the Visionary asked his questions . . .

And tell everything.

Marshall wondered how far they would go to get information from him. How much pain, how much time?

He had been tortured once. Captured by a small antigovernment tribe in the hills of Waziristan. Old school, they used their knives to keep him in agony for days.

They had been real amateurs. It doesn't quite work that way, he had wanted to explain to them. You got to go back and forth until it becomes clear to the subject that there was only one thing they wanted. For the dance of pain and remission to end. Nothing else mattered—the lives of friends, the safety of other soldiers, the mission, and even the fate of the goddamn world— you just wanted the pain to stop.

In the morning a squad of Rangers had parachuted nearby and raided the cave dwelling. The terrorists were dead in minutes; he had said nothing.

But now?

How long could he hold out?

One technique taught in Ranger school and drilled into the covert ops leaders was that you had to stay in the goddamn moment. Don't think about the past, of warm beds, meals, lovers . . . and don't think about the future, about what you want, how you want this to end one way or the other.

Concentrate on the small details in that moment.

Even amidst horrifying pain. One expert in counterinsurgency ops explained there can be good no matter what was happening. Focus on that.

Focus on the very fact of *existence*.

But no one in that room ever hoped to have to experience that, to have the need to try that technique. Marshall wasn't that lucky. What was happening now, he guessed, was a warm-up. Setting the stage for the morning's interrogation by the Visionary himself.

"We will stop this for now, Marshall. Want you fresh, alert, in the morning. But before you go back to your 'room,' you should know what the Visionary will be asking about."

The Visionary. It always came back to the Visionary.

A man Marshall knew. A bastard he hated a century ago, for what he did, for what he stood for.

Now he'd be questioned and tortured by that man.

"What is that? My name, rank, and fucking serial number?" Marshall didn't know this Authority officer standing before him, but all he could think about was how great it would be to make that sneering face squirm and twitch with pain.

He caught himself.

In the moment, he thought.

"Unlikely, considering your rank means nothing to the Authority. No, he will ask about your various secret bases. About the key people you work with, the settlements not to be trusted. Where you keep your supplies. In short, *Captain* Marshall," he snarled, "*everything* you, the pathetic Resistance leader, know."

In answer, Marshall spat on the ground.

The man turned aside.

"Take this piece of garbage away. Give him nothing. No food. No water."

The two Enforcers grabbed Marshall and began dragging him back to his cell.

Those guards disobeyed their orders, though, and thoughtfully gave him a boot to the head the next day. Not full force, but hard enough that Marshall saw stars as he awakened blinking, taking a few seconds to see where he was.

Right. It's morning.

He was curled on the floor of the cell, competely empty except for his battered body. Not even a hole in the floor for a toilet, as if making him as much of an animal as possible would help the process of interrogation. As far as he could tell, it wasn't working—he wasn't an animal yet.

But he was surrounded by them.

"Get up."

He could fight them, become a dead weight and force them to rough him up and then pull him to his feet. But what was the point?

To tell them they can kiss his ass, that's what.

But instead he pushed off his hands and got to his feet. If he still had nanotrites coursing through him, he'd be in a lot better shape. Not that it was a real possibility.

"Let's go boys," he said. "Guess your Visionary is waiting."

The Enforcers' helmets prevented Marshall from seeing if there was any reaction to his words.

Clever idea, making the people in uniform . . . faceless. Not only rendering them scarier than the freakiest bandit tribe, but also making it hard for them to ever see each other as anything but part of the army of the Authority.

And who were they, really? Recruited from settlements? Ark survivors who preferred life with the Authority rather than being on the run from them? Supposedly, more and more were choosing life with the Authority.

The Visionary's goddamn vision . . . coming true.

The Enforcers cuffed Marshall and then led him out of the cell. If he had been a religious man, he would have prayed.

And then, as he walked—despite everything—he did just that.

As Marshall entered the room, he was momentarily blinded by massive lights that dotted the ceiling and bathed the polished metal floor with a brilliant light.

It took him a few seconds to see what was here: a chair, a few tables, computer monitors—all probably removed from Arks. The monitors appeared to show different areas surrounding this building, the heart of the Authority.

He also noticed that one table had instruments on it. His eyes tried to make out exactly what those items were, and he found that his very inability to determine that made him anxious.

Steady, he told himself. *Don't let your thoughts race ahead.*

He saw someone sitting in the chair, two Enforcers on either side. The first inquisitor from yesterday stood to the left.

His two Enforcer escorts held his arms tightly.

"Anyone else coming to this party?"

The two guards holding him pushed him forward until he was meters away from the man in the chair.

The Visionary.

Or as he was known back in the day . . .

General Martin Cross.

"Colonel, see that he's uncuffed. He is a captain after all." Surprisingly, Marshall didn't detect any disdain when Cross said his rank.

The colonel signaled to the Enforcers behind Marshall, and one stuck a key in the cuffs. Marshall's hands slipped free and he rubbed his wrists, red and bruised.

"Am I supposed to kneel now?" he said.

The colonel walked forward and slapped Marshall with the back of his hand.

"You will speak with respect, Marshall. Or—"

"Colonel, please. *Really.* Marshall is not used to the ways of civility here in Capital Prime. No, Captain, you do not kneel. Or even salute."

"That's good, General. Since I plan on doing neither."

"You will—eventually, though—talk. That I can promise you. Just as others have."

Marshall knew that one of the key cell leaders—not an Ark survivor, but head of a small trading settlement to the north— had been captured weeks ago. He spoke. Good people were lost. In the end the Authority sent in Predators to torch the settlement. Killing everyone.

A message sent.

For some it signaled that the Resistance was dead. For others it signaled that the Resistance had just begun.

"We'll see, Cross."

Cross.

He had been hostile to the new President from the start of her administration, and then became a constant roadblock to President Campbell's foreign policy, until he was removed from that position by her. Then he was given responsibility for training, a bureaucratic job that took him far away from Washington, away from where he could stir up trouble and opposition to the President as she attempted to exit the wars that had spread to every continent.

That was her plan.

Was that how Cross came to be in charge of one of the Ark sites? Was that how the bastard got himself here? Who did him that favor, and did *that* bastard survive?

Because if he did, that was someone he would like to have some one-on-one time with.

The man who changed the future.

Or had Cross had his own network, planning this all along when the Ark Project became known to the upper levels of military brass?

Marshall didn't know. Perhaps he never would. He just knew that if there was one twenty-first-century maniac that should not be running anything, it was Cross.

"Colonel Casey, have you explained to the captain what I will want to talk about?"

"Yes, General."

Casey.

Marshall knew that name. That's how Cross made this happen. Casey had been a key security advisor to President Campbell. He would have had tremendous pull with any of the Ark sites.

If he had been secretly allied to Cross, everything fell into place.

"Good."

Cross stood up. He was dressed in a uniform similar to the Enforcers, save for insignia and medals. He walked closer to Marshall.

"You see, Captain, I know this can't be a rushed process. You know so much. And I must be patient to learn it."

Marshall thought of firing off something else to irritate Cross. But that would only trigger more punches and kicks, and he was sure there would be plenty of them without actually asking for more.

"So—we will begin today, and take our time. Everything you know, all the places, all the cells, all the people—everything. I will know it. It will be a great gift to the Authority."

He turned away and walked back to his chair as if to sit down and watch a show on television.

"Of course, there is an easier way. You tell me everything . . . now. No pain. No agony. You could even get a position of leadership. You . . . would get to enjoy the benefits of being a part of the Authority. The Capital, as you could discover, is not without its rewards and charms. There's food you haven't seen in decades." He laughed. "And women? Not those desert-worn types you find in the settlements. A different life here, Marshall. You should consider it."

"I have."

He felt the Enforcers on either side tense, ready to kick the wind out of him again.

"You can fucking keep it."

"So. The good soldier to the end. In a world that doesn't deserve one. Stupid decision."

Cross sat down.

"Now, let's begin. Tell me, who is in your cell?"

Marshall took a breath. He focused on the lights, the monitors with their images of the Capital fortress, the shiny metal floor, the nearby table with its . . . implements.

"Captain John Marshall, United States Army, serial number 9423382869."

Cross waved a hand in the air.

It was time to begin.

Marshall was on his knees, the lights not so bright anymore.

He was dripping sweat and blood, making his vision blurry again, his eyes sting. His shirt had been ripped off, and now his back was a mesh of welts and cuts.

And yet the worst part had been the hesitation before each blow landed.

Then two of the Enforcers started playing a game with his head, punching at it like it was a boxing bag, first to one side—followed by screams at him to get up—and then another smash to the opposite side.

Over and over.

He lost count of the number of times Cross had signaled them to stop so he could repeat his question.

Then, getting no answer to that, other questions.

Where is your base?

Who are the other leaders?

What equipment have you gathered that may prove dangerous to us?

Then more lashes to the back, more blood, more savage punches to the head that sent Marshall twisting to the floor, curling in on himself, his face smacking down hard on the metal.

It went on and on and on . . .

"Pull him up. To his feet."

Marshall could barely stand. His head throbbed from the blows, while his brain now dreaded more savage lashes to the back.

"All right. As I said, Marshall, I can be patient. Today was to show you just that. But tomorrow—Colonel, if you would—"

Casey walked over to the table and brought back a fistful of shiny metal objects.

"There you go, Captain. You see them? Each can have a different purpose. Some are narrow and sharp, others are broad and unfortunately dull. There are so many ways they can be used to produce pain. As you know, we learned some tricks from those we fought—back in the day. And here, *now*, we are no longer afraid to use them."

Marshall tilted his head at the objects. Looking at what Casey held in his hand, like so many lethal lollipops, was nearly enough to make him groan.

Today had been nothing.

"I will give you twenty-four hours. To remember things. To recall. And," he said, pointing at the tray of torture, "to think on what we have here for you. And know this—it doesn't stop there. When your body gets—what would be the word— *acclimatized* to the pain of metal on skin, we will move on to other things. In the end, you will talk. You will *beg* to talk."

Cross started to walk away. Marshall saw a door in the corner of the room open.

"Think on it, Captain. No need for it. No need for any of this."

Cross, followed by Casey, disappeared from the room, and the Enforcers holding him up dragged him in the other direction.

And as they did, Marshall thought . . .

How long can I hold out?

More importantly: *Did it matter?*

Because he knew one thing: if the study of dictatorships and prison and torture told us anything, it was that sooner or later, God, everyone talks.

And with his feet dragging on the floor as they pulled him away, Marshall tried to find something in his mind that resembled hope.

For now, he found nothing.

THIRTY-FIVE

ABOUT THE BASH

"You wait here until Mr. Stiles is ready to see you."

The man talking to Raine had a headset on and held a clipboard tightly, as though it contained the secrets of the universe.

Somehow, Raine doubted it.

The man spoke into the mic of the headset.

"Yes, yes, he's here, Mr. Stiles. He looks . . ." The scrawny man looked at Raine. "He looks set. No, sir. I will." Putting a hand over the mic, he said, "Mr. Stiles—"

"Is ready to see me?"

The man nodded.

"Lead on."

The assistant led Raine into a room lit by the glow of TVs all showing the same thing: a frozen shot of the words MUTANT BASH. In front of all these screens, people sat at control desks.

Sally had already told Raine that there was only one network. This was it, and Stiles ran its most popular show . . .

Where people battled mutants in an arena each week for money and for their lives.

Raine took in all the faces, finally settling on one that was familiar—he recognized it from the billboards he had seen around town. Stiles sat behind one of the control desks, at a good vantage point for all the monitors. He tapped one of the people sitting at the dials and whispered something as Raine came closer.

Like he's pointedly trying to act busy before he talks to me.

And what a guy.

Easily the fattest human Raine had met in this world. Layers of excess blubbery skin around his neck. And yet Stiles sat with his legs crossed as though he was on a throne and not a director's chair.

Raine stood there, scrawny assistant with a clipboard by his side.

When Raine looked away, the assistant rolled his eyes and gave him a nod indicating that he should give his full attention to Mr. Stiles.

The things one has to do just to stay alive.

Though Sally said this wasn't the wisest step in that direction. She had offered to set him up, get him a vehicle of some kind to escape to a settlement where they might not worry about newcomers.

He simply asked: "Does such a place exist?"

And she had no answer.

Finally, Stiles turned to him and he got to see the man's face, looking oddly inflated, with buggy eyes ready to pop out of his fat head. The man's fingers looked way too stubby to operate the controls.

"Greetings, Mr. Raine; J.K. Stiles."

For once Raine was happy that handshakes had gone the way of the dinosaurs and fast-food outlets.

Stiles pursed his lips as if that mouth wasn't happy without something to chew or suck on.

"New to Wellspring, I hear?"

"Yeah."

"Quite the show last night. Some race. Lot of unhappy people with that outcome, I can tell you."

Stiles began laughing, a deep, phlegmy sound that looked to end with the blubbery bear of a man rolling onto the floor, dead.

"Want to explain your show to me? This Mutant Bash . . ."

Stiles became suddenly intense, his eyes gleaming. "Oh, eager, are we? Well, this, right here, is where . . . the magic happens."

Christ.

"Not just the cameras, but all the surprises in the Bash are controlled from here. We like to keep the show fresh. Give the viewers something new, something that they haven't seen every week."

"Well, they haven't seen me."

Stiles let his smile fade. "Yes, but they've seen a lot of nobodies from nowhere walk into our studio arena before. And while they love newbies, they also love—" He cleared his throat, its product swallowed. "—seeing when they don't walk out."

"People like it when the mutants win?"

"Ohhh, no, Mr. Raine, no. *Nobody* likes mutants. Everybody wants to see the muties get theirs, and good. But not all at once, you see. They want"—he turned one of his paws into a fist and banged it down into the open palm of his other hand—"drama. Suspense. *Story,* Mr. Raine, story! Good over evil, human over beast. And you don't get that without our side—the humans, the normal—taking some hits."

Stiles's use of the word "normal," especially to include himself, seemed wildly misplaced.

Raine ached from the race. His body was still bruised and banged. He had felt the nanotrites kick in as soon as he lay down, and was nearly healed by morning, the dark purple bruises themselves all but faded. Yet there was still lingering pain.

Stiles leaned forward.

"From what I hear, you don't have much choice. About being here."

"That might explain my lack of enthusiasm."

Stiles looked at him, the producer's face now lapsed into a sneer. He wants to say something really nasty, Raine thought. But he's holding back.

For now.

The nastiness, Raine guessed, would come in the arena later.

Which brought another, more chilling thought: *This man might have the power to kill me.*

And then—

I better find out just what the hell I am getting myself into here . . .

"Want to explain to me what I will be doing?"

Stiles nodded, his scowl in place.

"Sure, why not? You're gonna be a star, Raine—at least for a night. Might as well show you how it all works."

Stiles had indicated a seat next to him, and then gestured to the largest monitor in the studio.

"What I'm going to do is show you some clips from a past Bash. A greatest hits, if you will. Just a taste . . ."

A porky index finger came down and the screen unfroze, and now Raine saw the arena, not much larger than a hockey rink.

Aerial cameras panned the area, showing boxlike structures painted with colors and giant numbers. Round beach balls the size of small trucks sat in one corner.

A playpen for a giant baby.

Then a cut—someone in the arena, holding something like a curved sword in one hand and club in the other.

"You can select up to two weapons of your choice from our stock. No projectile weapons, of course. See, that gives you an advantage already. Each mutant gets only one weapon."

This made Stiles begin laughing again.

The man in the arena went up to the nearest box. He smashed at the sides, hitting the numbers dead center.

"You see that—what he's doing there?—*that's* important. Each bash has a hidden message. It's a puzzle. You can't just go in, run to the other side, and get out. You have to figure out the *puzzle,* and do something. This guy—well he had a number puzzle. The audience loves it. They play along at home."

"But without the mutants? I thought—"

Another cut, and now the same guy was encircled by four mutants who moved around him counterclockwise.

"The better you do with the puzzle, the more muties get released. Or is it the worse you do?" The fat man giggled. "I can never remember."

But Raine was now focused on the guy in the arena. The muties had him spinning, turning, trying to keep his eyes on the tightening chain of mutants.

"Always one against a bunch?"

"No. You never know. I mean I do. But not the basher. Sometimes there is team play. But this one here is a newbie. He has to get through alone. Not experienced mutants, though. A new batch. He should have done—"

A cut. And one mutant had charged and smashed the guy on the back of his head.

Didn't knock him down.

Raine heard a cheer.

"—better."

"You got an audience in there?"

"Oh, yes, that's part of the excitement. A live studio audience. VIPs. Tell you, it's hard to get a seat to the live show. 'Course, you'll have the best seat in the house."

The guy in the arena spun and stabbed at an attacking mutant—exactly the wrong move, as now the other three had a clear shot at him.

More blows from a mutant behind him, and the guy went to his knees.

Raine wanted to look away.

"And you don't stop it? I mean, the guy lost."

Stiles shook his head. "And deprive our faithful viewers?"

Sick world, Raine thought. What exactly made it this sick?

"Besides, Mr. Raine, you see . . . when they witness what happens to that poor fellow, they now want *payback*!"

Stiles had raised his voice.

"They wait for the next bashers to enter, for the rest of the story, so the mutants will get what they deserve, live and in color!"

Raine now had the thought that maybe running to some other settlement, no matter where, might be the better option.

But then again, he had faced mutants. He had certainly killed them before.

He had a chance here. That is, if Stiles didn't rig the show against him.

Stiles killed the monitor.

"Okay, a few last details . . . then you can get ready, Mr. Raine."

• • •

Somehow Stiles had been able to get his mammoth body out of its chair and walk over to what turned out to be a model of the arena.

He waved a hand over the open, empty space.

"You won't know what's in there until you get in. Once you enter the arena, we give you the puzzle and you will have to figure out what to do. Shouldn't be too hard for someone smart like you to figure out."

"And when I've solved it?"

"*If* you solve it—and you can fight past the mutants and head to what we call 'home' "—he pointed at one end of the arena, where a door stood in the middle of the wall—"then you walk behind the outside walls and emerge in our studio for the post-Bash interview. Done by me, of course."

Raine leaned forward. It wasn't far from one end to the other. So that wasn't the challenge.

"Do I have to *kill* all the mutants in the arena before I go through?"

Stiles shook his head. "No. Once you have shown us the solution to the puzzle inside the arena, you are free to go 'home.' If you can get there."

Raine nodded.

There were things this bastard wasn't telling him, he was sure of it.

Stiles's nasty grin and piggy eyes did nothing to dispel that thought. "Nearly showtime, Mr. Raine; you best get ready . . ."

And suddenly the assistant was there, clipboard in hand, ready to lead him away.

THIRTY-SIX

THE TRAP

Raine looked at the table of weapons.

The selection didn't seem to matter, not when you had an array of clunky clubs and homemade bladed weapons. He picked up the longest blade he could find, more of a pike with a sharpened tip and not much of an edge. For a club—he gave each one a heft. He wanted something light that could be whipped around easily. He found one that felt right.

"I'll take these two."

The assistant wrote down something on the clipboard.

"You gotta take a jacket."

The assistant pointed to a rack with jackets, all bright colors.

"They all have tonight's sponsor on them: SuperStim."

"I have to wear one?"

"Yes. It's in your—" He flipped through some pages. "—your contract. Somewhere."

"I didn't sign one," Raine said. "Late addition to the program."

The assistant misunderstood, the dialogue exceeding his intellect.

"No, you will be on first. You are the *first* Bash."

"Which means—I guess—that I'm not expected to get out alive?"

At first the assistant said nothing, but then: "The outfits give you an extra layer. That could be helpful. Good way to think about it."

Raine went over and picked up a blue jacket with the words SuperStim! on the back. He put it on.

I feel like a race car with ads plastered on its side.

He zipped it up. Not much protection. But the guy was right. A few millimeters extra padding.

"And the puzzle?"

"Oh, Mr. Stiles will announce that when you enter the arena."

The guy put a hand to his earpiece.

"Yeah, right. Okay, we go live to air in three minutes. When that door pops open, out you go."

Raine waited for a "good luck" that didn't come. He guessed the guy had seen enough people walk out that door only to disappear.

And I guess "break a leg" would have a very different meaning today—if people even remembered it.

Raine turned to the door, pike and club in hand. He started taking steady breaths.

Must be how the gladiators felt.

A light above the door glowed red.

Then, suddenly, it turned green and the door popped open.

• • •

And with the open door, cheers erupted from the studio audience filling the hundreds of seats that ringed the arena. Raine walked out, watching how the aerial cameras moved to follow him. His hands clenched tightly, holding the weapons up a bit and ready.

"And welcome, for our first Mutant Bash, the winner of the White Rabbit . . ."

That was met with boos.

". . . Raine!"

He listened to Stiles, but also took in the layout of the arena, no longer the empty space shown in the model. But it was also different from what he saw in the video.

The arena held oversized statues . . . more like bizarre, giant dolls:

A clownlike figure holding a bottle of stim up to its oversized lips.

A beautiful woman holding a bag of money.

A bandit figure with a ball of fire.

A flying creature, wings outstretched—a dragon with a massive head, open mouth lined with teeth, one claw foot holding a gun.

Four figures, each near fifteen feet tall.

"Your challenge, Raine, is to show us the answer to this . . . our world needs order. What is the order . . . here?" The audience groaned, quickly stumped by the riddle.

Me, too, Raine thought.

What the fuck is he talking about?

"Show us the answer!" Stiles's voice boomed in the arena.

Raine started walking. The door behind him slammed shut. He kept looking at the figures, turning from one to the other, when the base of the woman figure opened and a pair of mutants ran out.

"A clue *to get you started,*" Stiles screamed.

Raine raised his weapon.

The two mutants came out of the woman first.

That might mean something. He didn't wait for them to charge to him, but he ran up, swinging his club with the biggest arc possible. One mutant reared back. The other kept coming.

Raine then shoved his pike into the still-charging mutant, skewering it.

He immediately discovered a downside to the weapon. Once thrust in, it didn't come out too easily.

But the thing writhed on the end of the pike, dead.

The other mutant now came at him, and, one-handed, Raine swung his club at it, the bash he delivered living up to its name.

Cameras catching it all.

Raine tried to think about the riddle. *Order.* With these statues.

What could it mean?

Distracted for a moment, the mutant smacked at his knee, making that leg buckle.

But Raine discovered as he reared back that the pike slid out of the dead mutie like a pin out of cushion, dripping with mutant blood.

Good for a close-up.

Focus!

Then, quickly spinning, he thrust it at the other mutant. The length of the pike worked well, giving him that extra few inches.

It went in, and Raine heard the audience cheer.

• • •

Standing there, thinking about the riddle, he heard a loud click, and another pair of mutants came out of the bottom of the clown holding the bottle of stim. They raced toward him.

This time he stood his ground. He had to figure out what he was supposed to do or Stiles would just keep sending damn mutants at him.

Order.

He looked at the figures, each paired with something.

Bandit. Fire.

Woman. Money.

Clown. Stim.

Dragon. Gun.

Mismatched?

Could be that was the puzzle.

But no . . . there seemed no logic to that. And the puzzle couldn't be so hard that the viewers would be totally stumped.

That is, unless they just gave the viewers the answer.

Raine was frustrated. *What the hell do I know about game shows?*

Especially this game show, which had the added difficulty of mutants constantly attacking.

He crouched and let one impale itself on the pike.

But the other didn't even use its club. Instead it leapt on him, knocking him flat, his own club rendered useless. He smelled the thing in his face; had to be the worst smell in the foul-smelling world.

The thing was trying to get at his neck.

Getting this on camera, boys?

The jagged teeth and the snapping, open maw of the thing so close.

Raine just hoped Stiles didn't open another figure and let out even more mutants.

He couldn't use his club. His pike was feet away, still buried in the other mutant.

With no weapon, he had no choice.

Classic hand-to-hand technique. Use what you had. In this case, one free hand.

He took his fingers, formed them into a claw, and jammed them into the eye sockets of the mutant.

And though the thing was more animal than human, that degree of blinding pain made it leap away from him.

It stood up, dropped its club, and raised its hands to its head.

Raine ran over to the pike and pulled it out of the thing he had skewered, and though the blind mutant was now no threat, he gave it a quick in and out with the pike where he guessed its heart should be.

It fell to the ground.

Good guess.

They were dead.

"Ladies and gentlemen, a round of applause for Raine! Can he solve the Bash, now that things are about to get . . ."

The audience answered, a show mantra apparently.

". . . even . . . harder!"

With no mutants attacking, Raine had a few moments to once again look at the giant figures. The odd mix of what they held, jumbled up.

The one clue . . . about "order."

He heard a clicking sound, and another large statue began disgorging its mutants.

But he kept looking at the figures, waiting for something to occur to him.

The bandit. The clown. The dragon.

Fire. Gun. Money.

And then—something came.

Could be too simple. But as he started running toward the bandit figure, he remembered thinking that the riddle had to be something that viewers at home could get.

Close now to the towering bandit holding a wooden gun.

He *smashed* the bandit figure.

Lights exploded from the ceiling, a siren went off.

He was either very right or very wrong.

Now he bolted for the eerie clown grinning down at him, the smile locked on its face as it held the bottle of SuperStim.

He knew that he had two mutants chasing him just behind.

I got time, he thought. I can get to it . . . before they get to me.

Another smash with his club, and now more flashing lights from the ceiling, the siren sound again.

He turned around. The noise and light show had the advantage of disorienting the two mutants.

But only for a second.

That's when he noticed they had him backed up against one of the sides of the arena.

"Okay. Come on. What the hell you waiting for?"

He was surprised to hear his voice echoing through the arena studio.

Got mics picking up everything I say. All part of the show.

One of the mutants snarled back. Raine raised his pike like a javelin. The other mutant took a step closer.

Then the sick clicking noise as another one of the figures opened, meaning more mutants.

Four against one.

The time for waiting was over. Raine threw the pike and it cut right into one of the mutants, but didn't kill it. Instead, it dropped its club to grab the pike sticking out of it.

Leaving Raine without his best weapon.

Have to get it back. Especially now that more are coming.

He moved toward the other mutant, who raised its club over its head and began waving it around, gathering momentum.

When the mutant brought it down, Raine blocked the blow with his club, the loud sound of the clubs smashing together picked up by the mics.

He saw—out of the corners of his eyes—two more mutants hurrying into the fray.

Shit . . .

Raine brought his club down, a move that seemed to confuse the mutant, then brought it quickly up again, like a knockout punch from a fighter.

It had the desired effect, kicking the mutant back on its heels.

He went over to the mutant still struggling with his pike and slid it out.

The audience cheered.

Giving them a damn good show.

But how many more mutants could they send, wave after wave . . . until he made a mistake?

One thing was certain—the riddle was more important than defeating the mutants. He had hit the clown. So now he ran to the dragon, just feet ahead of the mutants. Another smash, more lights, and this time he knew how to take advantage of the distraction.

The two mutants fell to their knees as he smashed them, using the flashing to cover his moves.

He was splattered with their blood. Its dark blue color matched the sick smell.

He might be able to hit the rest of the figures now. He smashed the fire held by the bandit and then, ignoring the mayhem from the roof of the arena, went to the dragon's gun.

Following the only order that seemed clear enough here.

The letters of the damn alphabet . . .

He went on to the bag of money, hit that, and then moved to

the stim held by the clown. He was trying to keep the letters straight and worrying about whatever surprises Stiles might have in store. He moved to the final pairing, the woman.

Which had been the first figure to open.

One last smash.

The sirens went off again, just as, at the other end of the arena, a bunch of new mutants raced toward him.

But now the door would be open at the other end.

"Home," Stiles called it.

He started running.

But as he ran he looked up, and now, so close, he noticed something. In the arena. All around the arena. Standing.

Enforcers.

Waiting. Watching.

And worse than any mutants. Raine wondered if they were here for him, or just here for security?

He got to the door that led out of the back of the arena.

He grabbed the latch.

Did I solve the Bash? he wondered. This would tell the story, with mutants only seconds behind him.

He pulled down the latch . . .

It *opened,* and he vanished into the dark space, the corridor that circled the arena and led back to the studio.

He pulled the door shut behind him.

And then—in the darkness, with only a scattering of pale yellow bulbs lighting the way back to where he had started—he felt someone grab him hard.

FOUR

INTO THE CAPITAL

THIRTY-SEVEN

DR. CADENCE

Raine spun to face whoever had grabbed him.

Cheers and sirens still boomed from the arena, Stiles milking his unlikely success.

The figure was barely visible, but it was definitely a woman—her eyes catching the scant light. She had a rifle slung over her shoulder and two handguns at either side.

Armed and ready to play.

"What are—"

"*Stop.* You can't go back there."

"Got an interview to do. And who are—"

"Did you see the Enforcers all over? They have a hovercraft outside ready to take you away. You're *dead* if you go back there."

"How do you know?"

"Look, I'm Dr. Elizabeth Cadence. I'm with the Resistance.

We have people in places and we got word that you were here. I came to pick you up right after the Bash."

The cheering outside had subsided. Stiles would be wondering where his new star was.

"You are dead if you stay. I can get you out of here if you come now. *Right now.*"

"Why should I trust you?"

She took a step closer, her eyes locked on his. "Because I'm an Ark survivor as well, Lieutenant. Sally said this was what you wanted."

"You know Sally?"

"She's a brave woman—she gave me your stuff." Elizabeth looked around, eyes nervous. "Can we go now?"

Raine looked at this woman. From his own time. From an Ark.

Suddenly—he didn't feel so alone.

He took a breath. "Lead on."

Instead of heading back to the other end of the arena, the woman took him in the opposite direction. Before he could ask, she whispered, "They have other exits down here."

"No guards?"

"Not when I came in. Here—"

Elizabeth stopped by a light and Raine could make out a door labeled SERVICE AREA 19. A recessed handle was the only other adornment.

She used a knife on the latch and the door opened up. He followed her in and she shut it behind them. Then they ran down a corridor with pipes and wires overhead, the innards of the TV complex.

Elizabeth led the way to another door, unlocked this time, and to stairs.

"We have to go down," she said as she raced ahead of him. "All these old cities have tunnels, passageways. Mostly abandoned except for the stray packs of mutants who hole up in them."

Down one level, then another.

"They let infrastructure go. But I guess you've seen that."

"That's not all they have let go."

"Yeah—okay—"

She stopped and froze. A finger on her lips. Listening. Raine also tilted his head, trying to pick up any sounds, but heard nothing.

"Okay—thought I heard something. They'll be hunting for you now. Are you okay to keep running?"

He didn't tell her how much he hurt.

She ran down the bottom level of this area, turning one way, then the other, a mad dash down corridors that seemed erratic and haphazard. But then one basement corridor led to an open sewer area, the gully dry now, though still full of the smell of whatever the Wellspring people dumped into it.

"Follow me. On the ledge. You don't want to fall into that . . . shit."

"Literally."

She threw him a quick smile.

The ledge was narrow, and it was hard for Raine to keep his balance. But seeing the piles of filth in the trench of the sewer below was plenty of motivation.

Elizabeth kept up a steady pace, moving full out, and it took all of his strength to keep up with her.

Got those nanotrites working overtime, he thought.

They came to an area with no light at all, but Elizabeth had put on a headlamp, and suddenly he had a speck of light to follow.

"We're close. Nearly outside the town's limits. You okay, Raine?"

"Fine," he lied.

And they kept up their brutal pace through the tunnels and sewers of Wellspring.

Finally she stopped at what appeared to be a dead end.

"Okay," she said, the headlamp aimed right at him, and he had to shield his eyes. "Sorry."

She switched it off.

"I'll go out first. Make sure the site is still secure. Then I'll signal you. You follow me, get in, and we're off."

Raine imagined she had a buggy waiting, and he wasn't at all sure how they could get away in one, not with all the Enforcers spreading out, searching for him. This was her show, though, and he was too tired to care.

He watched her climb up a ladder, then push at a manhole cover, grunting as she did so.

A few moments of silence followed, and then she took a step back down, looking at him.

"All clear. Let's go."

He started up the ladder.

When he got out, Raine could see Wellspring behind him, the area they were in dark and deserted, the bright lights of the inner city miles away.

This part of the city was abandoned, destroyed—more a piece of the Wasteland than anything else.

He turned to see where Dr. Cadence had gone . . .

And he didn't know what he was looking at. There was a strange blackish shape in the shadows, large enough that he had to tilt his head back to try to see the top. Somewhere in the middle, on an open space, he could barely make out the doctor running back and forth.

He hurried to . . . whatever it was.

As he drew closer, he saw what looked like the deck of a ship. Some kind of boat? But when he climbed into it, he saw exactly what the large black shape above the deck was.

A balloon.

Like a dirigible. Something out of a Jules Verne novel.

They had no jets, but they had this.

An engine roared to life. Dr. Cadence came up to him. "Okay," she yelled over the engine. "Boiler's running. We're ready. Just hold on—in case we hit any currents heading up."

Raine noticed then that she hadn't turned on any running lights. They'd be running dark—which was probably incredibly dangerous—but it also might let them slip away without being seen.

In a world of buggies and cars, it would be as if he had disappeared.

The thing began to rise. Raine firmly attached himself to the deck and held on tight.

The balloon ship wobbled on the way up.

A steady breeze turned into something choppy, and—like a dinghy in a rough sea—the ship rocked back and forth.

But then, when they were well above the ground, Wellspring fading in the distance, it steadied. The moon had come up, Raine again seeing the scarlike gash on it that he first saw in the Wasteland. A visual reminder that this world . . . had changed.

Stars glistened, though. Ancient, unchanged.

Suddenly he felt cool, chilly at the altitude. And he was aware that he was still covered with mutant blood.

After making sure the ship was running smoothly, Elizabeth came over to him.

"Let me get you some clean clothes. Some water."

"Thanks." He looked up at her. A dark figure, worried about him. It felt strange to hear that concerned tone.

Yes, she wanted something from him. But she was of *his* time. She *remembered*.

He told himself . . .

For Ark survivors that must be a special bond.

For those who had been there before it all ended.

Elizabeth nodded as if she had heard his thoughts, then disappeared into what had to be a small belowdecks area.

The ship sailed evenly. Raine drank water from a cup that she brought up, and he shed his jacket for a clean one Elizabeth had found.

He stood next to the woman as she steered the balloon ship, the engine producing a steady roar that mixed with the whistle of the wind moving over the balloon.

"Okay to ask where we are going, Dr. Cadence?"

"Tell you what. You call me Elizabeth, and I *won't* call you 'Lieutenant.'"

"Great. Just Raine will do."

She pointed ahead. "Out there . . . there are more settlements. Some closer to Capital Prime."

"Capital Prime?"

"The fortress city of the Authority. Those settlements really serve the Authority. They live and die . . . at the Authority's whim."

"And we're going to one of them?" he asked skeptically.

"No. We're not. I'm taking you to our main base. Underground, in a place called Subway Town—right under their noses. The Authority ignores it and hasn't learned that we hide there. Least, not yet. We will have to move soon. We always have to be on the move."

For a few seconds Raine just stood there, listening to the sound of the wind, feeling the breeze as they sailed through the night.

"Nobody down below can see us?"

"No. Just got the fire in the boiler. And it's pretty much covered by the deck." She looked off into the distance.

He looked at her. A woman from his own time. He couldn't even begin to think of the questions to ask her.

She turned and looked back at him. "You had a rough couple of days, hm?"

"Hasn't been easy."

"Going to take us an hour or so, Raine. And I know you've got questions. So let me start . . . from the beginning."

As she spoke, Elizabeth looked at the man she had rescued.

Already she wondered if he'd be up to what lay head. Amazing that he had survived the few days he'd been here.

But did he have the strength, the basic health, to do what had to be done in the next twelve hours?

Could one man—even with all his training, his experience, now battered by the Bash, shaken by the arena—do what she was going to ask of him?

She was not at all confident.

"My field is—was—molecular biology. I was one of the core teams working on the nanotrites project."

"They've been very helpful, by the way."

"Well, don't get used to them."

"I've heard—"

"My husband helped create them. We didn't know . . . what they could do. How they could change."

"Your husband? He didn't come with you?"

She turned away. "I was sent in an Ark with my husband—a physicist—and our son. The three of us."

"They let children go?"

"If they wanted us, our son had to go, too. That was our stance. And I imagine they thought the gene pool might be promising."

"And your husband is . . . ?"

"We were all picked up by the Authority," she said quietly. "My husband, son—they were taken away. I was sent to the Dead City to work. The deal—"

"They like deals here."

She smiled wanly. "The deal was, if I helped them, then we could be reunited. At first I was diligent. But there were rumors . . . rumors my family was dead. And the work I was doing, I didn't understand. It seemed . . . sick. Using nanotrites on the mutants. Yet I only dealt with a piece of the puzzle."

She took a breath.

"Hopefully, what you got on that hard drive . . . will explain what was being done. What is *still* being done." She looked right at him. "Could be very important, Raine."

"And so you left."

"I couldn't keep helping the Authority. I *had* to leave. And I didn't believe they would ever let me see my family again. If they were still alive."

Raine went quiet for a few minutes.

So much to take in, she thought. She'd had years. This world no longer held surprises for her.

But for him?

Raine broke his silence. "How did this all happen? The Authority, the Enforcers? What happened to the plan to rebuild humanity, to make a new world?"

This was the question she had been waiting for. "You know what they say about plans," she said. "This one had a flaw that doomed it from the beginning. That, and a big surprise."

She then told Raine about the asteroid, how its course had shifted, whatever was inside it reacting to the planet. And how General Martin Cross and Colonel James Casey had commandeered an Ark.

How they made sure they were the first out.

Made sure that *they* would run this world.

"Most of the survivors that came after them were either killed or captured. The ones that could be used were put to work. A few, like myself, escaped. But not many." She looked at Raine again. "Now, there's only one other like you that we know of."

"Like me?"

"A soldier. Captain John Marshall. Leader of the Resistance."

"I look forward to meeting him."

She nodded.

Not yet, she told herself . . . she wouldn't tell him yet. Instead, she simply said:

"Me, too . . ."

THIRTY-EIGHT

SUBWAY TOWN

She turned and looked at him. She had already decided on a slight detour before they came to Subway Town.

This survivor needed to see things.

"Raine, take a look down there."

The airship felt steady enough for Raine to walk to the edge and lean over. With the moonlight, he could make out the landscape below.

It reminded him of grainy photographs of the trenches from World War One. The devastated landscape, farmhouses burnt to the ground, the terrain turned into a series of long, desperate lines as men charged at each other, day after day, so many falling uselessly to their death.

"What is it?"

Elizabeth had to speak loudly to be heard.

"Used to be the Cane Settlement. It was independent, made

up of basically goodhearted people. But some of the Cane leaders started working with us. Supplies, information. They knew the risks."

Raine looked back at Elizabeth. He could guess the rest of the story.

"Someone—could have been one of their family, maybe another trader who overheard something—turned them in to the Authority. And instead of arrests . . . they did that."

"Killed everyone?"

"Every last one of them." She took a breath. "Then burnt it to the ground."

It made Raine remember something he was thinking about earlier, about the French Resistance: did the Resistance feel any responsibility for what happened?

It was a classic scenario . . . a resistance does something, and innocent people pay a heavy price. Was any of it worth it?

Historians debated that.

"They wanted to make an example. For all the other far-flung settlements. Cross us, and *this* is what will happen. I'd say, based on the level of cooperation we've been getting, it worked. We've had to be more careful, more underground than ever."

Raine kept looking down.

The landscape had been left as pure desolation.

"How many people?" he asked.

"Depends on who might have been in the settlement. There were always migrant traders passing through. Our guess . . . nearly a hundred."

Raine nodded. A massacre, taking its place in line with others throughout modern history. He stepped back from the edge, for a few minutes saying nothing. He noticed that the airship had turned now, returning to an earlier course, the moon sliding to his left.

"You brought me there . . . for a reason."

"Could be."

"To show me what you are fighting. And why."

She turned, her face determined. This woman from his time who didn't know whether her own family was alive or dead, prisoner or free.

"I hoped it would help you understand."

"And that I would join you?"

She held his gaze. "They did send you back with a mission, isn't that right?"

"Yeah."

"I have to figure . . . *this* wasn't what they imagined for that future. Slaughter. Fear. Terror. The goddamned Authority."

He looked away. "No."

"So—"

Back to her. "Say no more." Another deep breath of the chilly night air. "I'm in."

And Elizabeth nodded.

The airship began dropping in altitude well before Raine could see anything like signs of life.

Just more deserted buildings, chunks of metal walls, up-turned cars.

They now glided a mere hundred feet above the ground.

"What is this?"

"Crescent City. Ever been here? I mean, before?"

"Can't say that I have."

"The city got destroyed by Apophis. But they had built a small subway line, and people took refuge there. Lawless, dangerous; it wasn't a great place to visit before. Definitely not a great place now."

The ship dropped a few more feet.

"But it's a good place for us to hide. For now. Definitely a place where no questions are asked."

"This is Subway Town?"

Elizabeth nodded.

"And the Authority tolerates it?"

"They could wipe it out. But that would mean going through every square inch of the tunnels, into tight spaces where people have amassed a lot of weapons. So it would be a costly, deadly operation. Besides, Redstone—"

"And he is?"

"He runs Subway Town. Who knows why . . ."

"Love the political system in this world."

"Yeah. Another thing we want to change. For now, though, Redstone is in charge. Whether people are scared of him or need what he can get, it doesn't much matter. This is his place."

Now only thirty feet above the ground, Raine watched Elizabeth turn to the right, banking the craft slightly.

"So you are safe here?"

"Like I said, for now. No place is safe too long. We're already looking for a new place." She looked at Raine. It seemed to him that she wanted to tell him something more but stopped.

He could see that up here, at the street level, the city aboveground was completely deserted.

Everyone was living below, he realized. Like . . .

What was the word?

Living like troglodytes.

Elizabeth grabbed a lever and the engine slowed. Another lever let more hot air out of the sausage-shaped balloon above.

In minutes they came to a landing.

She pulled the engine lever all the way down.

The boiler went quiet, and as the balloon deflated she ran around, neatly catching the folds of canvas material as if wrapping a mainsail tight after a day at sea.

"Okay—ready?" She jumped off the ship, its hull now camouflaged amidst the scattered debris of the city. "We have people waiting."

Raine grabbed his guns and his pack with the hard drive. Would they be of any value to this group?

He guessed he was about to find out.

Down into dark subway tunnels. Once his eyes adjusted, he could see that stretches were dotted with lights. Slowly, he could make out the sound of voices.

"Just walk like you live here," Elizabeth whispered. "Nice and natural, okay?"

"Sure."

The passed people, some drinking, others haggling at a stand.

She leaned close to him. "Put your arm around me. Looks better."

Raine did so. Been a while since any human contact, he thought.

They walked close together now, as if out for a late night stroll.

Past a place with neon lights . . .

Jani's.

From a doorway, smoke and people poured out. Raine could see that everyone had a weapon—either a rifle slung over their shoulder or a handgun by their side. No, it wouldn't be easy even for Enforcers to clear out this place.

Elizabeth leaned her head into him.

"We turn up here. It's going to get dark. Then we get to a place the train inspectors used to use. No one goes there—too dark, too far from the action."

He followed her lead, and Elizabeth led him down a narrow

tunnel, leaving the tracks behind. The lights and sounds behind them faded.

He didn't know how she knew where she was going. Counting some kind of markers on the side?

But then she stopped. She pulled her headlamp on and turned on the light.

"Here we are."

Raine didn't see anything.

But she knocked, and he could hear that whatever she was banging on was hollow. She knocked three times. One time. Then twice . . . and a door opened.

She moved to go inside, but before she did, she turned to him.

"Don't be disappointed . . . but welcome to the Resistance."

Not the best welcome . . .

A burly man—no shirt, but a band holding a knife around one of his thick muscular arms and two full holsters—stood on the other side of the door.

Having the correct knock . . . probably pretty damn important.

No smiles at Elizabeth's return.

"Everything go okay?"

She nodded in Raine's direction. "He won the Bash. That helped. I had the explosives ready for plan B."

The man nodded.

"Raine, this is Jack Portman. He's our ordnance expert. Gets the weapons, keeps them working. Irreplaceable."

"Glad to meet you," Raine said.

"We'll see about that."

Another man hurried out from the rear.

310 • MATTHEW COSTELLO

"Does he have it? I've been waiting."

Elizabeth continued, "And this is Mark Lassard. Does what we used to call I.T. Except he's a real genius."

"Yeah, yeah—we don't have a lot of time, Elizabeth. Where is *it*?"

"He's talking about the hard drive you got."

"Oh." Raine dug out the incendiaries and the shotgun, then handed the pack with the drive from the Dead City to Lassard.

"Good. I'll get on this right away." He hurried away.

Portman still stood there, taking him in.

Trust had to be scarce.

Was he weighing whether he, newly arrived, was worthy of it?

"Seems to be in a rush," Raine said.

Elizabeth turned to him.

"Yeah. Well—"

"And your leader. Marshall. Is he here?"

"Bring him over to the table," Portman said. "Chitchat time is over."

Good conversationalist, that Portman.

They sat at a small metal table.

Behind them, Lassard was at a keyboard at what seemed to be a decent computer setup. The sound of typing accompanied their talking.

"Want some food?" Elizabeth asked him.

Raine shook his head.

Portman sat with his elbows resting on the table, his arms folded.

Elizabeth looked at him. "There *is* a rush."

"I see you got your I.T. guy working like crazy," Raine said.

Portman looked back at Elizabeth, ignoring him. "Let's get on with it. See if he's really with us or not."

Yeah . . . not much trust emanating from the weapons guy.

"Our leader isn't here."

Raine nodded, listening to Elizabeth.

"He was captured days ago and sent into Capital Prime. He'll be questioned, tortured, then questioned again. Eventually he will tell them what he knows . . . or die. Either could happen."

"Or both," Portman rumbled.

"He's in the Capital?"

Elizabeth nodded. "We know he's still alive. We got word about that. We also got word that he's close to breaking. Tomorrow will be the day they pull out all the stops and try to get everything they can from him. What he knows could destroy the Resistance. Expose our cells all over the Wasteland, our plans . . ."

She looked to Portman to see how she was doing. He made a slight shrug with his massive shoulders. She continued.

"If we don't get him out by then, it's disaster for the Resistance. And with what you brought, we could be close to a turning point in our war against them."

Raine kept listening but noted that was the first time he had heard the word . . . *war.*

War was something he understood.

"We can tell you about that. About what we are trying to do. But none of it—the Resistance, the data on that hard drive—means much unless we get Marshall out."

Raine looked around at the room. No one said anything for a few moments. A lightbulb came on, without anyone saying a word. Finally, he spoke up.

"And I'm guessing . . . that that would be my job."

And no one said no.

THIRTY-NINE

THE PLAN

Portman spread out a hand drawn map.

"This is the Capital. We've sent teams around there to do a recon. Some made it back. It's as accurate as we could make it."

"But where did you get this?"

"People who worked on the Capital buildings . . . a few deserted to us," Elizabeth said. "The ones that could get away."

"And we've had some people on the inside," Portman added. "From time to time."

Raine recalled what they said about learning Marshall's condition.

Elizabeth was nodding to what Portman had said. "Still, there are a lot of things we don't know." She put a finger down.

"Here, this is the prison . . . right under one of the Enforcer barracks."

"That's convenient." They didn't acknowledge his sarcasm.

"Marshall is there. Could be any cell. Our last informant never could find out where, and now we don't have any inside information at all."

"Been in situations like that before."

"Not like this one," Portman said. "The outer perimeter of the place has weaponized fences. Enforcers patrolling all over the damn place."

"You make it sound almost easy." Raine glanced at a digital clock above Lassard's bank of computers. It was just after twelve. He was tired of all this debriefing. Tired, and hurt, and drained from the hell of the last few days.

Couldn't they do this tomorrow?

But no—he knew they had no time.

Which meant that *he* had no time.

As if sensing his internal struggle, Elizabeth ignored his last comment. "One thing we know is that we can't send a bunch of untrained settlers in there," she said. "They'd get destroyed. It needs to be someone with training. *Your* training."

"What do you know about my training?"

"One thing we did get from an Ark were the dossiers on all the planned survivors, who's still buried . . ."

"And all those who have already been killed or captured," Portman added. "A lot of good people."

Raine nodded, and once again thought about the mission. "So it's just me?"

"No—just *us*," Elizabeth said. "I'm going as well."

Raine shook his head. "No, you won't. If I have any chance at all, it will be on my own, with as much firepower as you"—a nod to Portman—"can give me. Besides, if I don't make it, that means Marshall doesn't make it, and *that* means this group will need you."

"He's right," Portman said. Then to Raine: "But I can go."

"No. I need what you can show me here, on the map and any weapons you have, but you're not coming with me."

"I can damn well go if—"

"What were you, before joining the Resistance?"

He sniffed the air. "Worked on engines. Dabbled in guns. But I can—"

"They'll need you as well. And I need what you can give me. But if you've never practiced and carried out an infiltration, you'd do me more harm than good."

The two of them stared at each other. Reluctantly, Portman nodded.

And Raine suddenly realized that the power had quietly shifted from them . . . to him.

Leading.

Now—he thought—that's what the hell I was sent here for.

He rubbed his eyes. Fighting the fatigue.

"Got anything? To give me a boost."

Elizabeth got up and went over to a shelf, grabbing a metal case.

"I can give you a shot—a mix of primobolan and testosterone. Some pills for a quick boost later. Your nanotrites still working okay?"

"Doing fine."

She nodded. "As I said—don't get used to them. When you come back, we'll get them out. But you're okay for now."

"Good. Now—you say you have a plan?"

She looked back at Lassard, still tapping furiously at his keyboard. "Yeah. And it involves what Lassard is doing as well." Elizabeth smiled and lifted the layout map of the Capital, to reveal a bird's-eye view of the area from a distance . . . and what looked like . . .

. . . an aircraft carrier.

What the . . . ?

"Ready?"

Raine let her finish, the plan well thought out even if it sounded like it was lifted from a suspense novel: impossible, mad, no margin for error.

He shook his head.

"Lot of unknowns there."

"We did the best we could."

He looked over at Lassard. "And what if *he* doesn't finish in time?"

"You go without it. Get Marshall. Come back."

Abruptly, Lassard pushed his chair away from his monitors.

"Christ. I was close." He turned back to them. The digital clock above his head kept clicking off the milliseconds. "So damn close!"

"Keep trying, Mark," Elizabeth said.

He nodded and went back to his keyboard.

Raine said, "How did you know you could trust me?"

"Kvasir." She smiled. "He may not like to think he's with us. But he is."

Raine realized then that she didn't know.

About Kvasir. About what happened.

"Elizabeth—Kvasir is dead."

Her eyes went wide. She kept them locked on Raine.

Then he explained how he had been rescued by the old scientist, and how he found him when he came back, slaughtered by the Authority.

She didn't say anything as he spoke, but he saw her eyes glisten.

Hard to think of the crazy old scientist as a soldier of the Resistance. But it was clear that's what he had been.

"Fuckers . . ."

The curse took Raine by surprise, coming from Elizabeth. Actually made him smile. "Right."

She took a breath, the room so quiet now. "When he sent us word of you, he sent something else. Portman—"

Portman nodded, grabbed a crate pack and brought it to the table.

"Take a look," Elizabeth said. "Kvasir's last gift to us. And they may just keep you alive."

Raine took one of the things out of the pack, a long, narrow needle with a small sharp clip attached to one end.

"A dart?"

"He sent them along with word of you. Called them mind darts. Only got to make five of them, and we haven't had the chance to test them."

Raine fingered it, felt the pointy end with a fingertip.

"Easy there," Portman said. "Get that stuck in you and it floods you with nanotrites."

"That would be good, no?"

"No. That would be *lethal*. According to Kvasir, the dosage far exceeds what a human can handle. Renders your system under their control. And see that clip?"

Raine undid the clip from the back of the dart.

"You can use that to move the person stuck with the dart, put them—apparently—anywhere you want them."

Raine laughed. "Kvasir. Crazy guy."

"And brilliant," Elizabeth added.

"I don't doubt it." Raine looked in the bag. "These could be useful. Wish we had more than five."

"We will work on making them—but for now, that's all we have."

He turned to Portman. "And what happens later? You said . . . they're lethal."

"You get a bit of time to move whoever you control around. But then the nanotrites' buildup will make them explode. Literally."

"Nasty."

He looked up from the dart to the two of them. It was indeed a nasty weapon. They had been at this for a while and, as in most any movement, had reached the point where they would do anything to win.

Raine put the clip back on the dart.

"Okay." He looked up at the clock. "What else?"

"Don't want you weighed down too much," Portman said, "but I put together a good array of ordnance for you. Wait here."

When Portman came back, he put down four guns and a half-dozen roughly made incendiaries.

"These handguns fire hollow points. Better than what you had. Your M16 was okay, but this one features an expanded clip and autotargeting. More rounds, faster shooting, better aim."

Raine picked up the fourth weapon, a full-sized shotgun. A monster of a weapon.

"And this?"

Portman nodded. "In some situations, having something that can kick a door in or knock someone's head off is always welcome."

Then Raine pointed to one of the explosives.

"Homemade?"

"Yeah. Like grenades from your day. But no adjustable timer. Got about fifteen . . . twenty seconds—"

Raine laughed. *"About?"*

Portman didn't grin back. "Just pull the pin and throw it. Gave you a half dozen. Any more and you'll have too much damn weight. Especially with the ammo."

Elizabeth reached up to her head. "You'd be amazed how surprisingly rare these are." She handed him her headlamp. "If you get stuck in the dark."

He took the lamp, then looked over to the table with the drawings of the Capital. "I think I have to do another review of the Capital and the plan."

"You could do a quick sketch," Elizabeth said.

Raine stood up. "No—I best get it locked in my head. Doubt I'll have much time to stop and look at any notes."

He walked back to the table.

After what seemed too short a time, he felt Elizabeth behind him. A hand on his shoulder. "Raine, time you got going. I can lead you to where we got you a car. Will get you to your point of—what did you call it?"

"Infil."

"Yeah. Think you're set?"

Another glance down at the large drawing.

"Okay, let's—"

They heard a loud near-shriek from behind them, Lassard at the computers.

Then words.

"I got it! I fucking *got* it!"

They moved to stand behind him.

"You see, the Authority, *they* can communicate with all the Arks. Was built into every Ark computer. That was no problem for them."

He turned around, eyes wide with excitement. "But what they couldn't do, what they *wanted* it to do . . . was control when the Arks emerged. To override the Arks' internal controls and get them all up. The resources in the Arks, the people . . . all that stuff the Authority wanted. So even though they could check in on a buried Ark, they had no way to command it to come up."

"The Arks have operational autonomy?" Raine said.

"Precisely."

"What we have been trying to do," Elizabeth added, "was crash the Arks' systems."

Lassard pointed at a screen. "This is from one of the Arks—damaged, but with enough systems intact that it gave us a clue. But what you brought, in that hard drive—last piece of the puzzle."

"What do you mean?"

Lassard turned, looking annoyed.

As if it's obvious.

"The Authority was able to use their I.T. people, all survivors, all prisoners, to establish communication with the buried Arks. *That* program's built into all their computer systems, including the one in the Dead City that you brought us. But they still couldn't override each Ark's integrity."

"You're losing me, Lassard."

He rolled his eyes and looked at Elzabeth. He was beside himself.

"Don't you get it? The Authority couldn't crack each Ark's program, which made them totally autonomous. They tried, did they ever. But see"—Lassard gestured at his own machine, to all the screens surrounding him—"I did. We can override the Arks. That's what!"

"Great. Then you can get to them, get the resources? Right now?"

Just as quickly, his smile faded. He looked from Portman to Elizabeth. "We got the override. But what we *don't* have is the program—and certainly not the damn range—to reach all the Arks."

Everyone went quiet for a few moments while Raine played

catch-up and began to understand why Lassard was racing to get this thing down before he left.

"But the Authority does? You need to use the Capital's system to reach each Ark, to communicate with them?"

Lassard nodded. "Right. So now, if we can plant a hard drive with my control program in their system, we can—for a short time—operate from here using their computers."

"At least," Elizabeth added, "until they discover it."

"You mean," Raine said, "plant it tonight?"

"Your number one goal is to get Marshall out." She took a breath. "But as you do, you have to try and plant the drive."

"Captain Marshall," Lassard said, "well, he knows how the Capital's computers work. Not the most complicated system. Just need to find a main terminal. Link this"—he spun around and pulled out the drive, now altered, from the one Raine had brought back from the Dead City—"and once we get a signal, we can get the Arks rising."

"And at the same time, our cells can get into position. No way will the Authority be able to get to all of them."

Lassard held out the drive in his hand.

Raine took it.

"Want me to lighten your load a bit?" Portman said. "Take out one of the grenades?"

Raine gave the hard drive a heft.

"No. I think I'll keep everything you've given me." He turned to Elizabeth. "Now, it's getting late, Dr. Cadence," he said with a grin. "And you promised me a shot, some pills?"

She nodded, and went over to her medical case.

"All set? I'll lead you to the buggy. It's a Monarch. Fast. Reliable."

Raine nodded. Loaded down with his pack of bombs and weapons, he looked at the others, studying him.

Their hope for the future, recently arrived from the past.

He felt the injection that Elizabeth had given him doing its work. Though it was now near two in the morning, he felt ready.

How long before it wore off? How long would the shot last?

"All set. Thanks. Portman, Lassard."

Portman nodded. "Just bring our leader back."

Raine nodded.

"I will do my best."

Then, with a tug at his sleeve, he turned to follow Elizabeth out of the hideout, through the tunnels of Subway Town, and out to the cold, moonlit night again.

FORTY

USS GERALD R. FORD

The Monarch screamed through the night, a class of vehicle made for the rough terrain and speed. Driving with
no lights, the engine adequately muffled, Raine could
drive to the outskirts of the Capital with just the reflected
moonlight to worry about—and the car's black matte paint
minimized that.

And, possibly because this was a route used by the Authority,
no bandits appeared along the way to attempt to stop him.

He felt the chemical cocktail in his veins. His fatigue had
vanished, though he knew you could only push a body so far.
Drugs could mask when you'd reached that tipping point. Mistakes could be made. So as he drove, he reviewed the steps in
the plan again and again.

He knew one thing: he didn't have time to critique it. No. The time for evaluation of the whole plan was past, and he certainly hadn't been any part of that. The only thing to do now was think on each component. Think of them as separate entities, separate challenges.

Self-contained exercises.

Get to A, take care of B, and then move on to C.

And on and on, until it was completed.

All the while being careful to not fall into the trap of thinking about when it was over. When you might be safe.

So he stayed with reviewing the individual pieces of the plan, keeping them in their separate boxes, never once letting himself attempt to answer the big question . . .

Will I survive this night?

The night progressed, and then he saw it, straddling the great gorge ahead, leading up to a higher plateau.

A goddamned aircraft carrier.

It was like something a Greek god had dropped from the sky.

The USS *Gerald R. Ford* was one of the country's last carriers before the hammer fell. It had been state-of-the-art and named for a President whose biggest accomplishment was holding the country together when the shit hit the fan.

I wonder how much confidence that inspired in the sailors aboard her?

A road led up to the carrier, to where there'd be guards and electronic defenses.

But not the way he would gain entry.

The carrier's nuclear reactor powered much of the Capital. Whatever insanity brought it here, left its hull battered and dented, had somehow left the reactors working fine.

The Capital might have backups. Generators. Elizabeth didn't know how many, or how long they would take to kick in. But as best they could figure it, taking the carrier's power out would bring down their defenses . . . if only for a short time.

Raine stopped the Monarch.

He had smeared some grease on his face back at the Resistance hideaway. He had on a black jacket, his pack also dark.

From here he'd be on foot. He grabbed his weapons and started moving.

Climbing down, Raine stumbled in the darkness, handholds slipping as rock crumpled.

He'd always hated the mountains. Whether because he was clumsy or just couldn't get a good read for handholds and places to wedge his feet, he always felt out of his element on a mountain patrol. Here the rock was jagged, with razorlike slivers, slowing his progress even more.

Bad place to make a mistake.

Of course, this made the idea of trying to get in and out before dawn seemingly more impossible.

And was there any guarantee they wouldn't drag Marshall out before morning? That he'd find an empty cell, the Resistance leader dead before telling the Authority butchers anything?

He forced himself to hurry, even though that made him tear his hands on the rock. Nothing deep—just bloody scrapes—but it still made him realize that his body had taken more abuse over these few days than all the combined tours of duty from the past.

At the bottom, he looked up to see whether any guards monitored the gorge floor.

But all he saw was the incredible flat bottom of the carrier hull.

He started walking to the other side. The drawing he had

been shown appeared accurate, though the light was even more scant here, with the ship blocking the moon.

In one drawing the carrier had been lodged on the other side of the gorge at about the two-thirds mark. And there was a place in the hull where they dumped garbage out, whatever leftovers and junk were created by the garrison of Enforcers inside.

And how many Enforcers?

No intel on that.

Could be five. Ten. Twenty. A hundred.

He reached the other end of the gorge floor and started the difficult climb up.

He could see the opening in the hull. Though there didn't seem to be any nearby rocky perch that would allow him simply to slide in, there was an outcrop close to the opening. He'd have to jump.

Shit.

Yet, he still felt awake, alert. Muscles responding well. He could do this.

He looked at the rock, calculating his move. He could throw the pack in. Might create too much noise, though. Worse, he might even lose it. And he had to remember that even though the hard drive was wrapped up, it was fragile.

No. He'd have to jump with the pack. *Making life a little less easier.*

He made his way cautiously to the rock, as close to the hull opening as he could get. A ship the size of a city was above him, and he was about sneak into it like a wharf rat.

Raine could now see a bit of the inside.

Dark. He stopped, listened. No talking. All quiet on the good ship *Gerald R. Ford.*

He edged out on the rock some more, as far as he could without falling off. He crouched.

Eyes locked on the opening.

The smooth metal. No visible handholds within this garbage chute of an opening.

No time like the present, he thought.

He leapt.

His midsection slammed into the floor of the opening, his feet dangling, pointing straight down to the gorge floor below. His palms were flat, hands pressed hard against the smooth metal.

While being careful not to lose any of his precarious purchase, he slid first one hand, then the other, to the side, searching for something to grab. At first he felt nothing, and still dangling, getting into the carrier had turned even harder than it first seemed.

But then he felt an edge. He closed his left hand on it, and now in one great effort worked to pull and kick himself in. Wriggling, he slid into the aircraft carrier.

No alarms, no guards.

Sloppy damn security, he thought.

He started making his way forward to the generator then, and the cable feeds that led into the fortress beyond the carrier.

Raine knew he didn't have time to move slowly; he had to get through the maze of hallways as fast as he could.

He opened his pack. The muzzle of his M16 stuck out.

Time to take it in his hands.

If he met anyone, he would just have to deal with it fast.

As if on cue, when he turned the corner he walked into a pair of Enforcers, their helmets off, talking.

They didn't look all that intimidating with their robotic head gear off. But their weapons—they looked powerful.

They both did a double take seeing him.

Guess they don't get too many visitors down here.

Noise or not, he had no choice. He started firing, and the two Enforcers fell to the ground.

Now he began a steady jog, taking care not to go so fast as to slip into oxygen debt.

As Raine ran, he heard alarms go off. Had cameras picked him up? Were the bodies found? Whatever it was, they knew he was here.

Not something he didn't expect.

Ahead, four Enforcers started marching in his direction. Two stopped, took aim, and started laying down covering fire while the other two raced ahead.

Damn.

It was always a shitty procedure to field-test a weapon during an operation. In this case, he had no choice.

He reached up for one of the darts and, using the same stance he took with his wingstick, threw it.

It hit one of the front runners, who stopped as if someone applied the brakes. He reached up to his neck. His partner kept coming. Raine crouched down to the side, making himself as small a target as possible, blindly firing his machine gun. While still sending out a spray of bullets, he fingered the mind dart control device, and as soon as his fingers touched it, it must have sent a signal to the nanotrites now flooding the Enforcer's body.

He could hear more Enforcers arriving, creating a wall of shooters, filling the corridor with smoke and sending bullets flying all around him like a swarm of wasps.

Raine slid his thumb on the controller, and the dart forced

the Enforcer to turn around. Another slide, and the puppet moved toward his Authority buddies.

They recognized that something was wrong, and a few began targeting him.

Amazingly—the bullets did nothing.

Or, rather, they didn't stop him. The guy walked on, and then—in an increased state of agitation—both his hands went to his neck, then to his head, like a human marionette.

He would keep moving on his own; Raine didn't have to do anything more with him, so he dropped the control device. He took time to aim his rifle at the lone Enforcer still running madly toward him.

Points for bravery . . . none for strategy.

He riddled the guy with bullets, not knowing where the armor was greatest.

As that guy fell, the Enforcer with the mind dart reached the wall of shooters.

With perfect timing, he exploded, a human bomb of blood and bone—the bone shredded into deadly shrapnel, the nano-trites themselves apparently explosive.

When the pinkish fog cleared, nobody was shooting, nobody was moving. And the way to the cable room, to where the ship's power fed into the Capital, lay ahead.

"Thanks, Kvasir . . ."

Raine stood up and resumed his jog.

In the generator room he spotted the massive two-foot-wide cables that carried power from the belly of the ship, out through what had to be a hangar deck opening, and on into the fortress city.

He remembered what Portman had told him about the explosives he carried, the homemade grenades.

"Pull the pin, and toss it. Fifteen seconds. Tops."

Not much confidence about the devices' timing from Portman. He would just have to hope the big man knew what he was talking about.

Raine went to where the cables led out—then separated—heading in different directions. He scrambled on top of the giant cables, using them as if they were a bridge leading out to the city's perimeter.

Would two of the grenades be enough?

He'd probably get only one shot at this.

He looked up. A small device hovered above the area, a red light at the front.

Surveillance.

They know I'm here, and they will know I'm coming.

Let's hope they think this is just about sabotage.

Raine walked across the cable bridge, joining up with the other end of the road that led across the flight deck of the carrier.

He got two grenades out.

He brought his hands close together so he could pull out both pins at the same time, a tricky, fumbling move.

Not one I've done before, he thought.

He pulled the pins, and, without counting, tossed them into the cable room.

One landed in the crack between the two cables, the other rolled to the floor, feet away.

Close enough?

Raine turned and started running. Barely watching where he was going . . .

The two explosions, within seconds of each other, showed that at least the grenades worked.

He had barely gotten off the ship.

And still running, he risked looking ahead.

330 • MATTHEW COSTELLO

The Capital.

A massive structure, like nothing he had seen in the world before. Newly built.

And he also saw that parts of it had turned dark.

Did I do enough damage? Did I buy enough fucking time?

He caught himself. *A . . . to B . . . to C.*

He was on to the next part of the mission.

That one lay ahead.

Inside the Capital.

And that's all he let himself think about.

FORTY-ONE

3:20 A.M.

Raine looked at the fence in front of him, and at the gun
turrets that dotted each section of it. As he approached,
they didn't move at all, all pointing aimlessly at some
spot back by the carrier.

Power down. Good.

But for how long?

Inside, he saw the main buildings of the Capital, and they
were not the haphazard collection of shapes and leftover pieces
of Wasteland junk. These were stories high, forming a sleek
metal fortress.

Now dark.

No backup power kicking in?

If only he could stay that lucky.

He pictured the layout that Elizabeth had showed him, and
which building he had to get to.

Already he saw figures running all around the inner area. Enforcers kicking into action while the power got restored.

Raine had debated blowing a hole in the fence—but with the Enforcers already on the move, that would bring them right to him. So he took hold of the steel mesh and started climbing right near one of the inactive gun turrets. It dawned on him that the fence was probably electrified as well.

Without power, though, the way into the Capital lay open.

At the top, he swung over, climbed down the other side for a few feet and jumped to the ground.

Without light he'd be hard to see. And if anyone did spot him, hopefully they wouldn't at first be able to tell him from one of the scrambling Enforcers.

He started running.

To the prison building . . . and a massive shaft that pumped out exhaust from the kitchens below.

But the shaft was quiet at the moment, and if the plans were right, it provided a hole that led into the belly of this building.

Raine looked over his shoulder and saw Enforcers by the fence, guns lowered but on alert. Other Enforcers had to be heading to the generator on the carrier.

If there were power backups, nobody had thrown the switch yet—or maybe they were dedicated to the complex's vital, internal systems.

He turned on the headlamp Elizabeth had given him and climbed into the exhaust shaft.

It went down, then horizontal, wending its way deeper into the building.

He moved as quietly as he could, the space too tight for anything more than a crawl. And when he hit a part that led straight down, he wedged his legs and arms against the sides and painfully inched his way downward.

Back and forth, like navigating a maze, every now and then hearing sounds outside the shaft, knowing from the plans that he was cutting through the Enforcers' barracks.

Hoping they were all outside dealing with the crisis.

A few feet down, his arms and shoulders gave out and he slipped for a few frightening seconds. He pressed his legs to the sides and stopped the fall.

But this also produced a loud scratching sound. He paused, waiting to hear if this tight air shaft was about to be his final resting place.

Nothing.

A breath, then he went farther down.

When he hit bottom—when the shaft turned flat—that would be where the cells were.

If the layout that Elizabeth had was accurate.

It had been up to this point. But if it wasn't . . . who knew where he'd end up.

His feet touched bottom and he had just enough room to bring his head down and start crawling forward.

Now to find an opening, some place where the shaft could be kicked out and he could get out of the shaft.

He didn't let himself think that he'd gotten into the Capital.

But he couldn't help but think: *How the hell will I get out?*

Farther along, he came to a square panel in the shaft, his headlamp picking up the screws that held it in place. It didn't look large enough for him to crawl through.

But it looked like the only option.

He dug out a knife from his pack and went to work on the

334 • MATTHEW COSTELLO

screws, the pointed end of the knife chewing up the metal head of the screws as much as it unscrewed them.

But taking his time, slowing a bit so he didn't completely strip the screws, he got them out.

When the last screw fell to the floor of the shaft, he gave the panel a nudge.

It could be pushed free.

But where was he? Who might be there to see the panel fall out?

Surprise!

One thing he knew, one change to the plan: there was no way—if he did find Marshall—they would be able to get out this way.

Might as well just surrender.

Checking that he had a handgun in a side pocket, he wriggled the backpack free and nudged it down to his feet. His pack would have to trail behind him if he had any hope of getting out. He'd have to perform a circus trick to do it, pulling the pack along with his feet as he fell.

He thought of turning the headlamp off.

No, he thought. Better to leave it on. Could be a useful distraction.

If someone is down there waiting for me.

All right then, he thought. Time to go.

He gave the metal panel a firm push and it popped free, flying out, followed by him rapidly crawling through the newly made opening.

He tumbled to the floor.

Raine's hands broke his fall, the pack landing on his body. He quickly rolled and sprung to his feet.

To see: cells. The corridor dark.

The right place. *Jeez, the prison.* He did it.

Then, a voice.

"Hey, who's there? Hold on."

The headlamp rendered Raine the only bright spot in the blackness, but it also shot out a light that let him see—and made it difficult for anyone looking at him.

Such as the Enforcer holding a rifle standing in front of him, the light in his eyes.

Raine pulled out his gun. No time to worry if the Enforcer had anyone with him. He fired three quick shots, the sound echoing in the narrow corridor.

The Enforcer went down.

And then Raine heard an unexpected voice. A familiar voice.

A *female* voice.

He moved down the row of cells, whipping his headlamp left and right.

Coming to a cell holding Loosum Hagar.

"Loosum? How the hell did you—"

"I'll save the story for later, Raine. Go get that Enforcer's keys and get me out of here. Whatever took out the power, it won't stay down for long."

Raine ran back for the keys and returned to the cell, letting Loosum out.

"Thanks for the rescue," she said. "Didn't know you cared."

"Afraid I'm not here for you," he said unapologetically. "Is there someone else down here?"

Could the Authority have taken Marshall, begun the process of breaking him down in the middle of the night? Could the Resistance leader be dead already?

"There's someone down the other end. Looked like a bloody mess when they brought him back last time."

Raine ran there. A man was curled on the floor of a cell. The headlamp picked up the dried splotches of blood. The man's lips were cracked, bloody as well. He had been well worked over.

But he lifted his head up when he saw someone there, then opened his eyes.

Raine thought: *Good . . . he can move.*

"Captain John Marshall?"

"Yes." Despite his battered state, the man sat up, blinking at Raine. "Is it time? Already?"

"Captain, I'm Lieutenant Nicholas Raine." Then, as he had done dozens of times before—and because it seemed right—he added: "Reporting for duty."

And he saluted.

Loosum ran up to Raine as he got Marshall's cell open.

"We *got* to get moving. As long as we have this darkness, we have to take advantage of it."

On cue: the lights in the corridor flickered, then came on.

"Shit." He turned to Marshall. "*That* changes things. You okay to move, Captain?"

Marshall nodded. "Yeah. Got a gun for me?"

"One for me, too," Loosum added.

He handed the shotgun to Loosum and the rifle to Marshall. He'd make do with the handguns for now.

"Come on," Loosum said.

Raine gave her a look. "Hold on." He looked at Marshall. "Captain, one more thing. I brought a hard drive. From the Dead City. Lassard has cracked the Ark override code. It's on there. But we need to—"

Marshall shook his head as if trying to understand what the hell Raine was talking about.

Then a half smile. "God, yes. Have to get into their system.

That means we're not quite ready to leave. Good thing everyone must be outside looking for you."

"We're not leaving?" Loosum rolled her eyes.

"There's a terminal . . . down there." Marshall pointed up the hall. "It's gotta be tied into the central computer. If we can dump what you got on their computer system, that should do it."

Marshall started walking, limping even as he tried to hurry.

Raine shot a look at Loosum, both of them seeing that escaping with the captain wasn't going to be easy even without the detour.

But Marshall marched ahead, ignoring his pain, and got to the terminal.

Raine heard voices from above.

Someone has got to come down here, sooner or later.

"Give it to me," Marshall said. Raine dug out the drive. Marshall tilted it back and forth, seeing where he could connect it to the terminal.

"Okay. We got to get that cover off."

Raine took out his knife again and used it to pry open the metal siding of the computer. It popped free, exposing the terminal's insides.

Marshall leaned forward and stared at the array of boards and wires.

"All of this is our tech here," he said to himself. "Early twenty-first century. Meant for the future."

Raine stood by the captain's side as he continued to mutter. "God, I wish Lassard was here. Need to just get it linked so the terminal can read the drive. Then—maybe—we can upload it."

The voices from above were getting louder.

Loosum leaned close to Raine and whispered, "I'm going to go stand by the stairs." She gave the shotgun a shake. "In case we get company."

Raine nodded.

"All right. Just need a fucking USB port. Buried in here. There. See one. Okay, that should do it."

He watched Marshall pull out a wire and attach it to the drive. Then his eyes moved toward the terminal's monitor as it registered the attached drive.

"When it copies the data, it will go right on the main servers drive, then all through the system. If Lassard did his work well, it will act like a Trojan Horse."

"A virus?" Raine said. "Nasty. Good goddamn thing Cross doesn't have his hands on the best computer scientists that were buried. Not yet, anyway."

Marshall turned and gave Raine a smile, some light coming back into his eyes. "They're still to come. And now—maybe, with luck—we'll get them."

He hit some keys on the computer keyboard. A screen asked for approval of a data upload. Another click. No viruses found.

Lassard had created a clean program. And after a few seconds a welcome notice on the monitor:

Data Uploaded.

Marshall backed away. "That's it. Christ, that's it."

Noise from the stairs.

Loosum hissing at them.

"Here comes . . . someone . . ."

Marshall nodded at Raine, and they went to the stairs.

From the steps of the heavy boots on the stairs, there had to be at least three Enforcers.

Had the power come back on from the backups? Or maybe they had the main feed already up and running?

Going to be fun getting the hell out of here, Raine thought.

"On—" Marshall coughed, the sound too loud "Shit. On my go."

The boots started to hurry, hearing the voices.

The Enforcers came to the turn in the stairwell, and now the three could be seen racing down, guns at the ready.

But sitting ducks for Raine and his companions.

They all fired and the Enforcers went tumbling down the stairs like wooden targets.

"You okay, Captain?"

"Just get moving, Raine."

They began to hurry up the stairs, climbing over the soldiers.

When they reached an upper area, a half-dozen Enforcers were already taking position, firing at the opening that led out of the stairway.

"No fucking way," Loosum said as she kept leaning out and firing the shotgun.

They had no choice, though. Raine saw that they had to keep their cover, buried as they were under the Enforcers' fire.

Probably the only reason they hadn't tossed an incendiary was because they were under orders to keep Marshall alive.

But how long before their resolve to obey that order vanished?

Raine reached into his pack, ignoring the ping of bullets bouncing all around them.

He pulled out a dart.

"What the hell is that?" Marshall said.

"New toy, from Kvasir." He grinned. "Give me as much cover as you can."

Loosum and Marshall both started firing full out at the barracks room already filled with gun smoke.

Now or never.

He stood up and saw one Enforcer with a bit too much of his body exposed. He threw the dart.

And missed.

He quickly ducked down, reaching into his pack and yelling at the other two, "Keep firing!"

They kept up their covering fire, and once he had another dart, he let it fly.

This time it hit the Enforcer, who immediately stood up.

He made a gesture with his hands as if to remove the dart but then started stumbling around, the nanotrites' overload coursing through him.

"Wow," Loosum said. "That's something. Nice throw, by the way."

"Taught by the best," Raine said.

He fingered the dart controller, and now his pet Enforcer moved back and forth, soaking up shots meant for the three of them, Raine using him like a human shield.

Waiting until the guy was ready to blow.

"Stay down," he said to Marshall and Loosum.

They pulled back, and a second later he heard the massive explosion as the Enforcer exploded.

The bullets stopped.

The way to the outside was open.

He caught Marshall looking at him. Marshall was the captain. But for now, that look between them said that this was all his operation.

And Raine just hoped he didn't fuck it all up.

FORTY-TWO

4:25 A.M.

aine led Marshall outside, Loosum just behind, swinging right and left with her gun as though she had done a bunch of tours of duty in the hellish sandpits of the Middle East.

Raine looked up.

And he saw only a few Enforcers looking in the direction of the carrier, probably the still-suspected location of the attack. And why would they look back here, with a small army of Enforcers in the barracks?

That army the three of them had just eliminated.

But then one turned, and he saw the other two react.

"Never any wood to knock on," he muttered.

Loosum shrugged, not understanding. "I got the one on the left."

"I'll take the right," Raine said.

He started firing, and while Loosum's target went down immediately, Raine's shots went wide.

But Marshall, though he looked hardly able to stand, had taken a shot, and now there was just one Enforcer. Loosum took him out.

We're off the plan now, Raine thought. "We have to get to the gorge."

It was the only way he knew out of here. He saw Loosum look at him, perhaps weighing whether she should follow her own instincts or listen to this newcomer from the past.

Marshall spoke up.

"They'll have Enforcers all over the carrier. Protecting the main way in or out. Raine's right. The gorge is the only way. We have to hurry." He took a breath. "We've got a narrow window."

Raine looked at him as they kept moving. "You mean before they have their fences all armed, the turret weapons?"

Marshall looked at him.

"No. Something worse. Mutants."

Raine thought: *So what, mutants?* He had dealt with them before. Though why the hell they would be inside the Capital . . .

That didn't make any sense at all.

Loosum spoke, breaking him out of that train of thought.

"God. What the hell—"

The words were like a spear of ice hitting Raine's brain.

Before he even looked up, Loosum's voice had signaled that something was really bad.

When he *did* look up, he saw a line of attackers, moving together, in formation, armed, a *wall* of them. Some of them already firing.

Not Enforcers.

Not people recruited from the Wasteland and given a high-tech weapon and armored suit.

No—these attackers didn't need any armor.

Because they just didn't go down too easy.

The three of them started firing even as they backed away from the advancing line as fast as they could.

Marshall tried to make it on his own, but when he stumbled and fell a few times, Raine had no choice but give him an arm as he fired haphazardly. "Christ," Raine shouted, "how can they be mutants?"

"They're experiments," Marshall said. "What they were doing in the Dead City . . . they completed here."

Raine didn't need Marshall to explain what that was. It was right before his eyes. Mutants, controlled, *weaponized*. Ready to do the bidding of the Authority.

Raine looked around, to the buildings nearby. If they were being controlled, was someone watching, in charge of them?

"We gotta move," Loosum said.

Their own shots seemed to have little effect. There were so many of the mutants that even if they got perfect shots to their heads, there was no way they'd be able to take them all out.

They kept on firing as they turned and ran to the fence along the perimeter of the Capital.

The army of mutants gained on them.

The hopelessness began to hit Raine. To have come this far, to be so close.

You never knew when it was game over.

Now, with their dwindling ammo and the sheer numbers coming for them, he began to let himself consider other options.

Those options that one didn't voice, when the tide turned, when hopelessness became the reality. When you had to think of other things. About what you would do when the monsters finally fell upon you.

He looked back, the fence not far away.

"Leave me," Marshall said. "The two of you—you can get the hell away."

"You're the reason I came here," Raine said as he reloaded.

Loosum, still behind them, kept up her shots.

Raine reached into his pack, realizing that the mutant horde was close enough that he could use a dart.

One of the last two.

He threw it, and now aim didn't matter as much. The wall of mutants coming toward them was so *thick* he could hardly miss hitting one.

When the dart hit, he sent that mutant crashing into its brothers, tripping some up even though one quickly sliced off its head—

One, two, through and through.

—but still the nanotrite-overloaded mutant kept moving.

It exploded, and now there were five less of them. And the fence was a few meters closer.

Was the electricity on? Raine wondered. Turret guns already turning to them?

Or had they only restored power to certain areas?

They were close enough to the fence now that he could turn and see the carrier, covered with Enforcers. How long before they realized that the real intruders were back at the Capital buildings?

How long before they faced two fucking armies: Enforcers and a living shield of mutants in front of them?

Raine thought of a legendary battle. Thermopylae. The last stand of last stands.

He turned to the fence, dug out a grenade from his pack and tossed it at the fence.

The three stopped then, waiting for the hole to be kicked in.

The mutants seconds away.

Raine saw that—without his even noticing it—Marshall had taken a shot to the shoulder.

"I'm okay," he said, seeing Raine spot it.

Loosum kept firing with the shotgun.

At this range, not the most effective weapon.

Raine thought: *We're fucked.*

Then he pushed the useless thought away.

The grenade behind them exploded, blowing a hole. Raine had the delusional idea that if they got out and climbed down the gorge, they could get out of the sights of the Enforcers, the mutants, and the gun turrets.

About as an impossible dream as there ever was.

The only thing in their favor was that the mutants, as controlled as they might be, were wild shots. And only half of them had projectile weapons.

But what they lacked in skill and firepower, they made up in numbers.

The fence was open, but Raine didn't think they'd make it.

"Come on, you bastards!" Loosum yelled.

And as Raine fired beside her, he thought . . . with people like Loosum in this world, the future had hope.

Regardless of what was about to happen.

Loosum moaned. Raine looked down. A shot right at the kneecap. She fell forward.

Raine went to her. No way she could move, her blood glimmering even in the predawn darkness.

But she reacted quickly.

"Give me that last dart. The grenades. As much ammo as you can."

Raine didn't understand.

"*Give* me the fucking stuff, and get the hell out of here now. Get Marshall out."

And half lying down, half squatting, Loosum turned around and began firing at the line of mutants.

"Go!" she screamed, without looking back.

"We can't—" Marshall started.

But this wasn't the first time either of them had been in such a situation. The moment where a sacrifice is offered, where a decision had to be made. For the greater good.

And you moved.

Raine gave her the grenades, another box of ammo. The last dart.

"Loosum—"

"Get the hell out of here," she said.

Raine turned and led Marshall, bleeding badly from the shoulder, to the hole in the fence.

As they went through, shots echoed from below them, around the front of the carrier in front of them.

And from behind, Raine heard the steady firing of Loosum and the shotgun.

Fast. She was reloading and firing so goddamned fast. Then the sound of an explosion as she used the dart.

Raine kept lugging Marshall farther into the darkness, the turret guns on the fence not tracking them, still dead, not laying down a line of fire as he stumbled toward the gorge leading down.

He heard a grenade.

Another.

Raine didn't dare look back.

Every second counted if Loosum's sacrifice wasn't to be totally in vain.

Then just the shotgun, all explosives gone. Mixed with the sound of the rifles the mutants fired.

Perhaps Enforcers had arrived.

Then—

No more blasts of the shotgun. No more grenades.

Raine felt Marshall—this hero of the Resistance, the man who came from the same time as he did, and started this world fighting back—turn more and more into dead weight with each step.

Neither spoke.

They reached the edge of the gorge, rocks leading down. It looked hopeless. How the hell could he get Marshall down? And even if he could, did they have enough time?

"Okay, okay," Raine said. "We gotta, we just gotta—"

He knew that Marshall was too experienced a military man to not know the impossibility of what they had to do.

And yet they would try.

"Gotta get down."

When Raine heard something, it took a moment. But it was a noise he recognized. A wheezing engine sound. The sound of a prop turning.

And with no lights on, looking like a rock rising out of the gorge basin, floating upward . . . the same balloon craft that had brought him from Wellspring to the Resistance base.

There were two shadows on the deck of the clumsy aircraft. As it came nearer, Raine could see Elizabeth at the wheel and Portman at the front, standing next to what looked like a small cannon.

So close.

"Get in!" Elizabeth said.

The craft hovered, rocking back and forth, actually banging into the rocks, as Raine dragged Marshall closer. Had Loosum bought them enough time?

The mutants weren't firing—which meant that he and Marshall were hidden by the rocks here. But they had to be only seconds behind.

Portman had left his weapon to help haul Marshall in. Raine leaped without help, freed of the captain's dead weight.

Portman's two strong arms grabbed him at his forearms, pulling him into the ship.

Raine was surprised, then, to find that instead of rising, instead of flying up as he expected, the airship dropped down.

He thought: *Are we too heavy? Is the thing sinking?*

But as he saw Marshall sprawled on the desk, he caught Elizabeth talking to Portman. Saw that she was in control. And Raine could put together what was happening. They were dropping as far down as they could, to get lost in the jutting rocks of the gorge, to where they could level out . . . and follow the gorge basin away.

A plan. A goddamned plan.

But then Raine heard the familiar sound of bullets, now ripping into the deck. A few shots into the balloon of the ship and they would simply crash to that basin floor, and wait for the Enforcers to come down—if it even mattered at that point.

Raine looked up to see where the shots came from.

Something in the sky.

"Goddamned *hovercraft!*" Portman said. "Shit."

"Got to make us weave," Elizabeth said. "Hold on."

Raine looked over to Marshall, who really only had one hand to hold on. He saw that the captain had locked that hand onto one of the mastlike pieces of wood at the ship's center.

Raine held on to the ship's edge as it began to veer right and left.

He heard more bullets, landing dangerously close.

We're sitting ducks here.

But when he looked forward, he saw Portman at the weapon at the ship's prow, both the cannon and its user dark shapes. The bore of the small cannon now pointed up at a sixty-degree angle.

And finally Portman started firing.

The cannon produced shakes in the ship, a recoil that sent the airship knocking against the gorge's side. Portman kept firing, shot after shot.

Raine saw a bullet tear into the balloon; had to be a few there already. Was there enough lift in the balloon to keep this thing in the air, this flying technology ancient and absurd?

Like a rejoinder to his disparaging thoughts, an explosion from above them produced a brilliant fireworks display as the Authority hovercraft exploded.

While the balloon craft kept moving forward.

And for the first time in a long time, Raine didn't hear any gunfire.

They weaved their way along the gorge bottom, the only sounds the wind and the ship's boiler.

Portman had moved over to the wheel while Elizabeth crouched beside Marshall, tending to his wound. With the amount of blood he'd lost, there was no telling if he'd survive . . . even after all they'd gone through.

Raine thought of Loosum.

The feelings . . . overwhelming. Confusing.

He saw a bit of color in the east.

The dark night finally giving way to the first hint of the sun about to rise.

And finally he let himself close his eyes.

EPILOGUE

RAGE

FORTY-THREE

LEAVING

From the moment they reached the Resistance base, Elizabeth and Portman raced around, grabbing things, rushing.

Marshall, bandaged, sat in a chair to the side.

"What about the file cabinets?" Elizabeth asked the rebel leader, now back in charge.

Lassard turned away from his terminal. "Don't worry, Elizabeth. Got them all backed up."

"Then just blow that stuff," Marshall said. "Leave them *nothing*."

Marshall looked over at Raine.

"You all right, Raine? I owe you a big debt of gratitude."

"It's Loosum we both owe."

"Yes. And if Lassard can get contact, this whole world will owe her."

"Still nothing, Captain. I'm connecting with the Capital computer okay—they haven't found the drive and yanked it. That's good. But—damn—it hasn't let me in to send the signal."

"What's the problem?" Raine said.

"We're running out of time," Marshall said. "Lassard's program should let us use the Capital's satellite link to reach all the Arks . . . and send the message."

"To emerge? To come out of the earth?"

"Yes. We already have alerted our cells all over the territories. When the Arks rise, they will be there. Today could be the tipping point. To get all that tech, the caches buried with them, the people . . ."

Portman walked over, his arms filled with guns. "I'm gonna load up, Captain. We got to get going."

"The Authority will track us here that quickly?" Raine asked.

"After what we did?" Marshall laughed. "There will be no price on our heads that will be too high. This is about to be as unsafe a place as can be."

Elizabeth walked over. "Got my equipment packed. The essentials." She looked over at Raine, and he realized they were three survivors, standing together.

Three people who had been entrusted with rebuilding a future.

About to go on the run.

"What about the computers?" he asked.

"In our other bases we have more. If the Arks were to come up, having computers would be the least of our problems. The important thing is that we have all the data."

"And you'll leave? Without reaching the Arks."

Marshall looked over to the I.T. guy. "No. I imagine Lassard will stay. Until he hears the Authority is at the door."

Raine looked at Lassard, too. Staying with the ship.

This world isn't just about deals.

There was something else, besides the death, the brutality, the fear. There were people willing to sacrifice.

Marshall caught his look. Neither had to say what it meant if Lassard stayed.

Then the captain spoke.

Asking what probably seemed a redundant question.

"You'll come with us?"

Raine stood there. Then, shaking his head. "No . . ."

He saw that Marshall didn't believe what he was hearing.

Then he explained.

"There's something I got to do first," he said, the anger in his voice rising. This wasn't just about Marshall and his Resistance anymore. This wasn't just about the settlements and those who struggled to survive in the shadow of the Authority. This wasn't just about orders anymore, about a mission.

Not after what had happened only hours ago.

"I will go to the Hagars. If Dan is to learn what happened to his daughter, he will learn it from me."

The ancient, time-honored military tradition.

The lone knock at the door. The officer in a uniform standing there.

The message conveyed before that door is even open.

Marshall put his hand on Raine.

"Yes. That makes sense."

"And then, Captain, I'm with you. To bring these bastards down. To try and save something out of this . . . very fucked-up world."

Marshall smiled. "Don't think I could do it without you. Elizabeth can show you where we will be headed. Pretty far away. But we will wait for you."

"Don't worry. I'll get there."

Is anger useful in combat? Raine wondered . . . even as he felt it building inside him.

The death of innocent people who just wanted freedom, who wanted a life. The mindless and brutal slaying of Kvasir. The creation of an army dedicated to just one thing . . . killing. The fact that Loosum *had* to sacrifice herself.

Yes, rage might be exactly the emotion needed.

At that moment Raine also realized . . . he was no longer a stranger here.

This was his world, as much as anyone else here.

Marshall nodded his head at the big man packing things up. "Make sure Portman gives you any weapons you need. We also have a vehicle for you. Fast, even has some armor. But you know what it's like out there."

"Yes, I do."

Nothing else left to say.

When finally—a *whoop* from behind them, from Lassard.

"I got it!" Lassard turned around in his chair. Everyone in the room stopped, all eyes on him.

"Must have been as they got all their systems on line, full power, and it let the drive with the program connect and execute." Lassard was indulging in some analysis, an I.T. guy to the core. "But—"

He grinned. "We can use their system to reach the Arks."

And if what Marshall told him was true, if Lassard was really as good as they thought he was, the program he had inserted would override the Arks' systems.

Resistance cells waiting, spread out over a hundred miles.

Would the Authority be able to pounce on some of the Arks? Undoubtedly.

But they couldn't be everywhere. Lives would be lost, but now lives from the past would be saved. As well as information, learning, technology.

Marshall spoke.

"Okay, Mark. What are you waiting for?"

Lassard held the gaze of the captain.

"You mean . . . now?"

"Hit the button. Get them up. And then we got to get out of here, blow this place up."

As though intimidated by the implication of what he was about to do, Lassard hesitated before turning back to his terminal.

Had one key stroke ever had more importance?

They all walked closer to him for the fateful moment.

The I.T. expert took a breath.

Raine sensed that Portman, standing next to him, was about to gruffly bark, *Just fucking do it.*

It seemed to take that long.

"Okay," Lassard said. "Still . . . all good. And—"

His fingers hit the keyboard.

Nobody moved. Nobody said anything.

Then the monitor started to send a wave of information flying across the screen.

A last act for these computers before they were blown into more useless junk for locals to scavenge.

"That's it," Lassard said, his eyes moving left and right as he looked at the screens. "It's happening. Sweet God, it's *happening.*"

Marshall looked at Raine, then over at Portman and Elizabeth.

"Time for us to go."

They started moving as fast as they could out of the hideout.

Lassard lagged behind, as if his eyes couldn't believe what they were seeing, the result of his handiwork.

"Lassard! Move it!" Marshall yelled.

And finally Lassard backed away, stood up. He threw the switch on the timed explosive off to the side of his desk.

He turned and picked up a pack that seemed empty.

Hard for him to leave, Raine thought.

Then the four of them started out, into the underground tunnels and warren of Subway Town.

It wasn't long—minutes, actually, after they heard the thunderous explosion behind them—that they came to the place where they were to split up. Marshall and the others one way, Raine off to a tunnel that led to where they had left a car for him.

"Captain—"

"Just remember we'll be waiting for you, Raine. Don't let us down."

Raine smiled. Elizabeth came up to him. "And when you come back, we'll have to get the nanotrites out. For now, though, be glad you have them."

Portman stuck out his arm, a chunky finger jabbing the air. "And I want every piece of ordnance returned, Lieutenant. Resistance property." Then Portman grinned—as close to a goodbye as he could get.

Raine nodded.

Without a word he turned and started running down the tunnel, one last mission before he could return to the three of them again.

Before he could return to the battle, to this war that was now as much his as theirs.

FORTY-FOUR

THE RISING

I n each Ark—their computers never fully powered down—
something registered.

Each Ark had remained in communication with the
others throughout the century. They even could take note
when disaster befell an Ark somewhere, crushed by the shifting
of a tectonic plate, or desperately struggling to emerge to the
surface before being trapped by bedrock.

But though linked, each Ark was its own entity.

Each had dominion over its own planned time for emergence, its own response system to emergencies.

That had been core to the Ark Project.

No longer.

Something new registered as each Ark continued to get signals from the other Arks.

And the code being executed carried with it all the information needed for each Ark to act in self-preservation.

A false reading of danger. Mimicked in each Ark's computer, simultaneous, and not recognized as false. Danger—to which there could only be one instantaneous response.

To rise . . .

To begin what could be a perilous journey to an unknown surface.

And all the Arks of what had been the government of the United States—the ones still intact, those not already surfaced, not destroyed or hopelessly damaged—sent a signal to the great bore machines that sat at each nose, rock-chewing machines that could screw the Ark through any rock . . . to whatever world awaited.

The Arks began to dig their way out.

Some journeyed in a straight path, easily grinding through loose rock and debris.

Others faced mammoth chunks of bedrock that required a steady, endless digging that to a human would have seemed hopeless, but to the lifesaving brain of the computer was merely what it had to do.

Others became damaged during their emergence, crushed as rock shifted, quickly killing the still-sleeping survivors.

But whether successful or not, all the Arks struggled to be born into this world.

And as they came closer to the surface, as a reading signaled that the new world and the surface was only minutes away, revival systems began their process, readying the Ark passengers for what might have to be a quick exit.

And outside, for these Arks, people waited.

The Arks rose.

Bringing with them to the surface something the people outside had thought an impossibility: a chance to fight back.

Before these emerging Arks, they had been a mere resistance, with all the weaknesses and hopelessness that such movements can bring.

Now, on this new day, it turned.

It changed.

It was no longer a *resistance*.

It was a *war*.

For all those who had lived in fear, who were imprisoned or brutalized—for everyone who hated the Authority with a rage that seemed to consume their lives—on this day . . .

. . . it began.

ACKNOWLEDGMENTS

Rage, the novel written by me, couldn't exist without my having been able to work on the game. Tim Willits, the legendary producer of Doom 3, and now Rage, invited me to work on the game. Due to that, I was able to see Team id's vision grow and develop over the years. When it came time for a novel, Tim made sure that I had what I needed to jump back into that world and go from interactive to prose. Likewise, under a tight deadline, the book's editor, David Pomerico, showed patience and care as important questions and issues were resolved, and we took the reader deeper into that world. Steve Perkins at Bethesda Softworks graciously made sure that I was kept up to date as this project came closer to happening. For me, the writing and pages flew . . . and that is in large part due to all their support.

ABOUT THE AUTHOR

MATTHEW COSTELLO's award-winning work across all media includes groundbreaking TV, novels, nonfiction, and games in both the United States and Europe.

He has scripted and designed dozens of bestselling games including the critically acclaimed The 7th Guest, Doom 3, Just Cause (with Neil Richards), G-Force, and Pirates of the Caribbean: At World's End.

His novel *Beneath Still Waters* was adapted for film and released by Lions Gate. His novel *Missing Monday* was recently optioned for television. His latest suspense novel, *Nowhere*, was published by Putnam Books. He also wrote *Island of the Skull* (Pocket Books), an original prequel to Peter Jackson's film, *King Kong*, as well as two original novels based on Doom 3, which he scripted. His next novel, from St. Martin's Press, is the post-apocalyptic thriller, *Vacation* (October 2011). His children's titles include the Scholastic series *The Kids of Einstein Elementary* and *Magic Everywhere* (Random House), as well as puzzle and game books.

Matt has consulted and written episodes and created formats for broadcasters worldwide including PBS, The Disney Channel, SyFy, and the BBC, among others. He also speaks to, consults, and mentors transmedia teams around the world. He has not been to Antarctica . . . yet.

FROM THE CREATORS OF DOOM® AND QUAKE®

WINNER OF MORE THAN 20 E3 AWARDS

"RAGE IS AN ABSOLUTE STUNNER"
-G4TV.COM

AVAILABLE 10.4.11 · WWW.RAGE.COM

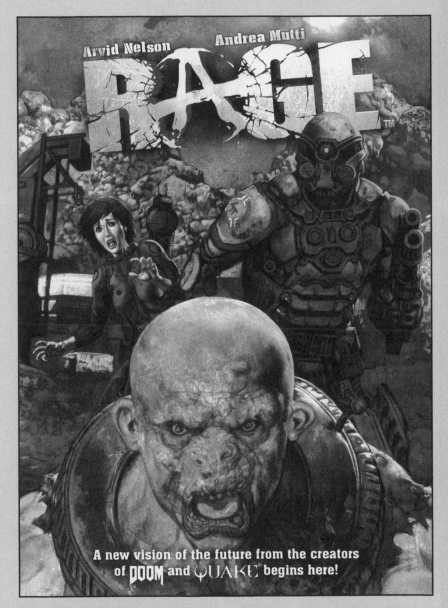

A new vision of the future from the creators of DOOM™ and QUAKE™ begins here!

AVAILABLE AT YOUR LOCAL COMICS SHOP